CASH MONEY CONTENT

D0052385

Get It Girls

A HARLEM GIRL LOST NOVEL

TREASURE BLUE

PREVIOUSLY PUBLISHED AS HARLEM GIRL LOST 2

CASH MONEY CONTENT

Book Layout: Candace K. Cottrell
Cover Design: Emily Mahon
For further information log onto www.CashMoneyContent.com

Library of Congress Control Number: 2011936943

ISBN: 978-1-936-39924-6   pbk
ISBN: 978-1-936-39923-9   ebook

10 9 8 7 6 5 4 3 2 1
Printed in the United States

Previously published as: HARLEM GIRL LOST 2

Dedication

This book is dedicated to Mr. Marvin L. Grant.

Our son, father, brother, uncle, and cousin. Words cannot express how your passing on has made an profound impact in our lives. Though we have moved on, you continue to have a place in our hearts, and all we have are those memories and wonderful times that we will cherish for the rest of our lives. Thank you for always being you and not changing who you were for anyone. You will continue to have life through us always and forever.

Until we meet again, RIP Marvin aka Shorty!

ALSO BY TREASURE E. BLUE

Harlem Girl Lost
A Street Girl Named Desire
Keyshia and Clyde
Flexin' and Sexin' Volume 2

CONTACTS

TreasureEBlue@yahoo.com
HarlemWorldPublishing@yahoo.com

Author's Note

would first like to thank all my loyal readers who expressed their kind words and praise for my very first novel, *Harlem Girl Lost*. You made it an instant classic, and I thank you from the bottom of my heart for your unwavering support since my debut.

Over the years, I've received literally thousands of e-mails and letters asking if there will be a *Harlem Girl Lost 2*. My initial response was that I doubted if there would be one because I killed off so many of the supporting characters in the first book. And to be even more candid with you, I also loved the happy ending and wanted to leave well enough alone.

I was at a speaking engagement at a local high school in Harlem, when I was posed this recurring question by a student during the panel discussion. After I expressed to her that I highly doubted if there would ever be a part two, she immediately posed another question:

"In your opinion, how would Jessica's life have turned out if she hadn't gotten pregnant with Silver at such a young age?"

I have to admit that it was an excellent question, and it was one of the first times in my life I was at loss for words. Over the next few days, the young girl's question continued to resonate in my mind, and that's when it hit me like a ton of bricks.

What *would* have happened not only to Jessica, but to her entire crew of Vonda, Tiny, and Lynn?

I then called up my good friend and fellow Harlemite, bestselling author and mentor K'wan, and ran the idea past him. He thought it was genius and said it would be considered an alternate reality. The rest is history.

So ladies and gentleman, without further ado, I proudly present to you, *Get It Girls*....

Enjoy,

TREASURE

Get It Girls

Chapter 1

APRIL 1981

HARLEM, NEW YORK

"Ay, yo, Jessica! Jessica! Come down before we be late for school," yelled Vonda.

She, Tiny, and Lynn stood impatiently in front of Jessica Jones's parents' three-family brownstone on 138th Street between 7th and 8th Avenue in Harlem. Jessica's was the only one out of the four of them whose family owned their own property in the upscale section of Harlem's exclusive Strivers Row, a block that housed well-to-do black professionals such as actors, doctors, lawyers, or businessmen. Though Jessica's parents had typical city jobs—her mother was a public school teacher and her father was a postal employee—they had the vision to sacrifice and invest in the neighborhood way before Harlem became cliché.

Vonda and Tiny, lived only two blocks away on 140th Street between Lenox and 7th Avenue in a tenement building. Their neighborhood was like night and day to Striver's Row because it was the ghetto. Lynn's family lived in Drew Hamilton projects on 142nd Street and 7th Avenue, and she developed a complex because of the stigma that only poor people lived in the projects.

Tiny sucked her teeth and scowled. "She does this same shit every day. We should just leave her ass to teach her lesson." Tiny looked toward Vonda to see if she would agree with her, but Vonda said nothing. "As soon as she comes out anyway her mama gonna call her back again like she always do. You watch," Tiny continued.

Lynn and Vonda continued to ignore Tiny as if she wasn't even there. They were more than used to her complaining, and everything Tiny said just flew by them.

Just then, the front door at the top of the stairs flew open and Jessica came rushing out as her book bag dangled precariously over her shoulder. Halfway down the stairs Jessica heard her mother call her, and she stopped her in place.

Tiny rolled her eyes and shook her head knowingly. "What I fucking tell you?" she said loud enough for Jessica to hear, but low enough so that Jessica's mother didn't.

Jessica closed her eyes and reluctantly walked back up the steps. Her mother stood at the doorway with her arms folded and said, "Jessica, what have I told you about sneaking out the house without seeing me first?"

"What, Mama?" Jessica sucked her teeth and sighed. "I'm going to be late for school, and I have a first period test."

"Don't get smart with me in front of your friends, Jessica, because I will embarrass you in front of them too."

Jessica decided to remain silent because she knew it wasn't worth getting into it with her mother in front of her friends. Mrs. Jones watched her daughter's three friends walk off toward the avenue and then squared her grim eyes back to her seventeen-year-old daughter.

"After school when you wait for your brother to get off the bus, I want you right back in this house. Take the food out of the freezer for dinner and then fix your brother a snack. You hear me?"

Jessica rolled her eyes, "But Ma, he's got his own key and—"

"But, my ass, now you heard what I said, Jessica. I want you home as soon as you get out of school waiting on your brother."

Jessica knew there wasn't anything she could have said that would change her mother's mind, so she just kept quiet and walked down the stairs in a huff.

"And I'm going to call at 4:30 to make sure you home too. You hear me, Jessica?"

"I hear you!" Jessica yelled in a tone she knew would infuriate her mother, but she didn't care any longer because the damage was done. Besides, she had already turned the corner and was too far out of sight to be reprimanded any more. When Jessica caught up with her friends a block away, she began apologizing for the tardiness. "I'm sorry, y'all, but my mom be bugging out and making me do stuff when she know I got to go to school."

Never to miss out on an opportunity to put Jessica on blast, Tiny added her two cents to it. "Yeah, but you be making us late and we the ones that got to pay for it."

Ever since Jessica befriended Vonda in their freshman year, Tiny despised Jessica for such an intrusion, because she and Vonda had been best friends since they were in Pampers. Since Vonda grew to be nearly six feet tall, and Tiny was barely five-feet-nothing, they were the consummate odd couple and sometimes received ridicule over it. Vonda was dark-skinned with a radiant, smooth complexion. Keen eyes on top of her statuesque body made her look like a beauty queen.

Jessica had a soft, light brown complexion and equaled Vonda in height and stature. Jessica was highly sought after because of her defining beauty wherever they went. To Vonda, it was refreshing to have someone take the heat off of her because boys, men, and even women would constantly harass her because of her looks, and Jessica bore half of the burden.

Lynn, who stood about five feet, five inches tall, was the thickest of the crew, and she came along about the same time as Jessica.

They attended an all-girls Catholic school in East Manhattan downtown called Cathedral High School. Over the four years that they attended Cathedral, they'd become inseparable. But Tiny never came to terms with Jessica seemingly taking her place and constantly tried to show Jessica up with insults. Jessica developed a thick skin and knew from past experience not to show Tiny her weak spots because Tiny would feed on it. So, she simply just checked her hard by talking about her physical attributes, which Tiny hated.

Jessica sneered and said, "I ain't ask you to wait for me, Tiny. You can do whatever you want to do. Nobody is stopping you."

Tiny quickly retorted. "Don't forget we letting you roll with us. So keep talking shit and we gonna leave ya ass next time."

Jessica chuckled. "Who is *we*? Like you speak for Vonda and Lynn?"

Tiny looked at Vonda for support and asked, "Yo, Vonda, ain't you getting tired of her shit?"

For the most part, Vonda tried to stand clear of Tiny's nonsense and learned to ignore her, but lately she'd been growing weary because of her constant bickering and scheming. "Why don't you shut the fuck up, Tiny? If you don't want to wait with us, you can go ahead without us. It's just that simple."

Tiny stood stone-faced. "Oh, you gonna play me over her, Vonda?"

"Playing you? No, Tiny, you playing yourself. How you gonna try to tell us who and who not to wait for?" Vonda waited for a response and heard none. "So you can make up your mind what you want to do, because you've got options."

Tiny was still unmoved by her comment and added, "Yeah, whatever, Vonda. But don't forget we got that biology test first period, and see what happens if they lock us out this morning. Don't say I didn't tell you so, and we'll see who you blame then."

Lynn snickered and jumped in. "Since when the fuck did you start worrying about a test, Tiny? All you doing is starting shit."

Tiny turned her attention to Lynn. "Don't even start talking, Lynn. We waited for your fat ass this morning too."

"Fuck you, Tiny!" Lynn quickly snapped. "My elevator was broke, and I had to walk down nineteen flights of stairs."

Tiny gave her a wicked smile. "You should be happy. Maybe you lost some weight in the process."

"Least I got some weight, Tiny, unlike your bony, malnutritioned ass."

"Don't even try it; all that shit is fat," Tiny joked.

Lynn stopped suddenly and said, "Yeah, but you wish you had a body like mines, you skinny toothpick." Lynn pointed her thumb at Tiny. "This bitch is so skinny, she could hula hoop through a Cheerio."

"Oh, you snapping, Lynn? At least my hair ain't so short that I use Rice-A-Roni to roll it."

Tiny and Lynn always snapped on each other every morning, and Vonda and Jessica couldn't help but laugh. These were the moments they enjoyed the most despite Tiny's constant nitpicking.

Lynn and Tiny went on like this for the next two blocks as they cracked jokes on each other. They were all laughing so hard, they were oblivious to the five girls standing on the corner. When they finally spotted them, it was too late to avoid them, so they all grew silent and braced themselves for the unexpected.

The group of girls, the Lenox Avenue Girls, was a bunch of hard heads who lived for fighting and starting trouble. Cookie, Denise, Tay-Tay, Nikki, and Kimmi preyed on most of the girls in the neighborhood. They were all in their late teens or early twenties, and particularly didn't like Catholic school girls. They thought all Catholic school girls were stuck up and thought they were better than public school girls. It wasn't uncommon throughout Harlem, though. Public school girls were frequently seen jumping and beating up a few Catholic girls coming or going to school.

Vonda, Tiny, Lynn, and Jessica had had more than their share of run-ins with The Lenox Avenue Girls during their four years together. Normally, they avoided them by taking the long way to the train station. But today they were caught slipping.

"Oh, shit, Tay-Tay, look what the fuck we have here," said the ringleader, Cookie. The group began walking in the four girls' direction.

Jessica and her crew tried to walk around them, but the five girls blocked them by creating a human wall in front of them.

Vonda tried to show no weakness. "What the fuck do you

want now, Cookie?" Even though Vonda was tall, she was small in comparison to Cookie in both height and girth.

"I don't know who the fuck you think you talking to, Vonda, but you better recognize who the fuck you talking to."

Vonda gritted down on her jaw and cursed herself under her breath for not carrying her knife or razor as she normally did. She wasn't afraid to throw down with Cookie one-on-one, but she knew if she got in the mix with her she would get jumped on by the four other girls. The only one in her crew she could really rely on was Jessica, because she knew from experience that neither Tiny nor Lynn would be any help. She weighed her odds and decided to use her head for now, but she wasn't going to be taken advantage of by any means.

Vonda looked her directly in her eyes to gain some respect. "So what do you want, Cookie?"

"Y'all bitches know what the fuck it is. I told y'all last time the next time I see you bitches walking on my avenue, you gots ta pay a bitch to pass."

Cookie's partner Denise interjected and said, "What? Y'all bitches thought we forgot?"

Cookie snarled and gained even more confidence when she saw the fear in Lynn's eyes. "What you got in your purse, Lynn? Come up off that shit right now."

Lynn began shaking so badly that she was unable to respond.

Cookie stepped directly in her face and screamed, "You heard what the fuck I said, bitch. Up that shit right now or I'm gonna bust your shit!"

Lynn began reaching for her handbag when Vonda and Jessica stepped between them to defend their friend.

Vonda stated flatly, "Yo, Cookie, I'm not going to let you take her money."

Cookie grimaced. "What? And how the fuck are you going to stop me?"

There was a moment of silence until Jessica spoke up. "She can't give you her money because she's a diabetic."

The five girls looked at each other, not getting the point.

"So the fuck what?" asked Nikki, who looked at Cookie, Tay-Tay, Denise, and Kimmi like they might have an answer.

Jessica shook her head. "Since she's a diabetic, she got to buy some snacks during and after school so she doesn't get sick."

The five girls all began looking at Lynn until Cookie joked, "This bitch look like she could stand to miss a few snacks."

They all began laughing—hard—in light of the joke.

Cookie turned her attention to Tiny and looked her up and down. "Look at this li'l bitch," she said, looking over her shoulders and pointing toward Tiny. "She looks like she's the one that needs to be eating some snacks because she ain't got no fucking titties."

The Lenox Avenue girls all started laughing heartily and slapping high fives to each other.

Cookie continued digging into Tiny. "This bitch must be one of the board members on the Itty Bitty Titty Committee."

They bent over in laughter as Tiny stood stoned-faced, clutching her fist.

Vonda and Jessica watched Tiny's eyes slant and each prayed that she wouldn't say a word because they knew her, and it would be nothing but trouble.

Cookie's crew was laughing so hard they seemed to have forgotten they were there until Cookie said, "All right, all right.

I'm gonna let y'all go this time, but the next time I catch y'all on my block or on my avenue," she paused, pulled out a switchblade from her hoodie, flicked it open, and licked the blade, "All y'all bitches is gonna come up with that loot. Y'all hear me?"

Jessica, Vonda, Tiny, and Lynn remained silent as the five girls parted and allowed them to walk through.

As the rough girls watched them walk away, Tay-Tay added one more insult toward Tiny. "Ay yo, Tiny. I know why they call you that. 'Cause you a chicken head with a chicken butt."

The girls began to mock her further by making clucking sounds. Tiny was clearly vexed, and Vonda, Jessica, and Lynn knew it by the way she was biting down on her lip. She was also slanting her eyes, and that was an expression they were all too familiar with. It had gotten them in more than their share of trouble in the past.

"Tiny, don't say a fucking word. Just keep on walking," Vonda whispered.

"Yeah, Tiny. Let that shit go," added Jessica.

Tiny continued to bite down on her lip and clutch her fist. Halfway down the block, Tiny couldn't take it any longer and lost it. She turned around and yelled at the top of her lungs, "At least I'm not a high school dropout like you, you dumb dyke bitches!"

That was it. Tiny had set it off, and the four girls ran as fast and as hard as they could toward the train station. Cookie and the four other girls were fuming as they yelled obscenities at the retreating girls' backs.

"Get in on 'em, girls. Get their asses! We gonna fuck y'all up. Get it in, y'all! Get it in on 'em!"

It was only in vain, as Cookie and her crew ran out of steam after only one block of pursuit.

"That's all right, bitches," yelled Cookie. "When I catch y'all asses it's fuckin' on!"

Jessica, Vonda, Tiny, and Lynn ran five more blocks and slowed down only when they were sure they were no longer in danger. When they arrived at the number 3 train at 148th and 7th Avenue, the four girls were out of breath and so furious that that Vonda threw Tiny up against the entrance wall and began digging into her—hard.

"You just couldn't keep your fuckin' mouth shut, could you? You just had to say something, Tiny, huh?" Vonda grabbed her by her sweater. "Now you got us in the fucking mix with them bitches and now we got to watch our backs!"

Tiny knew she was wrong and could not respond.

Vonda refused to let up as her eyes turned blood red from anger. "I fuckin' told you not to say nothing, but you don't listen."

If it wasn't for Lynn and Jessica pulling Vonda off of Tiny, she would have surely wound up choking Tiny to death. Tiny coyly eyed the ground like a child, only now realizing how much she had put them in jeopardy. Vonda's chest heaved in and out. She stared down at Tiny red-faced, awaiting an answer, but she never received one.

Forever the peacemaker, Lynn wiped the sweat from her brow. "Damn. I don't know about y'all, but I sure could use a snack, 'cause my diabetes must be acting up."

Just like that, the four of them laughed as they looked at each other's hair, which was now sweated out. Tiny walked over and lifted her chin toward Vonda. They stared at each other for a moment, and then they both grinned wickedly and embraced.

"Why the fuck do I keep you as a friend?" Vonda wondered out loud as she patted Tiny's hair back into place.

"'Cause without me, your life would be boring." Tiny snickered.

"No, because she would get that ass kicked every day if it wasn't for you." Jessica grinned as she playfully patted Tiny on her head.

They began to fix their clothing back into place and used their fingers to restyle their hair and walked down the stairs to the train station.

"They really wanted to get our asses, huh?" Vonda asked.

They all nodded, and Jessica asked, "Yo, was it me or did I hear that fat bitch Cookie yelling, 'Get it in, girls'?"

"Yes, she did," said Vonda. "'Get it, girls! get their asses, girls!' Shit, I felt like we were being chased by a pack of hungry wolves or something."

All the girls started cracking up. After their adrenaline rush subsided, reality once again struck them and Jessica said, "But, yo, them bitches is serious, so we can't walk on 7th or Lenox Avenue no time soon."

They all looked down and agreed with a nod.

"We could just catch the train on 135th instead of here from now on," Lynn suggested. "We only got two months left till we all graduate. We lay low for the summer, and after that we don't have to worry about them bitches forever."

They collectively discussed it for a moment and agreed to avoid their rivals by lying low. "So that's what it is," said Vonda. "Watch each other's back from now till we go off to college."

They all nodded. They watched the train pulling into the station and Vonda added, "We are now wanted girls, so we got to be on point."

Fear once again was in their eyes and Vonda saw it and joked, "We not just *wanted* girls, but we are the Get It Girls."

A smile instantly came across all their faces.

Lynn asked, "So, is that the name of our crew now? Are we the Get It Girls crew?"

All at once, the girls began to nod and agree. One by one, each stuck out her fist and put it together in the center. In unison they said, "Get It Girls!"

Chapter 2

When Jessica arrived home with her younger brother Jordan, she immediately began to follow her mother's orders and took out some frozen meat from the freezer. She paused for a moment and listened closely. "Jordan, cut that Atari off and get to your homework, now!"

The sound coming from his room instantly stopped, and she became suspicious. She knew her brother, and she also knew that he didn't take well to being told what to do that quickly, so she quietly began climbing the stairs to his bedroom. She listened at his door for a second and thought she heard the handling of the Atari controllers patting away. She rushed in his room. Just as she thought; he'd only turned the volume down on the television and continued playing the game.

"Aha!" yelled Jessica as she ran toward her little brother and snatched the controller out of his hands. "Jordan, you think I'm that stupid? You know Mama said you have to do your homework before you get on these games."

"Come on, Jessica," Jordan pleaded. "My friend at school let me borrow his game till tomorrow, and I'm just testing it out for a minute, that's all."

"Jordan, you know that if Mama comes home and finds you playing these games without your homework being done she's going to yell at me too for letting you."

"But, Mama ain't getting home for another two hours, and I'll be finished with my homework by then, Jessica."

"Mommy *isn't* getting home," Jessica corrected, "and I'm not going to get yelled at, so the quicker you get your homework done, the quicker you can get back to your game."

Jordan felt wounded and put on the pouting face. Jessica stared at her twelve-year-old brother and instantly felt sad. Jessica and Jordan always had a deep affection toward each other and were extremely close ever since he was born prematurely. He grew up sickly, and Jessica, as well as her parents, was always overly protective over him. Jessica would do anything to protect the little boy. She was closer to him than his own parents because she watched him most of the time.

After staring at her little brother slowly unzipping his school bag while pouting, she relented and said, "I hope that game has two players, because I'm about to whip that little butt of yours."

Jordan's eyes lit up and a huge smile came across his face and he said, "Yes!"

Later that evening, Vonda called just as Jessica was finishing up washing the dishes.

"Yo, Jessica, guess what?" said Vonda.

"I don't know, what?"

"No, guess," Vonda repeated.

"Bitch, I don't have time to be standing here guessing all night. Spit it out," Jessica teased.

"Aight, you know Stevo and them dudes that always be trying to holla at us from 143rd Street? Anyway, me and Tiny saw him walking through my block a little while ago and he said that he was throwing a big party this Friday and invited all of us to come."

"And?" said Jessica, like it wasn't that much of a big deal.

"And, we are going, right?"

"I don't know, Vonda. He's probably going to invite everybody from the neighborhood there, and you know we can't get caught up with the bullshit again."

"No, it's not that kind of party; it's a house party, and he's handpicking everyone to show up. He told me that no bum bitches are allowed at his party, and you know Cookie and them other bitches are straight-up chicken heads, so that's a wrap."

Jessica sighed. "I don't know."

"Come, Jessica. It ain't gonna be right if you don't come. I'm tired of going to parties with only Tiny and Lynn. Tiny always showing her ass, and Lynn's always complaining she ready to go because nobody be asking her to dance. I get tired of that shit. At least if you come I can have a good time because I don't have to be feeling so guilty."

They both laughed.

"Oh!" said Vonda. "I forgot to tell you!"

Jessica smiled and folded her because arms because she knew Vonda didn't normally get this excited over just anything. "What?"

"Guess who gonna be at the party too?"

"Who?"

"Fine-ass Kenny!" Vonda squealed.

Jessica was at loss for words and melted by just hearing his name.

Hearing Jessica's silence, Vonda knew that was the hook, line, and sinker. "Yeah, I knew that would get your ass open."

"No."

"Bitch, get the fuck out of here. Yo' ass is probably creaming your panties right now."

Jessica shifted from one leg to the other, embarrassed that she was right.

"So, you gonna go or what?" asked Vonda.

Jessica frowned and bit down on her lip and spoke in a low tone. "I want to, but I don't know if my mother's going let me go, though."

"Come on, Jessica, you almost eighteen. She won't mind you going to one little ole party."

Jessica shrugged. "What time the party starts anyway?" Jessica knew instantly there was a problem when she heard Vonda's brief pause.

"It starts at ten o'clock."

"Ten o'clock, Vonda? Ten fucking o'clock, Vonda?"

"Just tell your mother you staying over my house," offered Vonda.

Jessica shook her head. "No, she still won't go for it."

"Well," conceded Vonda, "You got by Friday to figure something out, ok?"

Jessica shook her head as Vonda gave her a reminder,

"Remember, we got a half a day on Friday too, so we could chill and change at my house till it's time to go to the party, aight?"

"Ok," said Jessica, "I'll see you tomorrow." She hung up the phone softly. Jessica immediately began formulating a plan of action. She smiled and walked into the living room, where her father was half asleep as the ten o'clock news played. Jessica sat on the arm of his La-Z-Boy chair, where he reclined, and planted a soft kiss on his cheek.

Mr. Robert W. Jones smiled immediately and asked, "What was that for?"

Jessica's forty-seven-year-old father was the absolute apple of her eye, as she was to him. Jessica would forever be his pride and joy, and he'd spoiled her since the day she was born. It was impossible for him to tell her no to anything, and she knew it.

"Nothing, Daddy . . . I just felt like giving you a kiss."

He eyed her suspiciously and said, "Ok, how much do you need?"

Jessica chided him and said, "Oh, Daddy, I don't want any money."

He displayed a surprised look. "Let me check your temperature."

She tapped him on the shoulder and smiled. "Why something got to be wrong with me, Daddy?"

"I know, baby. I'm just joshing you."

They stared at the television in silence until Jessica asked, "Daddy?"

"Yes, pumpkin."

"It's this premiere to a movie coming out downtown this Friday, and me and Vonda and the rest of us have free passes to see it, but the only thing is it starts at ten o'clock. You think I can go?"

He scratched his fading hair and said, "If it starts at ten, you won't get out till at least midnight. That's pretty late to be getting home by yourself," said Mr. Jones.

Jessica anticipated his answer and quickly stated, "I know. That's why we all planning on staying at Vonda's house so none of us have to walk home by ourselves."

He shrugged. "Ok, that makes sense."

Jessica jumped up and asked excitedly, "That means I can go, Daddy?"

He nodded his head and submitted, "Yes, baby, you can go with your friends."

Jessica began clapping and gave her father a big hug and a kiss. "Thank you, Daddy! I love you so much."

These were the moments Mr. Jones lived for, as he saw the joy in his baby girl eyes. She gave him another kiss on the cheek and then headed upstairs to her bedroom. Just before she went up she peeked back into the living room and asked her father, "Daddy, umm, what about Mama?"

Mr. Jones looked into his daughter's big doe eyes. "Now, you don't have to worry about your mother. I'm still the man around here, if you haven't noticed." He winked.

* * *

The day of the party, Jessica packed her clothes and shoes in an overnight bag before she went to school. She made sure her outfit for the night was looking fresh and hugged all her curves in just the right places. Jessica thought that she would have to be the most stunning girl at the party if she had any chance of getting Kenny's attention.

Kenny Duboise was a neighborhood teen who had it all— good looks, style, and a fierce reputation as a ladies' man. Girls and women alike flocked around him because of his magnetic personality and smooth demeanor. But what really set Kenny apart like no other were his deep, penetrating hazel eyes. Just one look into a girl's eyes would send them in a whirl, so Jessica knew the competition would be thick.

Even though Jessica herself was highly sought after, she was used to seeing Kenny with older and more sophisticated women. She had to at least try to stand apart from the other girls even though she doubted her chances of being with a person like him.

After the four girls got out of school at noon that day, they went over to Vonda's house to practice the latest dance moves. Vonda had gotten some weed from one of her older brothers, and she, Lynn, and Jessica were having a ball, smoking, dancing, and bragging on how they would rule the dance floor that night. Tiny, however, was disinterested in dancing and remained laid back in a chair as she smoked the weed and watched the three of them dance through her icy eyes. The more weed she consumed, the more she seemed to grow angry at the world— especially toward her arch nemesis, Jessica Jones.

Lynn and Jessica were doing their thing in the middle of the room and had just perfected an intricate succession of dance moves.

"Oh, snap," said Vonda, as she watched her two home girls twirl and spin to the beat. "Yo, let me learn that shit."

Tiny watched Vonda take Jessica's hand as she taught her the reinvented Hustle move. Even though The Hustle wasn't in style anymore, they still practiced the dance and used it from time to time at parties to showcase their style. Lynn changed records and put on what she felt was the ultimate Hustle song to dance to: "Trans Europe Express" by Kraftwerk. Vonda and Jessica immediately screamed their excitement and went into full dance mode. Tiny's glassy eyes turned into a slant as she watched the two tall girls groove to the song. The more she watched them, the angrier she grew and finally had enough.

"Wack . . . wack . . . wack! That shit y'all doing is straight up wack!" yelled Tiny, instantly breaking the girls' stride.

The three girls stopped in their tracks and stared at Tiny, who was now standing up wiping the marijuana ashes off of her clothes.

Lynn took the needle off the record player and immediately pressed Tiny. "Why are you always hatin', Tiny? You just mad because you can't do it."

Tiny only rolled her eyes. "All y'all doing are biting someone else's shit. But, me," she patted herself on the chest, "I'm gonna be original with mine, not like that tired played out shit Jessica be doing."

Jessica immediately rebutted, "I knew it. She's just jealous."

"Jealous!" said Tiny, exasperated. "Bitch, the day I'm jealous of you will be the day I die."

Jessica pulled Lynn and Vonda farther away from Tiny.

Perplexed, Tiny asked, "What the fuck are you doing?"

Jessica smiled cunningly and said, "We got to stand away from you because God is going to hit your jealous ass with a bolt of lightning if you keep lying."

Vonda and Lynn busted out with laughter.

This time, like any, Tiny hated to be clowned on. "At least I don't have to lie to my parents so I can go out to a party. Do I, bitch?"

There was complete silence for a moment. Vonda put her head down for violating Jessica's trust by telling Tiny how she'd gotten out to go to the party.

Jessica had to show control so Tiny didn't know she was hurt. She decided to check Tiny just as hard. "At least I don't wear my little brother's clothes." Jessica gave a sly smile.

Tiny quickly countered. "At least my li'l brother ain't slow."

Jessica walked right into that one, she thought, but she had to show no emotions or Tiny would feed off of it forever. Jessica decided to hit her where it really hurt.

"At least I don't have to put tissue in my bra to make it look like I have titties, bitch."

That was it. Tiny was livid as she looked at the only one who knew she put tissue in her bra: Vonda. Tiny's eyes began to slant, and she turned her anger back toward Jessica, who was laughing and giving Lynn a high five.

Suddenly, as if she'd had a revelation, Tiny silently sat back in the chair, relit the joint, and simply smiled wickedly at Jessica. The three girls knew Tiny was up to something, but they didn't know what. She would never have allowed anyone to out-talk her in her life. For her to walk away from verbal confrontation, they knew she was up to no good.

Breaking the tense atmosphere, Lynn put the needle back in the record. "Come on y'all, we got a party to go to tonight, and it's going to be nothing but cuties up in that piece. We got to show them other bitches who's the queens of the dance floor, so let's dance."

Lynn started shaking her body, clowning, making Vonda and Jessica crack a smile. She took them by the hand and started dancing again as if the incident hadn't even happened. But, one person in the room wasn't going to forget the incident by a longshot and already had plans for Miss High and Mighty Jessica Jones.

Suddenly, Vonda's bedroom door swung open, causing them all to stop in place and turn their attention toward it. It was Vonda's youngest brother, twelve-year-old Chubby. Tiny hid the joint she was smoking.

He stood with his arms folded over his robust stomach and said to Tiny, "Why you tryna hide the weed, Tiny? You think I can't still smell it?"

Vonda walked over to the door. "What I told you about busting in my room without knocking, Chubby?"

Chubby didn't have an answer and began shifting from one leg to another. It was what he always did whenever he did something wrong or when he would lie.

Vonda knew her brother so she just asked, "What do you want?"

He took the Tootsie Roll Pop out of his mouth. "I'm hungry and Mama ain't coming home till late and she left this note for you to fix me sumptin' ta eat."

"Ok, I'll cook you something later." Vonda attempted to push him out of the doorway.

"But, I'm hungry now," he cried.

"Make a peanut butter and jelly sandwich till I'm ready."

"Ain't no bread," he stated quickly.

Rolling her eyes, Vonda waved him off. "Then you got a problem, so you just gonna hafta wait. Now get out!"

"But, I'm hungry now!" he cried again.

Tiny jumped in and said, "Awww, look at the big baby crying."

Chubby frowned. "Fuck you, Tiny. Your bony ass need to mind your business."

Tiny only laughed.

"Watch your mouth before I tell Mama you cursing," Vonda scolded.

"And I'll call Mama and tell her y'all are smoking reefer."

"You do and I'll kick your fat ass," said Vonda.

"Watch me." Chubby attempted to go to the phone in the kitchen, but Vonda stopped him cold and threw him to the floor. Tiny ran over and helped her with the assault by shaking and patting his wide stomach.

"Let me go, let me go," he cried. "Jessica, help me."

Jessica ran over to aid him and helped him to his feet. "Leave my li'l man alone." Jessica smiled as she wrapped her arms around him protectively.

Vonda sucked her teeth. "Jessica, why you always helping this li'l nigga out? He's bad now just like the rest of his no good brothers."

"No, he's not," said Jessica, as she hugged him tighter. "He will always be my li'l cubby bear."

As Jessica hugged him, Chubby stuck out his tongue at the two other girls.

Vonda shook her head. "All right, you little fucker. Just for that I ain't cooking you shit, and I don't care if you call Mama; I'll just tell her you are lying. Now!"

"But I'm hungry," he submitted as tears began to flow.

All the girls except Jessica began chastising and taunting him.

"Aw, look at the big baby."

"Leave him alone, leave him alone." Jessica took him by the hand and said, "Come on, Chubby. I'll cook you something to eat, don't worry." She led him out of the room toward the kitchen.

Seconds later, he peeked his head back into the room and flashed a cunning smile. "Yo, Lynn, I'll settle for one of your big titties so I can make a big-ass titty sandwich."

They made an attempt to run after him, but he slammed the door in their faces and ran to Jessica.

Chapter 3

The party was being thrown in the St. Nicholas Housing Projects on 127th Street. Jessica, Vonda, Tiny, and Lynn arrived around 11:30 PM so they could make a fashionably late grand entrance. All the girls were dressed to kill, and when they walked through the door they immediately turned heads.

The host of the party, Stevo, was the first to greet them at the door, and he asked Vonda for the first dance. She accepted. Moments later, all four girls were side-by-side dancing with a partner to the latest dance craze, The Spank, and were enjoying themselves.

It didn't take long for Jessica's and Lynn's dance partners to realize that the girls were far superior in technique and flair. So, much so, that Jessica and Lynn found themselves all alone on the dance floor. All eyes fell on them as they switched up and did their new version of The Hustle. Jessica and Lynn knew they had everyone's attention and were really working it, putting and extra spin and twirl on every intricate move with accentuation.

All the boys watched with pleasure. The girls watched in envy, and hated them for it and began to whisper amongst themselves about everything from their clothing and shoes, to their particular hairstyles. Jessica and Lynn knew it and didn't care. One thing the girls knew for sure was that they were the queens of the dance floor at that moment. It was also right about that time when Jessica spotted Kenny lurking among the revelers.

Kenny Duboise was a twenty-year-old heartthrob, plain and simple. He was tall, slim and had the deepest hazel-silver eyes that you ever saw on a human being. He was the epitome of ghetto fabulous even before it became popular because of the way he dressed and especially because of the way he danced. All the girls, and women, for that matter, even some who were twice his age fell head over heels for him at just one glance. He carried himself well to be so young, many thought, handling everything with the smoothness in all he did. For Kenny to be so well known, he was still enigmatic. Nobody knew his family, and he wasn't born in America, but came from Haiti at the tender age of eleven. He was bilingual, speaking both English and French-Creole fluently, and one would have to listen very closely to detect even a hint of his native tongue. But when he did speak in French dialect, it would send any woman or girl into a whirl.

When Jessica caught a glimpse that he was in her midst, she purposely put her dancing in overdrive and inched closer to where he stood so he could get the perfect view. When the song was over, Jessica and Lynn received a rousing applause from the crowd. They had finally arrived, they thought.

Not everyone was clapping, though. Jessica watched Tiny's

grim eyes staring at her as if she wanted to kill her. She paid her no mind and decided not to let her spoil her moment of glory. Jessica and Lynn were sweating profusely and headed over to the punch bowl to get something to drink with Vonda in tow. The three girls were laughing and giggling all the while about their newfound status.

Suddenly, Vonda elbowed Jessica in her side. "Yo, Jess, don't look now, but Kenny and his boys are looking over here at us," she whispered.

Jessica turned to look, but Vonda stopped her. "Don't look over there, bitch. Play your position and let him think you not worrying about him."

Jessica nodded and asked Vonda, "So what's up with you and Stevo? He's been all up on you since we walked in here."

Vonda agreed, and said, "Yeah, I'm feeling that nigga too. I been talking to him for a minute, but I had to let him know that I wasn't no chickenhead and he got to respect me. You know what I mean?"

Jessica nodded.

Vonda continued. "Yo, Jessica, remember this. When you fucking with a nigga for the first time, you got to learn to say 'no' before you say 'yes.' You feel me?"

Jessica listened to all her words intently and nodded.

"That way, you separate yourself from all the other girls he's used to talking to, putting you in a class by yourself. And that applies especially to them pretty boys, you hear me?"

Just as she finished schooling her best friend, the latest dance song, "Square Biz" by Teena Marie came blaring out of the speakers and it instantly filled the dance floor.

Lynn said, "Oh, shit, y'all. Kenny is walking over here."

Everyone began patting their hair and straightening their clothing. All three girls grew numb with excitement as he stood in front of the three of them.

Tiny came up from behind him and asked, "Hey Kenny, you want to dance?"

He barely noticed her, as his penetrating eyes were locked in on Jessica's.

Tiny followed his eyes and then gently grabbed him by his arm, forcing him to look at her. She smiled, batted her eyes, and repeated, "Kenny, you want to dance?"

He smiled, exposing a set of perfectly white teeth. "I'm sorry, not now; but maybe later, ok?"

He turned his attention back to Jessica. He was definitely feeling her style, but didn't want to appear too pressed. He gave her one of his famous lingering glances right before he walked over to the punch, picked up the ladle, and poured some in a cup. He stopped before he took a sip and asked them, "This isn't spiked with alcohol? Does anybody know?"

Lynn was the closest, and she looked into his piercing eyes and got stuck.

He smiled and asked again, "Do you know if it's spiked with alcohol? Because I don't drink."

Lynn regained her composure. "No—I mean, I don't think so. It tasted fine when we had some a second ago," she stuttered.

He thanked her and began drinking it. When he finished, he looked at Jessica again and said, "Your name is Jessica, right?"

Jessica couldn't believe he knew her name and was totally speechless. He awaited an answer, but received none until Vonda elbowed Jessica in the ribs.

She regrouped and said, "Yes."

He nodded and smiled. "I saw you out there on the dance floor a minute ago. You were fly."

Jessica blushed and put her head down.

He turned and looked at the dance floor. "Hey, you want to dance?"

Jessica looked at Vonda and remembered what she'd said. "No, thanks. Not right now."

Kenny's smile instantly turned into a frown. Vonda and Lynn were equally stunned.

"What?" he stammered, not believing what he'd just heard. Never in his life had a girl turned him down for anything.

"I just finished dancing, you know, and it's so hot in here. Maybe a little later though, ok?"

This caught Kenny totally off guard, but he recouped well, smiled and said, "I understand." Kenny walked back over to where his boys were with his head down.

As soon as he was out of ear reach, both Vonda and Lynn grabbed Jessica, spinning her around. "Jessica, are you crazy?"

Jessica was confused. "What?"

"Bitch, what do you mean 'what'? Why would you turn down a dance from Kenny?" Vonda asked furiously.

"You told me that I should say no to separate myself from the chicken heads."

"Bitch, I didn't say to turn him down for a simple dance."

Lynn shook her head and said, "You stupid," then walked away.

Jessica and Vonda looked over at Kenny and his boys, who looked as if they were teasing him for being turned down by a girl—a young girl at that. It wasn't even twenty minutes before the girls watch Kenny walk away from his group of friends and back in their direction again.

He walked directly up to Jessica and said, "Jessica, can I have a word with you?"

Jessica looked at Vonda, who nodded. She smiled at Kenny and said, "Yes."

Tiny had just arrived back over to the group from dancing when she saw Kenny take Jessica by the hand and lead her over to a sofa.

She quickly asked Vonda and Lynn, "What's going on?"

Both girls smiled and Vonda said, "My girl Jessica just got Kenny open like a token."

The three looked over at the sofa where they were sitting. Tiny was livid as her eyes turned into a slant and she grew angrier by the second.

"I guess you won't be getting the man of your dreams tonight, huh, Tiny?"

Tiny remained silent as her frown suddenly turned into a smile. She turned around and said to her two friends. "Listen, I'm going downstairs for a minute. I need some air. I'll be back." She headed toward the front door.

Vonda and Lynn watched Tiny leave, then Lynn said, "That bitch is scheming. She's up to something."

Vonda squinted. She knew Lynn was right.

Outside, Tiny fished around in her pocket for some coins and when she found two dimes she searched for the nearest pay phone. She dialed the number and waited.

By the third ring, a voice answered, "Hello?"

Tiny cleared her throat and said, "Hello, yes, this is Tiny—" Tiny rolled her eyes and corrected herself— "I mean Claresse, Mrs. Jones. Can I speak to Jessica?"

"Young lady, it's awfully late to be calling for Jessica. She's not here anyway," said Mrs. Jones.

"Oh, darn, they must have already left for the party," said Tiny, fighting hard to keep from laughing.

Mrs. Jones sat up from her bed and asked, "Party? What party? She is supposed to be at the movies." There was a pause. "Hello?"

"Yes, I'm still here, Mrs. Jones."

"Claresse, is there something you're not telling me that I should know about?"

Tiny held her mouth to prevent her laughter from escaping. "Mrs. Jones, I can't lie to you, but, I don't know if I'm supposed to tell you that we are supposed to be at a house party tonight in the projects at 1132 St. Nicholas, apartment 3B. Please don't tell her I told you." Tiny hung up and began laughing so hard passing strangers thought she was losing her mind.

Meanwhile, Jessica and Kenny were vibing well together as they chatted about everything under the sun. Jessica forced her to eyes the ground; she could not bear to stare into his silver-hazel eyes without melting. He willingly admitted to Jessica that he wasn't used to being turned down, and it made him want to know her even more.

Jessica still didn't believe she was actually sitting with the most handsome boy in Harlem, and she kept having to pinch herself to see if she was dreaming. She'd heard all kinds of rumors about him, and he already seemed like a legend. Some people said he was the son of Ron O'Neal, the actor who played Superfly in the movie, and that he changed clothes at least three times a day. But whether the stories about him were truth or fiction, it was a reality that they were sitting together that night. It was truly a dream come true for any girl, Jessica thought.

"So what block are you from?" asked Kenny.

"Oh, I live on 138th Street."

"Lenox and 7th?"

Jessica paused for a second before she answered. She put her head down again, rather embarrassed. "No, I live between 7th and 8th avenue."

Kenny pulled back in surprise and asked, "Your family got an apartment in Strivers Row?"

Jessica hated to answer the question, because she didn't like being perceived to be wealthy. She didn't want everyone to think she was stuck up little rich girl. This was the reason she gravitated and became so close to Vonda and the rest of the girls. They were the first real friends she'd ever had. She wanted to lie, but told him the truth.

"No, my parents own the building on that block."

"So your parents are rich?"

She knew this would happen and grew uncomfortable. "No, my mother is a 5th grade school teacher and my father works at the post office. That doesn't exactly qualify us to be rich, you know."

Kenny detected her frustration and said, "Cool out, baby;

you should be proud to have parents that own their own home. My uncle was smart just like your parents and invested in real estate. He tells me all the time that I should think about buying a brownstone before there is no more left."

Kenny began to mock his uncle, French accent and all. "Kenneth, if you ever invest in anything, always invests in real estate, nothing else." They laughed. Kenny began to see that Jessica wasn't the average girl he talked to in Harlem and really found her interesting.

They stared into each other's eyes for a brief moment when Jessica broke the trance. "Can I ask you a question, Kenny?" She put her head down and blushed.

He smiled at her innocence and said, "Anything, baby. Just ask me."

Jessica smiled and put her head down again. "Is it true that your father is Ron O'Neal, the actor, and that you are super rich?"

He chuckled and shook his head. "No, Ron O'Neal is not my father, and no, I'm not super rich." Kenny searched her face and saw that she was still unsure about something. "What else would you like to ask?"

She giggled. "Is it that obvious?"

He nodded and said, "Yeah."

"How do you stay so fly? You dress in all those nice, expensive clothes. I mean, people say that you change up at least three times a day."

He paused, and replied, "That's true, but I don't change clothes three time a day; I just go out a lot. Parties, clubs, and things like that. My uncle takes good care of me."

"So you stay with your uncle?"

"Most of the time. He owns some buildings on Amsterdam Avenue, too, but my parents live in New Jersey."

Jessica nodded. "So, you don't live with your parents?"

Kenny shrugged. "Sometimes, but it is so boring out there in Jersey 'cause we the only blacks in the entire area. I'd rather be in Harlem around my people."

Jessica agreed with a smile and a nod. "What does your uncle do for a living besides owning buildings?"

Kenny's smile disappeared as he shifted his body on the sofa. He appeared to be searching for the right words while his eyes looked up toward the ceiling. He finally looked her straight in the eyes and confessed.

"Jessica, I usually don't tell people this, but my uncle does some bad things. He sells drugs."

He paused to see how she reacted before continuing, but he couldn't read any reaction.

"I mean, he's not a bad person; he just does bad things and he tells me all the time to stay away from it because of what it could do to a person and everything." He looked Jessica in the eye and got serious. "Jessica, don't ever use any drugs. I know what it does to people. He took me to a shooting gallery and actually made me watch these dope fiends shoot that shit in their arms, their legs, their necks, everywhere where there's a vein. That scared the mess out of me. I don't do any of that because that's how it all starts, he told me. So he gives me and buys me anything that I want, as long as I stay away from drugs and out of trouble. He told me I can be anything that I wanted, and I believe him."

Jessica never would have imagined a person like Kenny had such morals. Every good looking boy she'd met prior to him reveled in the fact that they used drugs. "So what is it that you'd like to become someday?"

He didn't have to think long about it. "A real estate developer. I want to be the biggest real estate owner in Harlem. That's why I respect you and your parents for owning their own property."

Jessica smiled and said, "So your uncle did teach you something good."

Kenny smiled and nodded. "My uncle drilled it into my head for so long, I guess it stuck," he joked. "What about you? What do you want to become?"

Jessica folded her arms. "Well, I like people—you know, helping people—so I'll probably get into the medical field. Me and my friends are all going away to college when we graduate this year. I'm looking forward to getting out of Harlem and maybe going to an all-black college down south."

"So, that means I'm going to have to come visit you someday."

Jessica was flattered. They both smiled and stared into each other's eyes momentarily, secretly hoping the night wouldn't end.

"Jessica, I know this might be too soon for me to ask, but do you think we can see each after this party? You know, maybe catch a movie or get something to eat?"

Jessica was so excited she wanted to explode, but she held it all in. She decided to take Vonda's advice again and separate herself from all the girls he was used to messing with.

"I'll think about it."

Kenny could not believe his ears again. For the first time in his life, he was baffled, yet intrigued, by a girl and wanted to get to know her even more.

Suddenly, the DJ cut the music and announced that guys should get their girls because it was time to slow dance.

Kenny looked at Jessica with uncertainty. "Jessica, you said you would dance with me later. Can we dance now?"

Jessica nodded. "Yes, I'd like to dance with you."

He stood up, took her by the hand, and led her to the middle of the dance floor. Pulling her into his arms, they danced like it would be their last chance.

While Jessica was dancing, she noticed her friend Vonda was in the arms of her newfound love, Stevo. When she and Vonda locked eyes, they winked at each other. Then Vonda gestured with her head behind her, and Jessica saw that Lynn was also dancing and getting it on with a boy as they slow danced to the love song.

When Tiny arrived back at the party, her eyes searched around for her friends, and when she spotted Jessica and Kenny dancing in the middle of the floor, she smiled cynically and had a seat in the corner of the room and waited—waited for all hell break loose.

After they danced and chatted through three love songs, Jessica's panties became so moist that she had excuse herself. She told Kenny that she had to go to the bathroom to freshen up. Vonda and Lynn did the same and followed her to girl-talk. They entered the tiny bathroom, locked the door, and began to scream and jump up and down for their new love interests.

"Oh, my God, Jessica. Stevo asked me out for a date."

Lynn quickly added, "Oh, shoot, the boy that I met name is Devin and he asked me the same thing."

Then they turned their attention back to their homegirl Jessica and she also nodded and said, "He said he wants to go out with me too."

The three girls hugged and jumped up and down a little more.

Vonda suddenly had a fantastic thought. "Oh, shoot! Maybe they can be our dates to our prom."

The girls were temporarily frozen in place until Jessica said, "They say dreams do come true if you only believe."

They all squealed and said, "I believe, I believe."

They finally managed to pull themselves together, regain their composure and fix their faces and clothing. After a brief inspection of one another, they were ready to seize their men. When they opened the door, the first thing they noticed was that the music was no longer playing and the lights were turned on. The second thing they noticed when they stepped into the living room stopped their hearts. It was Mrs. Jones. Jessica's mother.

The whole room was silent. When Mrs. Jones spotted her daughter, she walked straight up to her and said, "You lying whore," then slapped her viciously across her face.

Everyone in the room shuddered and cringed as her mother continued beating her while they walked out the front door. Sadly, everyone in the room began laughing loudly as Lynn, Vonda and Kenny stood by and felt responsible for her unfortunate incident. They were heartbroken.

Tiny however, stood in the corner reveling in Jessica's misfortune with a wicked smile.

Chapter 4

The incident at the party would long be remembered as a disaster, and the Jessica situation became the talk of the town. Jessica was so embarrassed that she became withdrawn and shallow and wanted nothing to do with the outside world—even Kenny. The fact that her mother put her on a two-week punishment suited her just fine, because, she thought, the fewer people who saw her face, the better.

Vonda and Lynn suspected Tiny had a hand in sabotaging their big evening. She denied everything at all costs, but they didn't believe her. Even though they still allowed Tiny to roll with them to school, she was treated like an outcast, especially from her longtime friend, Vonda. For the next few weeks, the four still went to school together, but none of the three girls said a word to Tiny.

Tiny felt really bad because she knew she took it too far this time. She knew that something had to be done to make up for her selfish behavior, but she didn't have a clue how to make things right.

During that time, Jessica's heart craved to see Kenny, but she could no longer face him because of the incident that left her so embarrassed. So she simply made up her mind to forget about him because he wouldn't want to see her either.

One day, the girls exited the building right after school let out, and there stood Kenny Duboise, in the flesh. Jessica was so surprised that she could hardly breathe, or move, for that matter. He stood proud and tall as soon as he saw her step out of the school. Jessica regained her composure and proceeded toward him. Vonda, Tiny, and Lynn stood by, watching it all unfold. In front of him now, Jessica smiled uneasily, still pretty much embarrassed about what had happened at the party. She was unsure of what to say and was glad when he finally spoke, breaking the uncomfortable silence lingering around them.

"Hi."

She asked, "How are you?"

He nodded and repeated, "I'm good, I'm good."

They both found it awkward for the moment until Jessica asked, "What are you doing down here?"

"I came to see you."

She searched his beautiful face. "I mean, how did you know where I went to school? I didn't tell you what school I went to."

Kenny gestured to her three friends who stood behind her and said, "Tiny told me."

Jessica was taken aback for a moment turned and looked at Tiny.

Tiny nodded back.

Kenny asked, "You think we can ride home together so we can talk?"

Jessica looked back at her friends, who must have read her mind.

Vonda walked up to them and said, "Hi, Kenny."

He smiled and answered, "Hey Vonda, how you doing? I hear Stevo is taking you to your prom. That's nice."

She blushed and nodded. "Yeah, he said he was going to take me." Vonda turned toward Jessica and continued, "Yo, me, Tiny, and Lynn gonna go ahead and go down to 34th Street to check out some shoe stores for the prom. We get up with you tomorrow, ok?"

"Ok." Jessica gave her a hug.

The three girls waved to the couple as they passed by, then suddenly Tiny stopped and walked over to Jessica but, avoided eye contact.

"Jessica, I'm . . ." She turned speechless and awkward until Jessica said, "It's all right, Tiny. Thanks."

Tiny looked up in Jessica's eyes and said, "Jessica, I may not always be there for you when you want me, but I will always be there for you when you need me."

Jessica nodded and they embraced. As soon as they pulled apart, Tiny ran off and caught up with Vonda and Lynn.

Jessica turned her attention back to Kenny and said, "Well, it looks like it's me and you."

He smiled, took her by her hand, and walked slowly toward the train station headed to Harlem.

Over the next couple of weeks, Jessica and Kenny were together almost all the time, as he met her at the train station on 135th Street and Lenox daily. Even though they hadn't been together long, it seemed like a lifetime to Jessica and she felt totally comfortable whenever she was around him. On this particular day, he asked her the ultimate question as they stood in front of her parents' building.

"Jessica, we been seeing each other for a while now, right?"

Jessica smiled and nodded, not sure where he was going with the conversation.

"Anyway . . ." He paused briefly and looked down at his feet. "I was wondering if you'd like to be with me. You know, be my girl."

Jessica was stunned. It was as if she was outside herself watching a movie. She was totally taken by surprise by the question. She knew Kenny liked her, but she never expected him to ask her to be exclusive so soon. She continued to search his face to see if he was joking, but there wasn't a hint of anything remotely close to being funny. He was serious.

He looked into her eyes and said, "Jessica, if you say yes, I'll make you this promise . . ." He looked at her with all the intensity in the world and spoke in French Creole. *"Mwin fe promes poum pa janm few mal, mwin pap janm few kriye, mwin fe promes poum pa janm baw kou. Se promes nan fon kem pou jistanm mouri!"*

Jessica didn't understand a word he was saying, but it sounded beautiful.

"It means, 'I promise I'll never hurt you, and never make you cry, I promise to you that I would never hit you, cross my heart . . ." He made a cross sign on his chest. "And hope to die!"

That was it. He'd stolen her heart forever, and there was no way for her to resist any longer. She knew from that moment on that he would play a major role in her future.

She said, "I just have one requirement if I was to say 'yes.'"

He immediately grew fearful, praying he could live up to her request. "What is it?"

Jessica smiled. "Will you take me to my prom?"

He chuckled. "Yes, I would love to take you to your prom." Kenny took Jessica in his arms and swung her around off her feet. When he let her down they looked into each other's eyes and slowly kissed for the very first time. They were in love.

❋ ❋ ❋

The week leading up to the prom, all the girls made heavy preparations for their big day. Even Jessica's mother seemed excited and helped her prepare for the big day by taking her shopping at Macy's. She bought Jessica an extravagant evening dress with coordinating shoes and accessories.

This is definitely going to be a night to remember, Jessica thought. She was with the right friends, the right man, and in the prime of her life. She knew that after that night she would no longer be a little girl. She would become a woman, and nothing would stop her.

Chapter 5

PROM NIGHT

JUNE 1981

The evening of the prom, the girls felt it would be better if they got dressed together and got picked up from Jessica's parents' house. Mrs. Jones invited the other parents over so they could experience and take pictures of their daughters' monumental moment.

Jessica had asked Kenny earlier if he could get one of his friends to take Tiny to the prom. He agreed and got one of his friends from the neighborhood named Calvin. Kenny even paid for Calvin's tuxedo, just so he could keep his girl happy. Tiny had never met Calvin before and was driving everyone crazy, worrying them all to death about if he was ugly or cute.

The time finally arrived when the doorbell rang. The gracious host, Mrs. Jones quickly walked over to answer the door. She looked back toward the other mothers before smiling and opening the door.

Standing at the door was Kenny, who was dressed to the teeth in a black tuxedo with a corsage in his arm. He flashed a bright smile. "Good evening, Mrs. Jones. My name is Kenneth Duboise, and I'm here to take Jessica to the prom."

Mrs. Jones was taken aback by the handsome, well-mannered young man. She thanked him and graciously invited him and the other boys, who had walked up behind him, into her home. The other young men introduced themselves as they entered and Mrs. Jones went about introducing them to everyone parents. Jessica's mother excused herself and told them she would tell the girls their dates were there.

Ten minutes later, the girls descended the stairs. It was if four angels were exiting the gate of heaven. All eyes followed their every move. Tears flowed freely from the parents, and the boys' mouths dropped agape.

One by one, each girl walked over to their respective dates. The boys greeted them and placed their corsages on their wrists. Cameras were flashing a mile a minute to preserve and immortalize the moment as a chapter of their lives.

Tiny instantly clung to Calvin. Her prayers were answered from God in the best way possible—he was fine. Not only was he cute, he was almost equal her size in height—with her pumps on, of course—making them look like the perfect couple.

Lynn and Vonda, equally content with their dates, were ready to show all the other girls at school what they were working with. And then there was Jessica. Nothing else had ever come close to how she felt at that present moment. Jessica felt like a real woman for the first time in her life as she stood before her mother and father with the first boy they'd ever seen her with, and she felt proud. They posed for another twenty minutes before they finally exited the house and climbed into the awaiting limousine the four guys chipped in to rent.

When they arrived at the Astor Park Ballroom in the Village, the four couples made a spectacular entrance as all eyes rained upon them. The girls proudly flaunted their dates in front of all their soon-to-be-former classmates. They became the envy of the night as they danced and romanced the entire night away. Nobody wanted the night to end as all the couples separated to their own little corners, their own little worlds.

As the night began to wind down, each girl knew they were coming upon the biggest moment in their brief lifetime—they would all lose their virginity. The girls had discussed this matter for months, some even for years, and in a matter of hours the elusive fantasy would finally come true. All the girls were so nervous they began to tremble. Finally, the night came to an end, and the girls met up in the bathroom to discuss their fate.

In a circle, each girl stood before each other in ominous silence as the reality of the matter materialized.

Vonda was the first to speak as she looked from face to face, "So, y'all, what's up? What we gonna do?"

Tiny spoke up and said, "I don't know about y'all, but I'm ready to get busy with that nigga Calvin, yo."

There were nervous smiles all around.

"I ain't gonna lie; I ain't never felt for a dude before like I'm feeling for that nigga Stevo." Vonda reached for her neck. "Look what this nigga done brought me, yo. An 18-carat solid gold necklace and pendant."

All three girls got up close and admired her new jewelry.

"Plus," Vonda continued, "all the money that them niggas spent on the limo, tuxedo, corsages, and everything. If ever a nigga deserved to get some, these niggas do. What y'all think?" She looked at Lynn and asked, "What's up, Lynn?"

Lynn still looked unsure and suddenly said, "I'm scared to death, but I think I'm ready to get it over with."

Vonda and Tiny smiled, and then all eyes focused on their remaining homegirl—Jessica.

"Well, Jesse? It's all on you now, what's up?"

The intensity at that moment was so thick that you could feel electricity course through the air, as they awaited the final verdict on what would surely change their lives.

Finally, Jessica said, "I think I'm ready, too."

All the girls were so happy that the decision was unanimous they could hardly contain themselves. When the weight of the unknown was behind them, they now had to plan a course of action to make it become a reality.

"Ok," said Vonda, "here's what we gonna do: We all gonna go to the same hotel and leave together. Since we won't have no limousine service after they drop us off at the hotel, we got to take a cab back home."

Jessica frowned and said, "That don't make no sense to take four cabs home."

"I know; that's why I said we all leave the hotel together. They take one and we'll take one. That way, we all don't have to wait till tomorrow to find out from each other what happened. Make sense?"

All agreed with a nod and a smile.

Vonda said, "We could ask the cab driver to drop us off on a neutral corner on Seventh Avenue, that way any of us won't have far to walk, bet?"

Everyone looked at her and said, "Bet!"

With a sly smile, Lynn stuck out her fist and said, "Get it girls?"

One by one, each stuck out her fist and said in unison, *"Get It Girls!"*

They headed out the bathroom in a single file when Vonda stopped short and said, "Remember, don't tell them we want to go to the hotel. Let them ask us first. We don't want them to think we that easy." She looked specifically at Tiny and said, "You got that, Tiny? Let them ask us first."

Tiny nodded quickly and they exited the bathroom.

One hour later, the limousine dropped the four couples out on 45th street at the Marriott Hotel in Times Square. Twenty minutes after that, the four young couples received the keys to their respective rooms and everyone went into Kenny and Jessica's room first to have a night cap of champagne and a little weed to calm their nerves.

Kenny was the only one of the boys who didn't drink or smoke. Neither did Jessica, but on that night Jessica had a couple glasses of champagne just to calm her nerves. They laughed, joked, and lived it up until Tiny and her date Calvin bid their farewells and were the first to retire to their room. Seconds later, Vonda, Stevo, Lynn, and Ronald said their goodbyes as well and retired to their rooms.

All alone now, Kenny took Jessica in his arms and slowly they began kissing. When they pulled away, they stared into each other's eyes and knew that this would be night neither one of them would ever forget.

Kenny slowly began unzipping her dress while his hand began rubbing her breasts. A tingling wave of electricity shot through her body and she'd already released her second orgasm before she even noticed. Jessica, nude down only to her panties, stood nervously watching the most beautiful boy she ever laid her eyes starting to undress. He switched off the bedside light, removed her soaked panties, and lay down next to her.

The warmth of their nude skin touching felt ever so remarkable, she thought. Kenny's hands and fingers began to explore every inch of her body as her breathing began to quicken. He used one of his fingers and penetrated her virginal canal as rivers of milky white liquid began to flow. At last, the moment had come, and Kenny began to mount her. At the same moment, Jessica stopped him and asked, "Kenny?"

Panting heavily, he answered, "Yes, Jessica?"

"Do you love me?"

He placed a soft kiss on her lips and answered, "Mwen remen ou."

Jessica took him by his waist and feverishly pulled his body into hers.

Chapter 6

The girls rode the cab back to Harlem in silence, and not a single word was spoken. Each was in her own little world because tonight was unlike any other—they were all now women. They remembered all the rumors they heard from other girls about their first sexual encounter—how the experience would be like no other. That it would be a moment to jump up and down about and tell their best friends that they were now a woman and share every intimate detail, right down to the size of their partner's penis. But, as they now knew, it was something much more than that. It was a personal memory that they would hold dear as they relived the tender moment, over and over again until the day they died.

When they finally arrived in Harlem, they paid for the cab and exited on 7th Avenue and 125th. The breezy pre-summer night air flowed pleasingly through their hair and faces. It was then that the first words were spoken. Vonda looked at her girls and asked, "Are you guys all right?"

One by one, a small smile came over their faces, and Tiny broke the humdrum and said, "I think I'm in love." It was now in the open, and each girl agreed that they too were in love. Now was the moment they began to shed tidbits of information about their new suitors as the spring in their step gave them an extra bounce and extra flair.

"So," said Vonda, "what was it like?" She looked at Tiny first, who smiled widely,

"Yo, when he first put that shit in, I said, 'take that motherfucker out!'"

All the girls began laughing as she continued. "But he kept telling me to calm down and I said 'I'm trying,' but that shit was hurting like a son of a bitch."

They looked at Tiny, who was still silent and Vonda asked, "Then what happened, bitch?"

Tiny snapped out of her fantasy and said, "Then, all of the sudden, I felt it going in and then he had all that shit in me pumping hard as hell, then after while, yo, I ain't lying, that shit began feeling good as motherfucker."

All the girls began to laugh again.

Vonda looked at Lynn. "What about you, Lynn? How was it?"

Lynn had a hollow stare then said, "It was kinda icky. I tried to get into it, but I wasn't feeling nothing but discomfort." She shrugged her shoulders and folded her arms. "It wasn't all what I thought it would be." Lynn then put on a sly smile and admitted, "But when he started licking it? Oh shit! I went crazy!"

Everyone stopped in place and asked, "He ate you out?"

Lynn nodded her head coyly.

Suddenly, they turned their attention toward Jessica and

Vonda asked, "It's on you, Jess? How did you like it?"

Jessica thought about it for a moment and walked as if she was walking on clouds until finally she simply said, "It was as endearing and as personal as I thought it would be, and I think I'm truly in love."

The girls waited for her to continue, but she didn't. She only added, "That's all I'm going to say about that."

"Come on, Jessica. This is pretty boy Kenny we talking about. Is he as good as all the rumors?" Vonda persisted.

"What he and I shared was really special, and I don't want to cheapen it by going into details." Jessica continue to stroll down the block as images of her first time swam around her head. Each time she thought about Kenny touching her, butterflies fluttered around in her stomach. She'd never imagined her first time to be so fantastic.

"There you go again," Tiny said with a smirk. "Jess, you with your girls. It's not like we're going to tell anyone. What's said between us stays between us."

"It's not just that. It's . . . it's just that I can't even seem to find the words . . ." she trailed off, looking toward the sky as if there she would find the answer there.

They nodded, choosing not to persist anymore and remained quiet until Tiny shifted her eyes over toward Vonda. "It's on you Vonda."

Vonda looked at Jessica before she answered and said, "Everything Jessica said."

All the girls began chiding her, but respected her secrecy. A sudden and mysterious feeling overcame them all as they now stepped through the threshold of womanhood. They held hands to show a form of liberation and began singing Evelyn "Champagne" King's song. *"Ain't no doubt about it, I'm in love!"* They were all in such bliss their common sense took a back seat to the elation they were feeling.

They rejoiced on their way home and felt as if they were now ready to take on the world. They finished high school and were looking forward to their graduation ceremony, finally being on their own, and living by their own rules when they would go off to college.

But their joy came to a dramatic halt when they realized that right in front of them was Cookie and most of her crew. Only Kimmi was absent. Panic overcame them all, and their first instinct was to run, but the long dresses and the high heels that they wore told them otherwise. Cookie, Denise, Tay-Tay, and Nikki had them surrounded in a matter of seconds and quickly pulled out switchblades. None of the girls could believe what was happening and couldn't even react.

"Look what the fuck we have here!" spewed the smiling ringleader, Cookie.

Before they could even make a plea, the four of them had the razor-sharp blades to their throats. The girls were shoved so violently that the heels on their shoes began to break away as the five girls pushed them into the closest building they could find. In the rear of the building's landing, they were pushed up against the wall with the deadly blades still pressed against their bodies.

Cookie stared at Lynn's cleavage lustfully before snatching her handbag from off of her shoulder. She rummaged through it in search of money, but found little. She came across a book of matches and read it. "The Marriott Hotel?" She leered at Lynn. "Y'all bitches just came back from fucking?"

She tossed the matches and the other unnecessary items to the floor and pocketed the money. Cookie turned her attention toward Tiny and sneered, unleashing a vicious punch to her face. Tiny's eye began to swell to the size of a small plum before she could hit the floor. Jessica and Vonda made an attempt to avenge their friend, but the knives pressed to their throats prevented them from doing anything.

"Talk that shit now, you li'l bitch," taunted Cookie. She spat on Tiny, who cradled her eye as she squirmed on the floor in agonizing pain. "Y'all bitches thought that this shit was over? Like you gonna talk shit and we gonna let you get away with it?" She stared at Lynn, who was already crying and trembling, and punched her too.

"Please, don't hit me," Lynn begged as she threw her hands over her face to prevent it from happening again.

"Yo, Cookie," pleaded Vonda, "why the fuck you got to be hitting my girls? They ain't do shit to you."

Cookie's frown turned harder, and she approached Vonda and put the knife in her face. "Who the fuck are you to tell me what I should do, bitch?" Cookie edged the point of the knife up Vonda's nostril. "Say one more motherfuckin' word and see if I don't cut your fuckin' nose off."

Vonda looked into her eyes, knowing that Cookie would make good on her threat, and chose to remain silent. It pained Jessica and Vonda to watch their friends being beaten, but there was nothing that they could do. Vonda vowed that when she out of her precarious position, she would get her brothers to track them down so she could whip each and every one of their asses for pulling knives on them. She was sure of it.

Cookie removed the knife from Vonda's nose and surveyed all four helpless girls. It seemed the more fear they showed, the more powerful she became. Cookie nudged her friend with her elbow and asked, "Yo, Denise, what the fuck you think we should we do with these bitches?"

Denise, who had a knife pressed up against Jessica's throat answered sadistically, "Let's cut one of their faces off and send a message to these other hoes."

Lynn squealed involuntarily.

Cookie folded her arm, tapped the blade against her head, and then smiled wickedly. "No, I got a better idea." She chuckled and looked down at Lynn with lust in her eyes then turned to her friends and stated, "Yo, remember what we made those bitches from the Eastside do?"

A sickening smile came over all their faces as they nodded their heads knowingly. Cookie turned her attention back to Vonda, Jessica, Lynn, and Tiny. Her eyes fell upon Lynn again and she demanded, "Get on ya knees and start sucking this pussy."

Lynn began crying louder at the thought of it.

Denise began to rub her pelvis up against Jessica, then placed her hand across her breasts and said, "Oh, Cookie, I want this one. She's the baddest one out of all of them," as she examined Jessica up and down.

"Not me," Cookie replied. "I like my bitches thick. Take that bitch into the corner."

Nikki grabbed Lynn by her arm and shoulders and tossed her down to the ground in the corner. Lynn called out to Vonda and Jessica for help, but they were powerless. There was simply nothing they could do at that moment with the knives at their throats.

Cookie told Tay-Tay to watch Tiny and walked over to Lynn, who had started to cry out of control. Nikki returned to Vonda, grabbed her from behind, and held the kinfe in place just millimeters from her throat.

"Shut the fuck up!" Cookie undid the zipper of her jeans and approached Lynn, who was on her knees pleading for her not to do that. "Start licking this pussy, bitch!"

"Please, don't. I'm begging you," Lynn tearfully pleaded.

Cookie suddenly unleashed a vicious slap to her face and threatened, "If I have to ask you one more time what to do, I'm gonna cut your fucking titties off!" Cookie grabbed a handful of Lynn's hair and buried her face into her crotch.

Jessica and Vonda squeezed their eyes closed, feeling totally helpless.

Moments later you could hear Cookie moaning. "Oh, shit, this bitch got it going on. Ooh, lick that shit, bitch. Lick it!" After few more minutes, she shifted her attention toward Tiny and ordered Tay-Tay, "Put her on her fuckin' knees too."

"No!" Tiny screamed in panic.

Tay-Tay attempted to grab her and force her to her knees, but Tiny's nimble body and small frame allowed her to slip free. Tiny quickly kicked off her heels and made a run for it out the building's front door with Tay-Tay chasing behind her. The diversion gave Vonda and Jessica enough time to catch their assailants off guard and make a grab for their knives. Vonda fought Cookie and Nikki at same time, proving to be too much for the both of them as she kicked and punched them as if her life depended on it. Jessica and Denise fought viciously for control of the knife. Jessica held on to the Denise's hand, refusing to let it go. As they fought, Jessica suddenly lost her balance from the high heels and they both fell backwards awkwardly to the ground with the Denise landing on top of her. The struggle came to an abrupt halt followed by a blood-curdling scream. It was so loud that it caused Vonda, Nikki, and Cookie to stop in their tracks and stare at the two girls on the floor. Denise slowly began rising to her feet. Jessica remained still as her face and white prom dress were saturated with blood.

Vonda immediately broke free of Nikki, went into panic mode, and rushed over to her friend's side. "Jessica!" Vonda screamed. "Oh my God, Jessica, tell me where she stabbed you at?"

Jessica said nothing and only stared back. Vonda continued to check her fallen friend's bodily injuries and that's when she spotted Jessica gripping a bloody knife tightly in her hand.

Everyone's attention fell upon Denise. It was then that she slowly turned around, holding her neck region. They watched in dread as Denise gasped for a breath with an overflow of blood spewing from her fingers like a water pump. The girl's eyes pleaded for help as she stepped drearily toward her partners in crime, but they were too shocked to offer her any assistance. It was obvious by the amount of blood streaming from her neck that her jugular had been severed. It appeared she wanted to speak, but the only sound that came out was sickening, gurgling sound as blood began to fill her throat and lungs. She stumbled to the ground and made a feeble attempt back to her feet, but lost her balance again and fell headfirst into a wall before finally collapsing into Lynn's arms.

Lynn screamed in sheer terror and panic from all the blood that began seeping on her. She pushed Denise's body away, backed into a nearby corner, and screamed as if she were losing her mind. Nobody moved or reacted, still too shocked to comprehend what was happening. They watched the fallen girl twitch violently before her body became deathly still.

Cookie and Nikki immediately retreated out of the building, leaving their fallen friend behind. As Vonda was helping Jessica to her feet, suddenly a door to one of the apartments opened and an elderly man yelled, "What's going on out here?"

Jessica and Vonda were still too shocked to respond, and the elderly man's eyes grew even wider when he surveyed the grisly hallway, with smeared in blood all over floor and walls. But, when he saw the bloodied, lifeless body sprawled across his hallway floor his mouth dropped. He turned to look in the other girls' direction and saw Jessica, with a bloodied face and clothing, holding a knife. He slammed the door immediately, locking it behind him and the girls heard him yell from behind the door, "Clara, call the police!"

The building's front door suddenly flew open, startling Jessica, Vonda, and Lynn. It was Tiny, who came back with a broken-off beer bottle in her hand. Tiny approached them cautiously, and it was then that she noticed the blood filled crime scene and body lying on the floor. Tiny dropped the jagged weapon as her hands flew over her mouth and she began to throw up violently.

When the police finally arrived they did a full investigation of the crime scene and spoke to all the tenants who lived in the building, including the 911 callers. As a squadron of uniformed police and detectives did their investigation, the coroner hauled the body of twenty-year old Denise Jackson to the city morgue. The detectives took pictures and blood samples from Jessica, Vonda, and Lynn's clothing for evidence to build a case against the four other girls being sought.

Soon after the police arrived, the four girls were taken the station to give their statements and go through mug shots. The girls were allowed to call their parents, who came down to the precinct immediately. Once the parents arrived, the police started taking their statements since they were all underage. They questioned the girls for several hours before they were finally released to the custody of their parents under the strict contingent they not leave town and would be available for more questioning as the need arose.

❋❋❋

Jessica's mother and father consoled her in the days following the incident and could never imagine how traumatizing the event must have been on her. Jessica was torn to pieces knowing she took the life of an individual no matter if it was an accident or not. She explained to them everything that led up to the event, only leaving out the part about the hotel.

Vonda, Jessica, Tiny, and Lynn talked on the phone daily and agreed to stay consistent with the story to protect themselves from their parents finding out they had sex in a hotel. They vowed that whatever happened, they would not tell the authorities or anyone else about it.

Several days later they were informed that the ring leader, Cookie, had finally been arrested and refused to give the authorities a statement about the two other suspects.

Exactly one week after that fateful night, Vonda, Jessica, Lynn, and Tiny attended graduation and received their diplomas. After the ceremony, they were outside taking pictures with their now former classmates and families when they were approached by the two New York City detectives who had originally taken their statements the night of the murder, along with two uniformed officers, who informed them that they were all being arrested for the murder of Denise Jackson.

The girls were at loss for words as the detectives produced their handcuffs to arrest them in front of their family, classmates, and onlookers. Each girl's family member grew alarmed and confused at what was going down and refused to allow the detectives to touch their loved ones, especially Jessica's father.

"My name is Mr. Jones. What do want with my daughter? She didn't do anything," he protested and moved in front of her.

"Sir," responded the tall white detective, "we have a warrant issued for the arrest of . . ." He paused and read the names on the arrest warrant. ". . . Claresse Maynard, Lynise Davis, Vonda Williams, and Jessica Jones."

Mr. Jones pleaded, "No, there's got to be some kind of mistake. My daughter did nothing wrong. She—"

The detective rudely cut him off before he finished. In his experience, it was better to make a quick arrest and let them deal with the court system. "Sir, what you need to do is step to the side before you are arrested for obstruction." He pushed Mr. Jones aside with a forearm, and the people in the crowd expressed their displeasure toward his callous behavior.

As the officers approached the remaining girls, Vonda's mother immediately cursed them loudly. "Don't even think about putting you fucking hands on my daughter, motherfucker!"

A loud cheer erupted from the crowd. The situation grew even tenser when the officers saw Vonda's three huge brothers surround their baby sister, ready to challenge the officers by any means necessary.

One uniformed officer had the good sense to radio in for assistance. The second detective, black and in his late forties, decided to play peacemaker to circumvent his partner's insensitive behavior. "We are only doing our job. If you want to be heard, you will have to see the judge at this point and all will be straightened out if they are innocent like you say. Trust me, you don't want to do this." He turned his attention to Vonda's mother and assured her, "I'll ensure that they are taken care of before their arraignment. The best thing you can do right now is get them a lawyer and arrange bail, and she will be out sooner than you think."

Mr. Jones searched his eyes and had no choice but to believe him. He nodded and hugged his daughter and told her she would be ok and he would get her out soon. The other officers then stepped in to handcuff them, but the black detective waved him off and, for the sake of their parents, simply escorted them to the cruisers.

Reality set in when Jessica, Vonda, Tiny, and Lynn were taken to the precinct and booked, photographed, fingerprinted, and thrown into a holding cell. Each girl cried and pleaded to the police officers that there must be some mistake and they hadn't done anything wrong. But their pleas fell on deaf ears as the robotic officers only told them to "Tell it to the judge."

After being processed, they were taken by van to central booking. It was if they were dreaming when they arrived handcuffed inside the huge ominous and decaying processing center. When they entered the bowels of the hub, it was then that they heard the deafening sound of screaming and threats from other women prisoners because they looked like easy victims.

Finally, they reached the end of the corridor and were thrown inside a solitary, dimly lit, primitive jail cell. As a promise to their parents, the detective arranged for them to have their own cell, away from the other women. Everything looked dirty and smelled horrible inside the tiny space, and the girls were horrified when they saw large rats roam freely in and out of their cell. For the first two hours inside the filthy cell, the girls refused to even sit on the dirty and dusty benches, but after several painstaking hours, they not only found themselves sitting on the uncomfortable benches, but they found themselves lying on the filthy floors as they took turns standing watch in case a rat approached.

Finally, after nearly nineteen hour straight hours, the girls' names were called.

"Claresse Maynard, Vonda Williams, Lynise Davis, and Jessica Jones!" bellowed the burly female officer.

The girls hurriedly stood to their feet in complete happiness and answered, "Here!"

An officer opened the cell door and escorted them through a maze of underground tunnels that seemed to go on forever. They were placed in yet another holding cell and were met by their lawyers a half hour later.

Vonda, Lynn, and Tiny had public defender, Isaac William

defending them, while Jessica was seen by a private attorney, Donovan Butler, hired by her family. As courtesy, the two lawyers took notes together with all four girls present to ensure that they would all have the same strategy anticipating bail, then spoke to their clients separately at the end. They decided that they had a greater chance of painting a clearer picture if the girls were tried together instead of separately.

The lawyers explained their charges and court procedures to them. The girls anxiously told the attorneys their side of the story, that they didn't start it and they were only defending themselves. They felt they were the victims. The attorneys wrote down everything they were saying and assured them everything would be ok. They were told that their names were already on the docket and it wouldn't be long before they saw the judge.

As promised, the four girls were led inside the court room only minutes later. The girls' terror-filled eyes darted and scanned the court room when they finally entered, looking for the familiar faces of their loved ones.

Ten minutes after entering the courtroom they were led in front of the judge. Standing before the judge with their lawyers standing beside them, the girls were trembling as they waited for the judge to finish reading the dockets. Finally he addressed them.

"Have you all been advised of your rights?"

The girls nodded. "Yes, sir."

"You have been charged with section 125.25-Murder in the second degree."

None of the girls could believe what they were hearing. Their knees suddenly became weak, and a shriek from their parents resonated from behind them, filling the air. Lynn lost the battle and collapsed to the floor. She had to be lifted back to her feet by her attorney.

Pandemonium ensued in the background as their parents lost control and tearfully voiced their displeasure. The judge called for order. Three court officers approached the offending parties and warned them that they faced expulsion if they didn't settle down.

When the room finally settled to his satisfaction, the judge turned his attention back toward the girls and continued. "Will each defendant state your name and enter your plea?"

In order, each girl stated their name and pleaded not guilty. "Ok," stated the judge, "in the matter of bail, Mr. Rickman, does the State have an opinion on bail?"

Mr. Rickman, a short, thin man with horn rimmed glasses, quickly responded, "Yes, your Honor, the State of New York request that bail be set at fifty thousand dollars each in light of the severity of the crime."

There was another brief outburst from the seats behind them where their parents sat, but it quickly waned.

Jessica's lawyer hurriedly stepped forward and made his rebuttal. "Your Honor, my name is Donovan Butler, from the law firm of Garret, Holden, and Butler, located at 189 Greenwich Street, representing Jessica Jones."

Vonda, Lynn, and Tiny's lawyer followed suit and entered his name for the record also.

Mr. Donovan continued. "Your Honor, my client comes from a stable home, and her mother and father are in the courtroom with her today." He turned and pointed them out to the judge before continuing. "My client has just graduated from a Catholic high school and received a partial scholarship to go to a prestigious college in Atlanta this fall. Her parents own their own property right here in the city, and both have been stable, productive city and government employees for over twenty years each. The fact that all the defendants, at the time of the incident, waited for the proper authority to arrive shows their character and innocence, I may add. I request that Miss Jones be released on her own recognizance."

Vonda, Lynn, and Tiny's attorney basically repeated the same thing and also requested that the girls be released on recognizance.

The judge stared sullenly at the four young girls, then at the weary eyed parents behind them. "Bail is set at five thousand dollars each."

Chapter 7

Since the bond was only five thousand dollars, the girls' parents only had to post five hundred dollars, which was ten percent of the bail. One hour later, all the girls were released.

Both lawyers told them that if everything checked out, the case probably wouldn't make it past the grand jury. Lynn asked what the grand jury was.

Attorney Williams explained it. "It's a body of elected jurors who are presented the information on the case and given facts. They then weigh whether or there is enough body of evidence to seek prosecution. In this case, it shows that the other parties were the aggressors, and that you were only defending yourselves at the time of Denise's death. If you've told us everything, there's an excellent chance of the charges being dropped and thrown out."

They were given their date to show up back to court, and the lawyers promised to stay in touch and that they could be reached by phone if they had any more questions.

By the time Jessica and her family got home that night, they were exhausted. Jessica never realized how good she had it until getting home and into her own bed. It was a far cry from the uncomfortable concrete floor or wood benches in the jail cell she was in for nearly twenty-four hours.

Since school had ended, Jessica spent the next few days home alone in bed. Each time she'd wake up hoping it was all just a bad dream and that it had never happened. But each time she would wake up and realize that she wasn't dreaming, she cried herself back to sleep again. Then one day, her mother told her she had a phone call—it was from Kenny.

"Hey, Jessica, this is Kenny. How are you doing, baby?"

Jessica paused and looked up toward the ceiling, blinking back the tears, unsure how to answer. "Kenny, I don't know if you heard, but . . . me and the rest of the girls got into an incident the night of the prom and . . ." Jessica's voice began to crack.

"I know, Jessica. You don't have to explain. Stevo talked to Vonda and she told him all about it. I'm just so sorry it had to happen. It was my fault. I should have made sure you got home like I was supposed to . . ."

Jessica leaned up against the wall closest to her and shook her head. "No, it's not your fault, Kenny. You had no way of knowing what was going on."

Kenny closed his eyes, genuinely concerned that he had a part in her predicament.

"But, I . . ." said Kenny as his voice cracked, "I should have been there for you, and I feel bad that it had to go down like that. I could've been there to protect you. You are my girl."

Jessica lost her fight to hold back her tears. "You still want to be with me even though you know what happened?"

He quickly answered, "Yes, baby. It wasn't your fault, and you got to believe that. It was an accident. An accident," he repeated. "The court's going to see that and everything will be ok. You'll see."

Jessica put her hand over her mouth and began to cry even more. She knew that Kenny really loved her and it made her feel better to know he was still in her corner.

"I love you, Kenny," she whispered into the phone.

"*Mwen remen ou*, Jessica."

Two weeks later, Jessica and her parents received the call that they were waiting for from their attorney, Donovan Butler. He told them that he had to meet with them in his office immediately to discuss matters surrounding the case. They scheduled an appointment for the following day. The expression on his face was somber as he welcomed them in to have a seat in his office.

He got straight to the point and said, "Mr. and Mrs. Jones, Jessica, I'm afraid to tell you this but that grand jury had voted to indict Jessica and the other girls on second degree murder charges."

They closed their eyes and shifted uneasily in their chairs.

Jessica's father asked, "How could that be? My daughter and her friends were the victims here, and they were being assaulted. This isn't fair."

"I know, Mr. Jones, but at this point the grand jury found enough substantiation to go forward in the case with the evidence that was presented to them."

Mrs. Jones inquired suspiciously, "What evidence?"

"Well," their attorney answered, "the police recovered the knife that was involved. It had Jessica's fingerprints on it, along with the deceased girl's blood type, and the dead girl blood was ot only on Jessica's person, but . . ." he put on his glasses and read from the indictment and continued, "Vonda's and Lynise's body and clothing as well. They even have a statement from the girl who was originally arrested and eventually cleared on all charges."

Infuriated, Mrs. Jones questioned, "What do you mean cleared of all charges? She was the aggressor! She was the one who started all the trouble. How the hell is she going to be cleared of all charges? What about the other girls that were involved in this? Didn't they find them?"

Mr. Butler paused, pondering how to tell them that it was the least of their concerns. He clasped his hands and simply told them the truth. "Well, the other girls that were supposed to be involved were never actually substantiated. The only eyewitness remembered specifically seeing a total of four people and a deceased body on the floor. It all comes down to your words against theirs and the evidence that was left at the scene. And the other victim in this case claims that you were the aggressors that originally produced a knife."

Jessica jumped up and said furiously, "That is a lie! We didn't start anything, and that was their knives." She looked at her parents and pleaded, "Mommy, Daddy, you got to believe me. We didn't start anything; they started with us by putting the knives to our throats and throwing us in the building."

Mr. Butler put his hand up and agreed. "I believe you, Jessica, but the fact remains that the State of New York found sizable and ample enough evidence to charge you, and now it comes down to her word against yours. That's what bothers me," he said. Then he added, talking more to himself, "They must have something more concrete." He looked Jessica in the eyes before continuing, "Now Jessica," he asked sternly, "is there something, anything that you haven't told me about the case that might be pertinent for me to know before we move on? Because if you're holding anything back, it may come out in court and blow up in our faces. I just need you to be honest with me to cover all the bases."

All three looked at Jessica, awaiting her response until she finally answered, "No, I told you everything. We had problems with them in the past, and they would always bother us coming from or going to school. We went to our prom, came home, and that's when everything happened. That's it."

Mr. Butler searched her face for a moment, smiled and said, "Ok, let's move on. We'll go through everything later." He turned his attention to a folder that already had her name on it and opened it. "I received information on the victim by messenger service, just before you arrived." He began scanning the papers and began to read the aloud. "The deceased's name was Denise Jackson, twenty years old, some college and stable home with no prior arrests. Her mother was deceased since she was five and her father . . ." His sudden pause soon concerned them all. He finally looked up at the Jones and repeated, "Her father is district Councilman Jonathan Jackson." He took off his glasses and began to rub his now weary eyes.

Mr. Jones asked, "So what does that mean?"

He looked at Mr. Jones and said, "It means he's got a lot of political clout and that Jessica is in for the fight of her life." He changed the subject and got down to business. "Mr. and Mrs. Jones, this would be a better time than any to discuss trial fees. And I can tell you right now that this will go to trial and could be very costly."

Mr. Jones sat erect. "Sir, my baby's life is on the line here, whatever the cost is I will get it, even if it means taking out a second mortgage on my home."

Mr. Butler smiled, just so, and said, "Good, good. I'll have my secretary give you some papers to sign later. In the meantime, Jessica, we need to go over everything from the very beginning again. Starting from the first time you ever had a run-in with the deceased and her friends."

Jessica exhaled and started from the beginning.

THE FOLLOWING EVENING

Ring...ring...ring...
Jessica picked up the phone and said, "Hello?"

"Yo, Jessica." It was Vonda, who immediately sounded as if something was wrong. "Turn to Channel 5. We on the news."

She dropped the phone and raced to the living room where her father sat, and she saw that he was already watching the news. She shifted her attention to the television and sure enough the corresponding reporter was in Harlem in front of the same building the incident took place in.

"It was here, on a cool and breezy night when two female friends were allegedly on their way home from bible study, and it was also then where four neighborhood toughs, also females, ended the short life

of Councilman Jonathan Jackson's daughter, Denise Jackson, twenty."

They showed a picture of Denise Jackson, possibly a junior high school photo which made her look much younger and innocent.

"It was inside here, in the rear of this dimly lit Harlem tenement, where the two girls were dragged into the building at knifepoint, robbed, and ultimately, where Denise Jackson lost her life."

The scene switched to the steps of City Hall, where Councilman Jackson stood grim faced before a press conference.

"My daughter was an innocent victim of a malicious street crime, and I will do everything in my power to bring all defendants to justice for my daughter. Crimes like these are far too common, and the police department must do more to clean up the streets and put criminals like my daughter's killer away to make our streets safer to walk again. But, I promise you this, I will be right there every day, front row, center to ensure justice is delivered so my daughter's death won't be in vain. Thank you."

The next day, all the girls met up in the park on 136th and St. Nicholas by the basketball courts to discuss the case and what they'd said to their lawyers. This was the first time they were all together since getting out of Central Booking, in downtown Manhattan. The park was still empty when everyone finally arrived, so they found a bench in the corner of the park and began to make small talk. It seemed like everyone waited for Vonda to start the real discussion, but she remained silent.

For the first time since Jessica met Vonda over four years

earlier, she saw actual fear in her eyes. Jessica decided to take lead and asked, "So, what went down with your lawyer?"

Vonda looked up from where she was sitting and shrugged. "He said that we could be sentenced to ten years. That's all I heard."

Jessica stared in her eyes and it was clear that she was afraid.

Lynn stood up and began pacing. "I can't do ten years in prison. We didn't even do anything. Why is this happening to us?" she said, almost hysterically.

Tiny remained silent and only stared at the ground.

Vonda stood. "How the fuck could they turn this shit around on us to make it look like we was the ones who was robbing them? It's just not right." Jessica watched her friend wipe a tear from the side of her eyes. "I mean, we coming from our prom, our fucking prom and they think we gonna look to rob somebody in our dresses? And why they never found Tay-Tay and the two other girls? That's some bullshit!"

Seeing their leader break down caused them all to feel hopeless, so Jessica added, "Don't worry, though," she nodded, "all this is going to come out in court and we going to—"

"Going to what, Jessica?" snapped Tiny, "Going to fucking jail, that's what gonna happen!" Tiny looked at each of her friends faces and said, "That bitch that you killed, Jessica, is the daughter of a big councilman, a councilman, Jessica. That means he got juice. It ain't gonna be nothing for them to convict our black asses just for a favor to one of his judge friends, so we fucked."

Lynn began to cry louder.

"No, my lawyer said—"

Before Jessica could finish, Tiny snapped, "What, your high

paid lawyer?" She stared Jessica down. "We got a court appointed lawyer because none of our families is rich like yours, Jessica."

Jessica turned and put her head down. "Shit, who knows, your lawyer might cut you a better deal and our asses are fucked, and you was the one who killed her. We didn't do shit and we still got caught up in the murder charge for just being there."

Just hearing Tiny remind her that she actually killed someone made Jessica cringe.

Vonda had had enough and finally said, "Tiny, we wouldn't even be in this situation if you had kept your fucking mouth shut in the first fucking place. Don't forget we was trying to save you when they tried to get you on your knees. Also don't forget you ran and left us hanging. Don't think I forgot that shit!" Vonda snapped.

"I came back to help!" Tiny screamed.

Jessica held her attitude in check and tried to keep order, despite the accusation from Tiny. "Yo, we don't have time to point fingers, y'all. We got to make sure we come out of this shit as if our lives depend on it or we are all fucked, plain and simple."

Tiny took a seat and put her chin to her chest.

Seeing everybody calm, Jessica continued, "Now, the only thing I'm worried about is when my lawyer asked me to tell him everything that went down that night leading up to the incident."

Vonda looked up and asked, "What did you tell him?"

All three girls looked at Jessica for an answer and she said, "I told him everything that we did, except the hotel part."

All the girls seemed relieved. Vonda spoke, "So did we."

Jessica questioned, "But, do you think that was a good idea to leave it out? Because my lawyer said that if I left anything out it may turn around and backfire on us."

Tiny answered, "How the fuck can it backfire on us? I, mean what do us getting fucked that night got to do with what happened, Jessica?" They all thought about what Tiny said. "Shit," Tiny continued, "I don't want my moms knowing I was out fuckin that night, do you?"

Everyone seemed to agree with her rationale.

Vonda looked at Tiny and Lynn. "So we all agree, we stick by what we said, ok?"

One by one they all nodded in agreement.

"Besides, they would never find out where we were if we don't tell them," added Vonda. She stuck out her fist and said, "Agreed?"

The girls all stood up and stuck out their fists and said, "Agreed."

Kenny and Jessica met up later that day and went to Times Square to catch a movie. They were now in a barbecue restaurant having dinner. For the most part, Jessica figured Kenny was abstaining from talking about the incident until she was ready, so she decided to get it out in the open.

"Kenny," Jessica said nervously, "I know you're wondering what's going on with everything, and you have the right to know."

He looked her in the eyes and she put her head down, searching for the right words. He took her hand to show her comfort and support.

She slowly lifted her head and said, "Kenny, they charged all of us with murder, for the incident that went down that night, and we're going to take the case to trial." Jessica searched his eyes to see his reaction before continuing. "I want you to know what happened that night was not our fault and it was an accident. They pulled these knives on us and—"

"No, Jessica, you don't have to explain. I just want to let you know that I will be by your side all the way and that if you need me I will be right there for you. All you have to do is call."

Jessica just looked at Kenny with amazement. To have a man like him to still be in her corner overwhelmed her and soon she became teary eyed.

"Jessica, I love you, and if you are going through something I want to go through it with you. But you got to believe that everything is going to work out for you and the other girls. I pray for you every night since it happened, and I want you to do the same because prayer really works, but you got to have faith."

Jessica attempted to hold back her tears, but failed pitifully. Kenny stood up and sat next to her and put his arms around her for assurance. Jessica felt a deep sense of security as his strong arms filled her with warmth and confidence. She closed her eyes, hoping the moment would never end.

Chapter 8

THE TRIAL

TEN MONTHS LATER – APRIL, 1982

The girls were so nervous about the trial, none of them had slept for days leading up to their court date. The only good news they'd received since the time of the arrest was that their charges were downgraded from murder in the second degree to involuntary manslaughter, which made a significant difference in years if sentenced. This was only because Cookie had a robbery charge before as a juvenile, but her record was sealed.

They got through the first day without any problems because it was only jury selection. Their lawyers were happy about the jurors that were selected because most were parents and that could work in their favor. But, they were warned that it could also work against them because the jurors, as parents, would be sympathetic to any parent that lost a child.

Seated at the defendant's table, before a judge, fighting for their life seemed so surreal for the girls. They felt uncomfortable as all the potential jurors eyed them with disdain, probably wondering how these four young girls could have possibly committed such a heinous crime. No one but their parents occupied the rear seats as spectators, giving them a sense of security for some reason. They adjourned the trial for the next day and would be ready for opening statements.

The second day of the trial was night and day from the first because the entire courtroom was now filled to capacity as spectators and court staff milled about, waiting for the judge to enter the courtroom. Councilman Jackson was at the entrance of the courtroom just as he said would be along with a small army of reporters who took his picture as he gave his opinion of the case. Councilman Jackson purposely grandstanded the case not as a politician, but as a grieving father who was only seeking justice. Behind closed doors, he reached out to everyone who owed him a favor to ensure that the judge and district attorneys knew they were not dealing with your average murder case. Everything now would be scrutinized down to the smallest detail, and the defense knew that all the evidence and statements would play critical roles in the case. In other words, if they made one mistake, the girls would go to jail for a long time.

It didn't make the girls feel any better when Councilman Jackson shook hands with the district attorneys like they were old friends before the start of the trial. The girls looked around at all the people in the courtroom—the reporters, spectators, and court officers—and began to feel very small. Jessica's nerves were so shot that she hadn't been able to hold down an ounce of food in three days.

Finally, the judge exited his chamber as one of the burly court officers barked, "Please rise for the Honorable Harry S. Gillard."

The no-nonsense judge simply waved his hand and said in a low tone, "Be seated." He sat down in his oversized chair and went straight to his docket and opened it. He surveyed the courtroom briefly and saw that the defense and district attorneys were in place. "Are we ready to proceed?"

The D.A. smiled. "Yes, your Honor. The State is ready to proceed."

"Yes, Your Honor. Defense is ready," Vonda, Tiny and Lynn's lawyer said.

"Yes, Your Honor," repeated Jessica's lawyer, Donovan Butler.

"Ok," said the judge, "bring out the jurors."

One of the court officers went through one of the doors and seconds later, all the jurors marched out and into the juror's box to take their seats. The judge introduced himself to the jurors and briefly explained their duties as a juror and the matters surrounding the case.

After the matters were explained, the judge went straight to the case and said, "Is the counsel ready to proceed with opening statement?" He looked down at the prosecutors' table.

"We are, Your Honor. The State is ready to proceed," said the tall, thin state prosecutor, Andrew Steinberg.

By the time the prosecutor finished with his opening argument, all the girls were looked upon as monsters. He didn't hold his tongue as he sarcastically spewed his verbal venom, calling Jessica and her friends time bombs waiting to explode. He totally switched everything around and made it look as if the girls were seasoned troublemakers who went around causing havoc on anyone or anything that crossed their paths.

Jessica turned around and looked at her parents' strained faces and felt even worse as he called their daughter a killer with no regard for life. She looked to the left of her parents and even saw her man, Kenny, with his head down. It was then that she realized the state was playing for keeps and that she could really lose and go to prison for a long time. Her stomach began to bubble loudly.

Jessica's lawyer delivered his opening statement, but it did little to make her feel better. This was only the quiet before the storm, she thought.

The district attorney called upon witness after witness, mainly the police officers and detectives who showed up to the murder scene the night of the incident. Then finally, the state called Constantine Wallace. None of the girls knew who she was, but when they escorted her out, all four girls' jaws nearly dropped to the floor. It was the one and only Cookie, who'd started it all. They barely recognized her because she now wore an ankle-length dress and glasses. Her cornrowed hair was now unbraided and hung neatly down to her shoulders. She had a white prayer cap placed on top of her head. All the girls sat up in their chairs and looked at each other, baffled. They could not believe what they were seeing and grew more uneasy by the second. If they'd had any shadow of doubt on how serious it had become, it was instantly removed by seeing what length the state had gone to get a conviction. Cookie was escorted to the witness chair and sworn in by the bailiff.

"Do you swear to tell the truth, the whole truth, and nothing but the truth, so help you God?"

"I do," she said, almost in a whisper.

Mr. Steinberg walked over to where she sat and smiled. "Good afternoon."

Cookie returned the smile and repeated, "Good afternoon."

He nodded. "Can you state your full name for the record, Ms. Wallace?"

"My name is Constantine Wallace," she answered politely.

"Ms. Wallace, can you tell us what you do for a living?"

She cleared her throat. "I work at St. Mary's Church on 127th Street in Harlem."

"And what do you do at the church?"

"I organize a lot of events for the youth program we have at the church, like trips, local events, and bible study classes."

Mr. Steinberg looked at the jury to get a greater impact on the revelation. Shortly after the murder of his daughter, Councilman Jackson had strategically found the unemployed Cookie a job at the local Catholic church, thanks to a favor from a priest in his district.

Steinberg continued. "Ms. Wallace, do you know Denise Jackson?"

Cookie put her head down and played a powerful performance in front of the crowd. After a long pause, she finally answered. "Yes, she was my best friend."

Mr. Steinberg paused to let the jurors feel the volume of her words. "Are you ok, Ms. Wallace?"

She nodded.

"Do you recall an incident happening on the night of June, 10th, 1981 that involved you and Ms. Jackson?"

Cookie cleared her throat and slowly answered, "Yes."

"Can you recount to us everything that happened leading up

to that incident, Ms. Wallace?"

Cookie put her head down as the court sat in complete silence. When she lifted her head a tear could already be seen falling from her eye. "Me and my best friend Denise were returning home from bible study class at the church where I now work. We were getting home a little later than usual because we stayed behind and helped the sisters clean up and stack the chairs." She paused again. "Well," she continued, "we were walking home on 7th Avenue, talking, and that's when we were confronted by four girls."

Mr. Steinberg shifted his eyes toward the jurors. "Ms. Wallace, do you see any of the girls who confronted you that night in the courtroom today?"

"Yes."

Mr. Steinberg looked at the jurors as if he was astonished. "Ms. Wallace, can you point out to the court where they are sitting at?" For the first time she looked at the girls and raised her hand slowly and pointed them out to the court.

Mr. Steinberg snapped to attention and turned to the judge. "Let the record reflect, Your Honor, that the witness pointed out the defendants."

"Noted," said the judge.

Mr. Steinberg continued. "Ms. Wallace, was that night the first time you ever came in contact with the defendants?"

Cookie shook her head. "No, they have been harassing us for years. They even took our money before and said they going to make us pay them every time they see us."

The girls could not believe their ears. They moaned their displeasure as they listened to Cookie tell an incredible lie. Tiny could not hold back her contempt any longer, so she stood up and yelled, "She's lying!"

The court officers immediately approached her and placed her back in her seat.

The judge then warned, "Young lady, if I hear one more outburst like that I will have you removed from this court and thrown in a cell. Do you understand?"

Her lawyer spoke for her. "Yes, Your Honor. She understands."

Mr. Steinberg proceeded. "Ok, Ms. Wallace, can you continue telling us what happened after you and Ms. Jackson were confronted by the defendants on the night of the tragic incident?"

She closed her eyes and said in a slow, strained voice, "After they confronted us, they pulled out a knife and they shoved us in the building. They pushed us in the back of the building and demanded our money. I gave them mines, but Denise refused to back down to them."

The girls grew angrier by the second as they listened to her calculated lie. All of them wanted to yell out, scream, or just tell someone that she was lying, but they were helpless—again.

"That's when she," Cookie looked over at Jessica, "put the knife to her throat and . . ." Cookie lips quivered as she began to cry.

"Do you need some time, Ms. Wallace?"

She wiped her eyes with her hand and shook her head. "No."

The judge handed her a box of tissues, and she took one and said, "That's when she put the knife to her throat and pushed it in."

The courtroom let out a loud gasp.

Mr. Steinberg waited until the courtroom died down to ask, "Let the record reflect that the witness pointed out Jessica Jones, one of the four defendants, who, for the record, is wearing a white shirt and red ribbons in her hair."

Mr. Steinberg went on to ask Cookie a series of questions that directly incriminated all the girls. By the time he finished with her, she was painted as an angel who'd never done any wrong.

By the time the girls' lawyers cross-examined Cookie, the damage had already been done as Cookie resorted to single answers and denied everything they asked. The lawyers were careful to not press her too much because a sympathetic juror could turn on the defense if they felt she was being harassed. Since all the girls had clean criminal records, it was still a matter of Cookie's word against theirs, so the lawyers decided to let the girls' creditability speak for its self.

One by one, Vonda, Tiny, and Lynn told their side of the story to the jurors and answered all the questions asked by both the defense and the prosecution. The girls had done an excellent job on the stand so far, and Jessica was expected to be called last. Mr. Butler couldn't help but wonder why the prosecutor let all the girls get off so easily during the questioning. The only things he'd asked them was if they were drinking, did they do drugs, and where they were coming from prior to the incident, all which they answered.

Finally, it was Jessica's turn to testify.

"Do you swear to tell the truth, the whole truth, and nothing but the truth so help you God?"

With her right hand in the air, Jessica confidently answered, "I do."

After Mr. Butler asked Jessica to run down her version of the story, Mr. Steinberg swaggered over to her and smiled. "Good afternoon, Ms. Jones. How are you?"

Jessica smiled lightly. "I'm ok."

Mr. Steinberg nodded. "Good. Now, Ms. Jones, I have just a couple of question to ask you. Is that ok?"

She nodded.

"Prior to the incident on the night of June, 10th, could you tell the court where you were?"

Jessica edged closer to the microphone. "I was at my prom."

Jessica's lawyer had told her to keep her answers short and to the point only.

"At this prom, were you drinking any alcohol?" Mr. Steinberg asked.

"No," she answered quickly.

"Were you doing drugs at this prom?"

"No," she said, growing uneasy.

He nodded and slowly walked closer to her. "Were you and your friends, your co-defendants, drinking or doing any drugs when you were at the hotel the same night of the murder, Ms. Jones?"

The girls' eyes lit up as their mouths fell wide open. Jessica suddenly felt sick as she stared at her parents and Kenny, who had his head down. She was speechless, but Mr. Steinberg would not let up.

"Ms. Jones, I ask you again, were you and your co-defendants at a hotel, drinking and doing drugs the night of June 10th, 1981 right before Denise Jackson was murdered?"

Jessica could not move or speak. She looked toward her lawyer, who only stared back her with a dumbfounded look on his face.

Mr. Steinberg walked over to his table and picked a plastic bag and removed the contents. "Do you recognize this, Ms.

Jones?" He held up a book of matches, the same matches that were dumped from Lynn's pocketbook to the floor when they were being robbed by Cookie and her crew.

Jessica just stared at the matchbook with *Marriott Hotel* inscribed on the cover.

Mr. Steinberg held the matchbook high in the air for all to see. "Your Honor, I'd like to enter this into evidence as exhibit A-9." He turned his attention back to Jessica for the squeeze play. "Ms. Jones, were you or were you not at the Marriott Hotel having sex, drinking, and doing drugs on the same night you murdered Denise Jackson!"

"Objection, Your Honor!" yelled her lawyer as he shot to his feet.

"Sustained," said the judge. "Strike that from the record."

"Sorry, Your Honor. I'll rephrase," Mr. Steinberg said with a smile. It was already too late. The damage was done, and he knew it.

Jessica sat shaking and crying as she wrapped her arms around herself like she was holding herself from falling apart.

Mr. Butler requested, "Your Honor, can I have a few minutes with my client?"

The judge nodded. "Ok, the court will have a twenty-minute recess." He banged his gavel and hurried off to his chambers.

Jessica felt dizzy and caught between a rock and a hard place. Her worst nightmare was unfolding before her eyes as a million regrets swirled through her mind. She was caught in a lie and exposed in front of her parents and jurors. A personal and endearing secret now could put her away for years. Her parents were confused and wounded as they stood next to her lawyer who asked her what is this thing with the hotel, drinking and drugs—and he wanted the truth. Jessica closed her eyes and told her parents she was sorry and that she didn't think the hotel thing would matter.

Her lawyer exploded and said, "Wouldn't matter? Jessica, that one omission can make the difference in the whole case. We are at that point now where you may come off as a lying drug addict who committed a murder. I want you to tell me everything that happened that night without leaving so much as the color the hotel room out. Do you understand?"

Back on the witness stand, Jessica stared at both her parents and Kenny as they sat sullenly in their seats sensing the worst.

The judge ordered, "Mr. Steinberg, proceed."

Mr. Steinberg stood to his feet and continued where he'd left off and walked over to the witness stand.

"Ms. Jones, on the night of June 10th, of last year, did you and your co-defendants go to the Marriott Hotel in Times Square to have sex, do drugs, and consume alcohol?"

"Objection, your honor. Irrelevant," said Mr. Butler.

"Your Honor, I'm showing the state of mind of the defendants as well as their condition leading up to the murder."

"Overruled," said the judge.

Mr. Steinberg smiled and repeated. "Ms. Jones, I say again, on the night of June 10th, of last year, did you and your co-defendants go to the Marriott Hotel in Times Square to have sex, drink alcohol, and use drugs?"

Jessica stared at Vonda, Tiny, and Lynn's dreadful faces, then at her parents. "I didn't do any drugs."

There was another loud gasp as she watched her parents put their heads down shamefully.

Mr. Steinberg wasn't finished there. "Are you saying that you, Jessica Jones, and your three other co-defendants were at the Marriott Hotel together the same night of the murder?"

"Yes," answered Jessica.

"So, when I asked the three other co-defendants the same question they lied under oath?"

Jessica paused and looked at her friends, then at her lawyer, and finally answered, "Yes"

Mr. Steinberg smiled to the jurors and said, "Ms. Jones, I have one final question to ask you. What was the full name of your escort you to the prom?"

Her eyes quickly shifted to Kenny and toward her parents. She reluctantly answered, "Kenneth Duboise."

Kenny, sitting right next to Mr. Jones, wanted so badly to be invisible at that moment.

"Your Honor," said Mr. Steinberg as he walked over to his table, opened a folder, and pulled out a sheet of paper and continued, "I have in my hand records from the Marriott Hotel, dated June 10th, 1981, at 9:38 pm, stating that four separate rooms we rented out by a Kenneth Duboise and paid in cash." He held up the records for all to see as all the girls sank deeper into their seats.

Councilman Jackson beamed wickedly at the girls, who he felt took his only daughter's life.

As the trial continued, the D.A. presented bloody crime scene pictures, the photos of the bloodied clothing they had on that night, and lastly, the eyewitness testimony that positively identified each girl.

It only took the jury two hours to deliberate. They walked back into the courtroom in single file from out the jurors' chambers.

After they were seated, the judge asked, "Ladies and gentleman of the jury, have you reached a decision?"

"Yes, sir, we have," answered the jury foreman.

The bailiff walked over to the foreman, who handed the decision to the bailiff, who then handed it to the judge. The judge took the note and studied it, showing no emotion.

The judge looked at the girls and said, "Will the defendants please rise?" The judge handed the note back to the bailiff, who returned it to the jury foreman.

"Please read the verdict, Mr. Foreman," the judge announced.

The foreman looked at the four and unfolded the paper. "In the case of manslaughter in the first degree, we jury, find the defendants, Jessica Jones, Claresse Maynard, Vonda Jamison, and Lynise Davis—guilty!"

Chapter 9

The girls were grief-stricken when they were all sentenced to a seven-year bid in a state prison, and there was nothing anyone could do about it. They were immediately taken into custody as their loved ones watched in horror to see their children—their babies, their loves—walk away in handcuffs for the next unforgiving seven years.

The girls walked out of the courtroom with their heads up because there was no longer any tears in them to cry. Between the arrest, the trial, and the conviction, their innocence was lost somewhere along the way and they were numb to it all and wanted nothing more but to face the challenge that they surely had ahead of them.

They spent a month on Rikers Island Correctional Institution for Women prior to being shipped up north to Bedford Hill Correctional. Rikers was the first dose of reality they received, which was only a prelude to the conditions that they would be getting in a state correctional facility. For the most part, the month that they spent on Rikers Island was nursery school compared to what they would soon face ahead.

Though Jessica and Vonda never been to prison before, they maintained their poise throughout their tenure there, but the same could not be said for Lynn and Tiny. Lynn remained quiet and wide-eyed the entire time there and showed her weaknesses openly. Jessica and Vonda told her many times that she couldn't show any weakness and she had to snap out of it. Lynn didn't care and simply couldn't help it, so they protected her all the same.

Tiny wasn't as bad as Lynn, but her nerves were completely shot. Even before the trial, Tiny had been consuming more and more weed and alcohol just to keep from shaking. She began worrying herself to death and the more she worried, the more she stayed high. But, now that she was locked up, she shook and shivered like a lost, wet puppy in a rainstorm because she had nothing in her system. Jessica silently thanked God that they didn't go sent straight to Bedford for all their sakes. They needed time to adjust to prison life and put the outside world behind them.

Whenever the four of them got time alone, they planned and went over the course of action they would take when they arrived at the big house. Vonda took lead because all her brothers took time out and schooled her on what to do when they got there.

1. Don't Rat. If you and another inmate have a problem, you settle it amongst yourselves. You do not go to the CO. If you see something going on that shouldn't be, keep it to yourself. It's none of your business. You are an inmate, not a cop.

2. Nobody is your friend. Having a friend on the street and having a friend in prison is two different things. Prison will expose

you to who you really are, and you never know who you will become once you get inside. It is a jungle mentality once you get to prison, and it becomes survival of the fittest. Your best friend could be the one who sets you up to the police, so watch everyone, and trust no one—because everyone changes.

3. You only got two days in prison that really matter: the day you walk in and the day you walk out. Everything in the middle doesn't count, so do what you have to do to survive.

4. Fight or get fucked. If an inmate exposes you to be weak when you first get to prison, you will be fucked over your entire time there. In other words, if an inmate takes something of yours when you first get to prison, they will be taking from you till the time you leave prison. It's no two ways about it.

5. If someone disrespects you in any way, try your very best to take their fucking head off and have no mercy when you do it.

6. Never accept anything from an inmate, because it is never free.

7. When you first get there, don't look away from anyone, because they are trying to read you and betting on how long it's going to take them to cop you. Don't give them anything to bet on.

They went over this hundreds of times in their two weeks at Rikers, and by the last day before they were to be bussed upstate, Lynn and Tiny had finally seemed to pull it all together and now they were all focused. Ready for whatever lay ahead for them the next seven years.

BEDFORD HILLS CORRECTIONAL FACILITY

Bedford Hills Correctional Facility was a maximum security prison that housed some of the most notorious and dangerous women in New York State. When the girls arrived through the gates of the facility, the first thing they noticed was watchtower that housed armed officers with shotguns. The second thing they noticed, and were very surprised to see, were inmates walking around the compound like they owned the place, gawking at the bus of new arrivals.

Whether it for was mental torture or was just procedure, the officers kept them sitting on the bus for what seemed like an hour after they arrived. Then, finally, the officers started calling off names. All four girls knew that it was already showtime because the betting was about to begin. They put on their game faces with the evil eye to boot. They were met with a lot of kisses and cat calling, but for the most part, all four girls did exactly as they were told and kept their heads up and didn't look away.

Inside central processing was even worse as officers, male and female alike, barked orders at them as they monitored their every move. Speak only when spoken to, move only when they said "move," and jump when they said "jump."

Nothing was worse than when they had finished processing their paperwork and had to be strip searched. All stood as naked as the day they were born, and they were told to bend and squat. They had every part of their body cavities inspected. Jessica was amazed as she watched some of the other girls stand and act as though it was a normal occurrence. She and her friends stood awkward and uneasy as they tried to cover any private parts they could humanly cover. Jessica wasn't at all happy about the setting and especially the smell that emanated from some of the women—it smelled of corn chips and dry, rotted fish.

After they were strip searched and had absolutely every material item taken from them, they were given state-issued clothing and bedding. The color green would become their color of choice for the next few years. Then the moment had finally arrived; the four girls were assigned to their housing area: 121 B, the back building—a.k.a. the Jungle. The jungle was where all girls were sent with a five or more year sentence, and it was definitely the most dangerous house on the compound. To get to the back building, you had to walk through a long tunnel from the front to the back. Many things had happened in the tunnel over the years, and the area was made famous for killings and the most common place for robberies. It became common knowledge to never walk the tunnel alone, and above all, watch your back.

The girls got lucky by all being assigned in the same housing unit. As they walked up to the last gate waiting to get into their unit, women began milling around awaiting the first dibs on the fresh new meat. The hardened women in 121B were more blatant than the ones in the front building with their sexual innuendos and taunts toward the new girls.

Just as they were let in Vonda turned around, her eyes on fire, and she said, "Y'all ready?"

Each girl was afraid, but ready, and they nodded back. Even though they carried bulky clothing and linen, they still managed to stick out their fists, unite, and say, "Get It Girls!"

Buzz.

The gate finally opened, and each knew that this was the first day of the rest of their lives. They would never be the same person they once were when they walked through those gates. As soon as they walked in the house, the inmates were lined up and in their faces, haggling which one of the girls would be their bitch.

"Oh, shit . . ." one girl said when she spotted Vonda. "This tall bitch is definitely mines." She caressed Vonda's ass.

Like a streak of lightning, Vonda dropped all her items and tore into her molester with all the fury of hell. Jessica followed suit and dropped her items and came to her friend's assistance by punching the girl in the face. The beaten prisoner's friends came to her aid by the dozens and began whipping and stomping Vonda and Jessica as if they were rag dolls.

Sheer reaction caused Tiny and Lynn to follow suit, and they pounced into the melee to help their fallen friends. But they too fell victim to the same beating as Vonda and Jessica as a barrage of stomping and fists rained upon them as well. The Get It Girls refused to submit, and a huge circle had formed as the inmates watched and cheered in a bloodlust frenzy at the lopsided assault on the new girls.

The girls didn't even hear the alarm go off as they continued fighting as if their lives depended on it. The police came busting through the crowd and broke up the melee. Bloodied and battered, none of the four girls gave the police an easy way to go as they cursed and struggled all the way out of the house and into solitary confinement for the next thirty days. The girls adrenaline-filled bodies smiled wickedly all the way to the hole, because they knew they'd won a small victory. They'd all fought back valiantly and violently despite being outnumbered five to one. They knew that the other inmates would think twice before they tried putting their hands on one of them again.

When the girls finally got out of solitary confinement, they were welcomed back into the house with evil stares or light nods. At that point, they were either hated or respected. That suited the girls just fine, because above all, at least everyone now knew that they would not be easy prey. The entire house also knew, most importantly, that if you fucked with one of them, you had to fuck with all of them. Over the next few days, the girls kept to themselves. They ate together, showered together, and walked the yard together. None of them wanted to be caught out there alone if anything would have jumped off. They knew that it would only be a matter of time before they were tested again, but they never expected it to go down so soon and by whom.

Corrections officers had three tours, morning, evenings, and overnight shifts. They had four officers on each tour. Two in the bubble, which was inside the control room, and two who actually walked the dorms. Most of the officers were there to do their jobs and go home, but you always had the ones who took their job too seriously or loved it too much. The others tried to get everything they could out of it by taking advantage of the weak. The latter would be Officer Clooney and Officer Landry, who worked the graveyard shift.

Officer Clooney was third generation, uneducated poor white trash, and the entire prison hated him because he showed no mercy or respect for inmates. His tall, wiry body and short, close-cropped dark hair made him look like the local rednecks who'd settled in the area since the prison was built in 1918. Without these state jobs, and the business that it brought to the area, Officer Clooney would have definitely been an inmate in some other prison in New York State long ago.

Officer Landry was female and gay, and she definitely fit in the category of loving her job a little too much. She was a butch woman who favored a man in every sense, down to prickly hairs that sprouted from her chin and upper lip.

These rogue guards ran everything from drugs to prostitution and loved to take advantage of all the new girls, especially the young ones. The new arrivals—Vonda, Jessica, Tiny, and Lynn—definitely fit the bill. When Clooney and Landry landed the job together over eight years ago, they were in pussy heaven and quickly learned they had something in common and personally requested floor duties, which required them to personally escort and watch the girls take showers. It would be only a matter of time before they would take the liberty and taste the product sooner than later. They were also the biggest supplier of drugs inside the Jungle, and had handpicked workers—all inmates—to sell it for them. Together, Officer Clooney and Officer Landry wreaked havoc for years by raping, extorting, or anything else inhumane or against their oath, as they walked the floors of the dorm.

It was 6AM, and the girls stood in the chow line for breakfast. Clooney and Landry had breakfast duties, monitoring the movement of the inmates.

Landry walked over to Clooney and gestured in the new girls' direction as they stood on the line holding their trays. She whispered, "Look what we got over there." Landry leered over in their direction and said excitedly, "Holy fucking shit! Look what the cat just dragged in."

"They can't be but barely eighteen," Clooney said, as saliva started foaming on the side of his mouth. Clooney's eyes narrowed as he honed in on Tiny. "Oh, my God," he said in a slight country drawl, "look at that little one. She don't look but thirteen. She's mine," he said quickly, staking claims on her.

"That's fine with me," said Landry. "You can have the guppy." Her eyes peered on Lynn's huge breasts and ass. She licked her lips. "Because I want the big game."

After the girls collected their food from the chow line, they began walking to a table in the rear. As they passed a table, an inmate stuck out her foot and tripped Lynn up, making her fall to the ground and causing her tray of food fall everywhere. Vonda, Tiny, and Jessica helped her up and stepped in front of the girl who'd done it.

The girl's name was Dear Mama. Mama, as most people called her, was a huge woman, and she ran the entire Jungle with an iron fist. She was Landry and Clooney's designated top dog and ran the three biggest rackets in prison—drugs, prostitution, and protection. She was the consummate gorilla pimp, who ran her stable of women with sheer brutality and violence. She was considered untouchable, not only because she ran the drug game for the officers, but because was considered the most violent and dangerous inmate the facility had ever had and had spent two thirds of her life behind bars. The battle scars on her face and body told the tale of a survivor in every sense of the word.

"What the fuck is your problem?" Lynn screamed, holding her own.

Mama stood up from the table to intimidate her with her six-foot height and her two-hundred-and-fifty-pound frame. "What the fuck did you say, bitch?"

Vonda jumped in front of Lynn. "You heard what the fuck she said!" Though Vonda was tall, she was small in comparison to Mama.

Mama reached behind her back and pulled out a huge shank. "I'm not that bitch y'all jumped when y'all came up in here. You better ask somebody who the fuck I am."

The girls saw the huge knife, but held their ground.

Suddenly the girls heard the officers shout, "Ok, break this shit up!" It was Clooney and Landry. Mama quickly passed off the knife to the other inmates, who followed suit.

Landry looked at the floor and saw the mess of food scattered everywhere and asked, "Whose tray is this?" She looked at Lynn's stained shirt and smiled. "What happened here, sugar?"

Lynn looked at everyone and said, "Nothing, I slipped."

Officer Landry looked at Mama and knew better and frowned. She shifted her eyes back to Lynn and smiled again and said, "Listen." She touched her shoulder and said sweetly ,"You pick up your tray and that food off the floor and go to the head of the line and get a fresh tray. Okay, sugar?"

Lynn nodded.

Landry looked at Mama and said, "Watch your ass, Mama."

Landry walked away and Lynn proceeded to pick up the remains off the floor. As Lynn began walking back to the chow line, Mama said, "Fat, stupid bitch!"

Lynn suddenly snapped, and without warning, she smashed the tray in Mama's face and began pounding her with it. Vonda,

Jessica, and Tiny all dropped their trays and began fighting Mama's clique, preventing them from jumping Lynn. Mama could only protect her face, because her legs were caught between her seat and the table, and she was unable to fight back or maneuver. Lynn got the best of her before the guards pulled her off and out of the mess hall.

"I'm gonna kill you, bitch! I'm gonna kill you!" Mama yelled, as oatmeal spilled down her face.

For the second time within a month, Lynn was put back into solitary confinement, but this time without her friends. She grinned and laughed hysterically all the way to the box from the mess hall as if she was losing her mind. Vonda, Jessica, and Tiny knew she was losing it, and they also knew at that moment that she would never be the same.

Mama looked at the three girls. "As for you bitches, this shit ain't over, that's for damn sure."

Vonda quickly responded as said, "We right here, we ain't going anywhere, so bring it!"

This infuriated Mama. She walked straight up to Vonda, ready to tear into her. Vonda threw up her hand, ready for whatever and wasn't backing down.

Just as they were to come to blows, Landry yelled, "Mama! Mama!" she repeated. Landry walked straight up to Mama and said through gritted teeth, "Goddamn it, Mama, I done told you one time to back off, and I'll be damned if I tell you twice!" Officer Landry was angry that Mama had ruined her chance of making a play for Lynn that night. Now she would have to wait thirty days till Lynn got out now that she was sent to the box. "Now get a fucking broom and a mop and clean up all this shit off the floor!"

Mama stared her down, but obeyed. She looked at Vonda and her two friends and said, "This ain't over," and walked off.

Landry looked at Vonda, Tiny, and Jessica and growled, "As for you three, come with me." She took them to the back of the kitchen and ordered them on kitchen duty—washing pots for the rest of the day.

By the end of the day the girls was exhausted. They cleaned the pots for breakfast, lunch, and dinner that day and wanted nothing more than to get back to their cells and go to sleep, and that's exactly what they did. But in the wee hours of the night, Vonda and Jessica were awakened by the screams of a familiar voice—it was Tiny! Officer Clooney didn't waste any time on his conquest of the tender-loined Tiny. Vonda and Jessica jumped from their bunks and yelled out to Tiny.

"Tiny, what's going on?" screamed a frantic Vonda.

"They taking me, they taking me!" she screamed. "Help! Help me, Vonda, they—" Her voice was followed by a muffled sound as the girls in the other cells started cheering.

"Oh, shit. They got the new one."

"It's gonna be some smooth fuckin' tonight."

"Clooney's horny again."

Jessica and Vonda screamed out for Tiny, but there was nothing any of them could do. Their faces stayed pressed against the bars, crying for their fallen friend.

Three hours later and still awake, Jessica and Vonda heard the opening of a cell door, then the faint sound of a body hitting the bunk. Softly, Vonda called out her name, but there was no answer. She called again and again and still, no answer. It wasn't until six o'clock that morning did the cell open up and almost simultaneously, Vonda and Jessica jumped out and ran to Tiny's cell. When they got there, they gasped as she lay half naked and passed out, bleeding from her vagina and anus.

Tiny had been brutally raped that early morning, and it would not be her last. The worst part about it was that there was nothing any of them could do about, and it killed Vonda to be so powerless—she couldn't save her. Clooney took such a liking to Tiny that she became his personal sex slave every night. She was put on untouchable status, and inmates knew that Tiny was protected and not to be touched. Tiny became like a zombie and stopped fighting and resisting. She found it easier to let him have his way with her. She did have one perk, and that was all the drugs she wanted. First he supplied her with her drug of choice, marijuana. But after a while, the marijuana no longer did the trick for her, so he introduced her to something more powerful— heroin—and she instantly fell in love.

Chapter 10

When Lynn finally got out of solitary confinement, Landry didn't waste any time making her midnight visit to Lynn's cell. At first Lynn would fight and resist the rapes by Landry, but over time it wasn't any hollering, wasn't any screaming, nor was there any crying. When Lynn passed by her friends cell she was as calm and serene as the morning was blue, and she nodded to her friends that she was in fact all right. After a while, they sat down to eat breakfast without a word being mentioned from either Lynn or the other girls. It became far too normal for the girls to any longer ask about the incident. Lynn began to enjoy the midnight trysts with Officer Landry and soon began to turn the tables on her rapist.

Lynn was immediately taken under Landry's wing as she became the property of the officers. Over the coming months, Lynn changed into a person that none of them knew, as her appearance and manners changed from feminine and ladylike to manly and butch. Out of all the girls, Lynn would have been least likely to turn into a dyke because she was always sensitive about her hair, nails, and appearance. This was the primary reason they were always late for school; she had to have her entire appearance in order before she came outdoors. Then one day she came out of her cell and her hair was cut off into a short close cropped afro. She became all into the "life" as she called it, and began having relationships with more and more other girls in the prison in addition to Landry. There was no turning back for her.

Over next few months, Mama kept good on her promise and fought and harassed the girls every chance she got. She began to hate them with a passion. But the Get It Girls refused to be intimidated and began arming themselves with homemade weapons as well. By this time, the house was beginning to split into two groups: Mama and her crew and Vonda and hers, neither crews backing down an inch. Because Vonda, Jessica, Tiny, and Lynn had stood up to Mama, other girls began to choose sides because it was only a matter of time that someone would have to die in this situation. Vonda and Jessica became their unofficial leaders. Vonda and Jessica also knew that something had to be done and soon, if they wanted to live because word around the cell block was that Mama had already hatched a plan to kill them and that bets were being taken.

Kenny would write Jessica often, and she would write him back just the same, until one day Jessica received news that would rock her whole world. Her father had died of a massive heart attack.

The State allowed Jessica to attend his funeral and since then Jessica had turned cold. She felt responsible in some ways for her father's death, and from that moment on she no longer cared about life as she knew it. No longer would she accept mail sent to her from her family or Kenny. She decided to leave the outside world behind her and finish her term so she could survive. After a while, her biggest supporter on the outside, Kenny, no longer wrote her letters, after she no longer responded back to him.

※ ※ ※

Tiny turned into a full-fledged junkie and began to stray off and hang out more and more with other addicts as they scored their dope and used together. Above all, Tiny was still part of the crew and ate every breakfast, lunch, and dinner with them and was right there with them whenever there was a beef. She resented Officer Clooney with a passion as he continued to use her as his personal sex slave. He got off because of her childlike body, and he too, became smitten by her and began to develop feelings for her. Any time she resisted he would threaten to cut her off of her drug supply, so she would submit to all his sexual whims.

Lynn no longer hid the fact that she was gay and hung around other butches and femmes that she took on as lovers. Officer Landry resented the fact that Lynn had gone off on her own, since she was the one to turn her out, and made her life miserable.

In addition to learning about the death threats, Jessica and Vonda learned of the entire operation Mama had from the drugs, prostitution, and protection. Vonda became obsessed and paranoid about the death threats and Mama's operation and decided it was time to make her move. She called a meeting with the three girls.

RECREATION ROOM — EVENING

The four girls sat around the table and pretended to be just playing some spades. They talked loudly as if they were going to kick each other's asses in the game just to throw Mama and her crew off their scent. After an hour passed, and they were sure that no one was interested, Vonda began to lay out her plan.

"Everybody knows that Mama is gonna be gunning for us real soon," she said as she threw down a card.

Everyone nodded and continued to play their hands.

"One of my girls that fuck with Mama's number two in charge told me that they going after you first, Vonda, and that it will be this week," Lynn mumbled, as she picked up and shuffled the cards.

Jessica spoke next. "So what we going to do about it?"

"What do you think? We gonna have to take that bitch out, that's what we going to do," Lynn quickly answered as she passed out the cards.

No one questioned her and knew they had no other choice. A death warrant was issued.

Tiny spoke next and asked, "Why not take them all out?"

There was an eerie silence as they looked at Tiny.

Vonda answered, "We don't have to take out her whole crew, Tiny. Slay the head, the body will follow."

Tiny looked up from her cards and she had a blank gaze as if she was looking through them. "I'm not talking about them."

The rest of the girls were confused until Tiny gestured with her head behind them. Officer Clooney and Officer Landry had just walked in for their evening shift. They turned around and looked to see if Tiny was joking.

"Tiny," Jessica chuckled and said in a whisper, "you can't be serious. We can't kill no cop."

They stared at Tiny for a response, but none came. There wasn't a smile on her face—she was deadly serious.

"This bitch is sniffing too much dope," said Lynn.

"Yeah, least I ain't eating no pussy," countered Tiny.

Vonda quickly squashed the beef before it got started and asked Tiny, "Come on, Tiny. I know you twisted about that shit Clooney do to you, but that nigga is a fuckin' cop. Nobody kill cops." Vonda stared into Tiny's eyes to see if she got the point, but Tiny wasn't backing down.

"Fuck that! You ain't the one he fuckin' raping, Vonda!" Her eyes began to water. "Do you know what he makes me do? Do you know how that shit makes me feel to have this white motherfucker fuck me in my ass? Kissing me with his nasty, stinking tongue down my throat when he on top of me? I hate that shit!" Her eyes pleaded for them to understand what she was going through. "I know y'all have eyes. Don't you see what I turned into? A motherfucking junkie, that's what the fuck I am. An eighteen-year-old junkie, and I'm fucked up for the rest of my life and that motherfucker turned me into one!"

The three girls remained silent.

"I just don't know if I can take it much longer, I just don't know."

The girls felt torn and hadn't a clue on how to answer her.

"Sometimes at night," Tiny admitted as she wiped the tears from her eyes, "I just feel like tying my sheets to the gate and just ending all this bullshit now before my mother sees what I turned into. " She no longer could control her tears, and Jessica stood up and put her arms around her and Tiny reciprocated.

Jessica lips turned into a sneer and she said, "She's right, all them fuckers got to go." Jessica shifted her focus back to Vonda and Lynn. "And I got just the plan for all their asses."

She looked at Tiny and said, "In order for me to do this, Tiny, I'm gonna need your help, so you got to be strong, ok?" Jessica caressed her hair and she nodded.

"Good," said Jessica. "Now let's get busy."

Chapter 11

Lynn worked in the mess hall, compliments of Officer Landry. The very next morning she started her shift at 4:30 AM, went straight to the rear of the kitchen, hopped on the table, and used a rolling pin to smash the ceiling light bulbs. She looked over her shoulder and paused to see if anyone was coming. Satisfied that no one had heard it she leap down and used a broom to clean up the mess and kept the larger shards of glass. After cleaning up and disposing of the ruins on the floor, Lynn found an apron and put the remaining glass in it and began folding it. She then took the rolling pin and began to roll and pound the apron. She repeated this process till she was satisfied that the glass was minuscule enough that the naked eye couldn't see it—almost crystallized.

She had more than enough to get the job done, so she exited the back room. On the way out she spoke to each and every one of the girls who would be on the chow line serving that day, who happened to be part of her clique, and set the final piece of the puzzle in place.

Like clockwork, Mama and her clique came into the mess hall at 6AM on the dot, loud and obnoxious as usual. Shortly after they came into the mess hall, Jessica, Vonda, and Tiny entered behind them. When they spotted Lynn who was serving the bread, she gestured with a slight nod that everything was in place and they nodded back.

As Mama and her crew moved down the chow line, they threatened each girl who was serving for larger portions. They were now close enough to count Mama's position and it was then that one of the girls on the chow line began to unravel the apron that held the crystallized glass and stealthily poured all of it into the oatmeal and began mixing it in. Lynn watched the girl's every move as she mixed it into Mama's food. The server looked at Lynn, whose eyes was now widened, and mouthed the words, *I said half.*

The server shrugged her shoulders as if there was nothing she could do now.

When Mama got up to the girl she was handed her tray. Mama looked down at the tray and sneered, "You think I'm stupid?"

Lynn, Tiny, Jessica, Vonda, and the girl who served her the food held their breaths.

"I saw you gave everybody else more than me. Give me some more."

The girl breathed again, smiled, then said, "No problem, Mama," and served her an extra portion of oatmeal on her tray.

The girls sat back and watched their victim eat and chat with her friends as if she didn't have a care in the world. But, soon, very soon, the broken and crystallized glass would be slowly traveling down her esophagus, through her small and large intestines, slicing the lining of each, making millions of tiny incisions as she began to bleed inward. Then finally, because of all the holes, acid and bile from her intestines would cause the hole to rupture even more and she'd begin to bleed outwardly from her mouth, ears and eyes, until finally she would die from choking on her own blood.

Mama turned around from her table and saw the four girls staring at her and stuck out her middle finger at them.

Mama skipped lunch that day, and by dinnertime she was sweating profusely and asked the officer on duty if she could see a doctor. It was then that the officer see blood coming from her ears and rushed her to the infirmary, but by then it was too late. Unfortunately for the rest of her crew, it would be the last time anyone would see the infamous Dear Mama ever again.

Jessica, Lynn, and Tiny wasted no time putting the second phase of their plan in action as they stood guard outside of Dear Mama's cell while Vonda frantically searched it. When she found what she was looking for she exited the cell and all the girls walked off unseen in different directions.

They decided to take no chances and plotted to take out Mama's number two in charge, Precious, who would certainly pose a threat and continue with her boss's orders to jeopardize their life by fulfilling the contract that was on their heads. Better safe than sorry. The girls waited till Precious returned to her cell and all four girls rushed in and stabbed her repeatedly until there was no longer any movement. They then showered and got rid of all weapons and clothing before the C.O's would find her lifeless body.

Shortly after the Mama and Precious incident, the girls spun their web and awaited their next victim—Officer Clooney. And just after two in the morning, like clockwork, the cat came for his kitten and led Tiny away. An hour and a half later Tiny came walking gingerly back toward her cell and grinned to the girls as she passed them by. She'd hit the jackpot.

That night Jessica wrote a note that read:

Dear Warden,
This is a used condom wrapper that Officer David Clooney used to fuck me with last night. If you are not sure if it's true, I also included the used condom with Officer David Clooney's sperm in it. I tied it up nice and tight in case you want to do some kind of test on it or something.
P.S. If you are receiving this letter that means that he done already killed me somehow.

Signed,
Eartha Lee Jenkins, a.k.a. Dear Mama.

The girls dropped the envelope off in the Warden's suggestion box.

Three days later, just as officer Clooney was about to get off, the Warden, six guards, and two representatives from the state police came into the ward and read officer Clooney his rights then handcuffed him right there. The girls watched from their cells as all the women in the unit began to clap and shout their happiness that karma had finally caught up with him.

Tiny simply lay back in her bunk and smiled for the first time in months.

With three major problems taken care of, the girls decided to go for the quadruple play and they set their focus on the final piece to their problem. They set up the impromptu meeting up inside the recreation room.

The girls sat in the recreation room well past the cut off time and awaited the overnight guard to clear them out—Officer Caroline Landry.

As suspected, she made her rounds, walked into the recreation room. When she saw the four girls still inside the room, she barked, "What the hell are you bitches still doing in this recreation room? Get your asses to your cells right goddamn now!"

None of the girls even flinched.

Officer Landry couldn't believe what she was seeing. "Did you hear what the fuck I said?"

Vonda only smiled and said, "We heard you, and we ain't going no-fucking-where!"

Landry was taken aback for a moment and placed her hand on her baton. "What I want you all to do is—"

Jessica cut her off and said, "What you gonna do is close the door and shut the fuck up if you don't want to end up like your friend Clooney."

Landry was instantly silenced just hearing her partner's name and was smart enough to at least hear her out. So, she complied with her order and closed the door behind her. She shrugged and challenged them, "I'm gonna give you five seconds to tell me what it is you want to me talk about."

Vonda approached her. "And I suggest you shut the fuck up and listen to the people who hold your whole fucking career in their hands."

They were now face-to-face, and Officer Landry thought better to hear her out. "So what is it that you all want?"

Lynn saw her opportunity, ambled over and said, "You do remember ol' Mama, don't you? It's too bad she and her friend Precious ain't no longer around to run your business for you."

Officer Landry remained silent and let her continue.

"Well, to make a long story short, we want control of her whole fucking operation—the drugs, the prostitution, and the protection."

Officer Landry was unmoved by the request. She needed someone take over the operation anyway since Dear Mama was killed, so if that's all they wanted, things were working in her favor, she thought. "Ok, if that's what you want, you got it," she finally said with confidence. "But if all of yous fuck me on this, I have enough guards on the payroll to ensure that none of you will make out of this prison alive," Landry threatened.

Vonda stepped in front of her and said, "You must ain't hearing us correctly. *You* ain't running shit no more. *We* are running this shit, and you taking orders from us."

Landry snickered. "Oh, yeah? How is that?"

Jessica spoke for the first time and began reading from a piece of paper. The more Jessica read, the more horrified Officer Landry became. By the time Jessica finished, Landry had her head down and was ready to faint.

Vonda smiled wickedly at the officer and said, "Yeah, Mama may have certainly looked dumb, but she was very, very detailed oriented when it came to names of officers, dates, and times. I say you and about nine other officers could get up to twenty-five years in prison for all the shit y'all did so far. She even went as far as to take out an insurance policy on herself just in case she didn't make it out of here alive by finding out the names and addresses of your whole family—your mama, your daddy, your sister, your brothers, grandparents, everybody."

Vonda paused to let it all sink in to her.

"Well, guess who got all that information now?" Vonda nodded her head. "You guessed it." She waved her hand around at her three friends and continued, "And don't get any ideas of shaking down our cell and looking for the original copies that we stole from Mama's cell the day she died, because we sent them off two days ago to our people on the outside."

Vonda paused to let her gain her bearings. "Now you got two options: either you take your chances by killing the four of us and live on what's left of what you and your entire family have left, or you can roll with us and continue with the operation and retire with a fat pension and eat all the pussy you want to for the rest of your life."

It didn't take Officer Landry to realize that the four girls had her over a barrel, and she quickly made her decision with a nod.

Vonda smiled and said, "Good." They began to walk out of the recreation room when Vonda turned around suddenly and added one more thing, "Oh, yeah, the split is now seventy-thirty. Us seventy, and you thirty."

Over the years, the Get It Girls ran the prison with the organization of any top corporation. The violence and fear that once ruled the unit no longer existed so as long as you conformed to the Get It Girls' rules. They made a massive amount of money and sent every dime home to ensure that they would be on their feet when they would ultimately be released.

Chapter 12

After five and a half years, all the girls with the exception of Jessica were released on parole. Jessica received too many infractions that took away from her good time for not following staff orders. Tiny, Vonda, and Lynn were released six months before Jessica, but stayed in contact with her until she was ultimately released. In the letters, they told Jessica how much the neighborhood had changed for the worse due to a new form of drug that everyone called crack. Jessica caught a glimpse of how bad this drug must have been, because of the influx of all the girls that were coming in at a record breaking rate. Most of them came in looking like they were near to death, especially when she ran into a girl she knew from her neighborhood and she looked like she'd aged twenty years. They sat down at lunch one day and she told Jessica all about it.

"Yeah, Jessica, it's called 'beaming up.' You know, like they do on *Star Trek*, beam me up Scotty!" she joked. "That shit has you feeling good, yo. It's like having multiple orgasms over and over again."

She tried to understand as she looked at the girl's buttery yellow and rotting teeth. "So you smoke it from a pipe?" asked Jessica curiously,

"Pipe, stem, whatever. It's like freebasing but not as expensive. It comes in little rocks, like pebbles. That's why they call it crack rocks."

Jessica was still confused and frowned. "If it's so inexpensive, why you get arrested for prostitution? What happened to your job?"

She shrugged and said, "Well, that's the one thing about crack; you can't stop once you get started, and when the money run out you start out selling little things like your jewelry, clothes, and stuff like that. After a while, you ain't got nothing else to sell and you get stuck cause you don't want to do nothing but smoke. Your job and your appearance go first. So, after you stole enough from your family and borrowed all you can borrow, or stole all you can steal, you have no other choice but to start selling you body to get that next hit. But I ain't get arrested for prostitution. I got it for possession of a damn ten-dollar cap." She shrugged her small shoulders again and said, "And here I am, in prison again."

Jessica frowned, "So they gave you two years for only ten dollars worth of crack?"

"Something like that. When I was arrested the first couple of times they usually give you an option of going into one of those drug programs, they call them T.C, or Therapeutic Community. That shit is like being in the Army, and plus you got to do like a year and a half, two years to complete it. The judge said either go into the program or go to prison."

"You choose to come to prison instead?" Jessica asked.

"Hell no, you think I'm stupid? I took the program, but I found out that that shit was awful and I couldn't take that shit, so I left. I got arrested on a humble and they found the dime cap of crack on me and arrested me. You want to know the bullshit?"

"What?" Jessica asked, fascinated by her story.

"After I came out of central booking, I stood before the same judge who gave me the choice of the program or prison and the motherfucker remembered me and threw the book at me and that's why I'm here. I should have stayed in the program, yo."

Jessica shook her head and changed the subject, "So, you say everybody is doing it, huh?"

"Yep, damn near. See, a lot of people start out by smoking it in a wulla, that's when you cut open a cigar and replaced the tobacco with some weed. You crush up the crack in a dollar bill or something and sprinkle it on the weed and wrap it back up and smoke it. That's how a lot of people get hooked. After a while, it's only a matter a time when they hit the pipe and when that happens," she shook her head, "your life is over. I'm serious, Jessica; I wouldn't wish that shit on my worst enemy. I seen women sell their own children to men just to get a hit. I saw men—and I ain't talking about gay men, real niggas—get down on their knees and suck another man's dick, yo!"

Jessica was shocked by what she heard and couldn't help but think of her neighborhood amongst other things. Since Jessica didn't have her girls there with her anymore, she thought about her brother, her mother, and Kenny most of the time. With her time dwindling down, her days began feeling like months, and she decided to take some correspondence courses to make her days go by quicker. Since she already had her high school diploma, she didn't have to take any GED courses as required, so one day she saw a language course being offered in English, Spanish, or French. She smiled and thought of how Kenny used to talk to her in French and decided to take the French course for some strange reason. She found it to be very hard, but stuck with just in case it would come in useful one day.

The day Jessica got out prison, she was met by Vonda at the bus station in Times Square. Jessica thought Vonda looked like a totally different person because of the fresh new hair style and fashionable clothing she now wore. They were so excited to see each other that when Jessica stepped off the bus, Vonda screamed and gave her a huge hug, sweeping her off her feet.

"Welcome home baby girl."

"Thanks," said Jessica, and she closed her eyes and felt her first warmth of real freedom.

They pulled apart and Vonda inspected Jessica's clothing and frowned immediately. "I'm taking you shopping because I ain't having my girl seen in borrowed shit."

Since Jessica's father had died, her and her mother's relationship suffered. Jessica really felt that her mother still blamed her for her father's untimely death of a heart attack because of the stress that he gone through over her arrest and sentencing. Jessica only called home for birthdays or when she wanted to talk to her younger brother. She wouldn't ask her mother for a dime after she lost the house, and it'd been like that ever since. So Jessica had no choice but to wear borrowed clothes from the State to come home in.

Vonda smiled at Jessica and joked, "I still got a reputation to maintain, you know."

They hugged again and Vonda looked around and asked, "Where's your stuff?"

Jessica shrugged. "You're looking at it." She patted her body to show her that was all she had.

Vonda grabbed her by the arm and said, "Let's go shopping."

When the girls finished shopping they went to an outdoor cafe and had a late lunch. Jessica looked and felt like a totally different person after she was stripped of the worn and borrowed clothes and into something new and chic. While they ate their food, they laughed, joked, and caught up on everything from old classmates to old flames.

"So what's up with li'l man?"

Vonda frowned and said, "Who, you talking about, Chubby?"

"Yeah."

Vonda rolled her eyes, "Girl, please, ain't nothing little about him no more. He is big, and when I say big, I mean real big."

Jessica laughed. "So what is he up to these days, he working or what?"

"He ain't doing shit but trying to keep his ass out of jail. He was getting himself in so much trouble that the judge was tired of seeing his face in the courthouse. They on his ass too and his P.O said that if he violates one more time or don't get a job soon, they gonna have to give all those years back to the state. So he's walking on thin ice."

Jessica looked around at the scenery. "Yo, it's nice to be out and around normal people, but it ain't nothing like being up in Harlem around my people." She smiled added, "and plus I want to see my baby brother. I miss my li'l man. I can't wait to see him." Jessica smiled as she reminisced. "Shoot, I didn't talk to him in over a year; every time I called home my moms told me he was out." She smiled again. "He must be enjoying his freedom since he turned eighteen. Probably found himself some new friends or girlfriend or something."

Jessica watched Vonda face sadden, followed by her putting her head down. She grew suspicious and inquired, "Vonda, what's wrong?"

Vonda appeared to be gathering her thoughts and finally confessed. "Jessica, remember when we wrote you and told you that the neighborhood changed? How everybody is doing this new drug called crack?"

Jessica stared at her, dreading the worst. "Yeah, what about it?"

Vonda let out a sigh. "Well, your li'l brother is hooked on that shit too."

Jessica was dazed for a moment and didn't want to believe what she had just heard. In her mind her brother was still just twelve years old and she couldn't see him smoking a cigarette much less doing some kind of drugs.

The initial shock wore off and Jessica said, "Don't worry, his big sister is home now I'll straighten him out." She nodded, trying to convince herself. "He'll listen to me, and I'll make sure he stops fucking around with that shit. You'll see. I'll kick his li'l ass if I have to."

Vonda shook her head. "Jesse, your little brother is not so little anymore. He is big now; he changed." Vonda looked her deeply in her eyes. "That crack shit," she shook her head again, "is unlike anything you saw before. That shit has all of Harlem changed in the worst way. Either you are getting rich from selling it or you losing your mind from smoking it. That shit got women selling their bodies for two fucking dollars just to get a hit, Jessica, and they will do anything to get it—anything!"

Vonda paused to see if she was getting through to her. "It like everybody is zombies or something. Even four of my brothers got hooked on that shit." She read Jessica's eyes and said, "No, Chubby is the only one who's not on it, but he sells it from time to time and shouldn't be doing that. That shit even got Tiny's moms strung out and Lynn's sisters." Vonda shook her head again. "That's why I met you before you got uptown to prepare you for what you are about to see."

Jessica remained silent as her words resonated in her mind.

Vonda reached in her purse and pulled out a roll of money and handed it to her and said, "Here, this is a thousand dollars."

Jessica looked at the wad of money with apprehension.

"This just part of the money that we earned while we were up. Come by my house anytime you ready and you can get the rest of your share."

Jessica looked at the money again and shook her head. "No, Vonda. I didn't earn this."

"What do you mean you didn't earn this?" asked Vonda. "We were crew, and that's what we vowed before we even went in there. All for one and one for all, remember?"

Jessica was still reluctant. "I told you from Jump Street that I didn't want to deal drugs and wanted no part of that."

Vonda got serious and said, "Jessica, you know as well as I do that nobody on the outside was sending us any packages or filling our commissary. We had to do what we had to do, remember? Now we made it out and we are alive and that's the only thing that matters." She pushed the money back over to her. "We only did two days in prison, the day we entered . . ." Vonda waited for Jessica to complete the rest.

"And the day we leave out," Jessica finished. "And everything in the middle doesn't count."

When Vonda and Jessica got uptown to Harlem, Jessica was surprised to see how much everything had changed. It seemed like everywhere they walked, young boys were yelling, "Jumbos, y'all. Jumbos, two for five."

The strange thing was how openly they were doing it, like they didn't have a care in the world. All the guys seemed to wear huge gold chains around their necks and all had fancy cars and pagers on their hips. They also seemed more disrespectful to women. A group of guys hollered at Vonda and Jessica as they passed, trying to get their attention by offering them some money or drugs to talk to them. And then, with her own eyes, Jessica saw one of Vonda's older brothers that she'd known since she was kid, pushing an old rickety shopping cart collecting cans. When he saw his sister and Jessica, his eyes lit up with excitement.

"Oh, shit, is that you Jessica?"

The minute he walked up to them, Jessica smelled a strong, musty odor emitting from his body. The clothes he had on were well worn and tattered, and he looked as if he hadn't showered or changed his clothes in months. "What's up, sis?" he said to Vonda, as he jumped nervously from toe to toe. He shifted his attention back to Jessica and smiled, revealing his yellow, decaying teeth.

Jessica couldn't believe what she was seeing. Since she known him he was always a sharp and immaculate dresser and was always the first person to offer her and the other girls money for school.

He saw Jessica's reaction and conceded to shame. "I know I look a li'l bad right now, but I'm gonna get myself together this week and go in one of them programs," he said, trying his best to reassure them. He looked away and said, "Listen, Jess, I know you just got out, but you think you can spare a couple dollars to get something to eat?"

Vonda could no longer look at him because she knew he was lying. Many days he'd made such promises to his sister only to disappoint her by lying and taking the money she gave him to buy some more drugs. She tried in vain to get him to go in a program, only to have him not show up at all. She'd lost all trust in him and it hurt her deeply.

Jessica immediately reached in her pocket and pulled out a hundred-dollar bill. He looked at the bill as if it were a poisonous snake. She extended the bill out to him and he quickly snatched the bill and walked off in frenzy in case she realized she had made a mistake.

"Oh, thanks Jess," he hollered, "I'm, I'm gonna pay you back too, soon as I get my welfare check."

They watched him with sadness as he rounded the corner, knowing exactly what he was going to do with the money. All Jessica could think of at that moment was getting home to see her little brother.

Jessica's mother had lost the family brownstone years ago because of the second mortgage, and Mrs. Jones now rented a two-bedroom apartment nearby on 142nd Street between Lenox and 7th Avenue.

Vonda walked Jessica to 142nd Street and gave her her number and promised to get up with her the next day. They said their goodbyes and Jessica reached in her pocket and pulled out a small piece of paper with 141 W 142nd street written on it and proceeded down the block. When Jessica finally got to building 141, she immediately grew uneasy. Never in her life did she recall living in such squalor. She watched a group of men standing menacingly on the stoop as people walked in and out of the building. She reached in her pocket for the address that she had written down and looked at it again, somehow hoping that she had it wrong. She cursed. She took a deep breath and walked toward the building and up the stairs.

She was immediately accosted by young thugs, who asked her, "How many you want, baby?"

"What's up baby, you want a hit?"

Some were even more blatant and asked, "How many of these thangs you want to suck this dick, baby?"

Jessica didn't say a word and proceeded up the staircase to apartment 3F. Along the way, she passed a female addict giving another man a blow job right on the staircase landing. Jessica walked past them with disgust—they didn't even have the common courtesy to stop what they were doing and continued as if she wasn't even there. Jessica arrived on the dank, barely lit third floor and looked around in anguish. She paused and looked at the decaying walls and worn floors and searched for apartment 3F. When she found it, she inhaled deeply and smelled the pungent odor of dried urine and immediately wanted to vomit. She wiped her nose, closed her eyes, then knocked on the apartment door. Jessica knocked harder after no one responded, and that was when she heard her mother's voice.

"Get away from my door, Jordan; I'm not letting you in. Now go away!"

"Ma, it's me, Jessica." Jessica heard footsteps approach, then the peephole latch slide.

"Jessica?" asked Mrs. Jones, who still didn't fully recognize her only daughter.

"Yeah, Ma, it's me."

Jessica heard her mother unlatching a multitude of locks. Finally, she stared in her mother's face, which she hadn't seen in over six years since her father's funeral. Her mother had aged badly, she thought. They stood in the doorway unsure of what to do next, so Jessica made the first move and put her arms around her mother. They hugged briefly and pulled away just as fast.

Jessica smiled awkwardly until her mother opened the door wider and said, "Well, come on in."

When Jessica walked in the apartment, she looked around and noticed that it was sparse, but clean, just as her mother had always kept her home. She showed her to the living room and offered her a seat on the sofa and sat across from her on what Jessica recognized as her father's favorite chair.

There was an uncomfortable moment of silence until her mother inquired, "Why didn't you let me know you were getting out? I would have had things prepared for you."

Jessica only shrugged. "I wanted to surprise you."

Her mother nodded.

Jessica looked at an old picture of her and her family on the wall and asked, "So, where is Jordan?"

Her mother shook her head wearily, exposing a valley of worry marks on forehead. She let out a huge sigh. "Jessica, I don't know where your brother is. He done changed for the worse by getting himself messed up on drugs."

Jessica could see that it was very hard for her mother to talk about him, but she needed to know everything.

"So, he doesn't stay here anymore?" Jessica asked.

Her mother shook her head and admitted, "No, I put him out over six months ago and won't let him back in until he gets himself some help."

"So, you had to put him out, Ma? You couldn't just, you know, let him stay here instead of being on the streets with nowhere to go?"

Her mother stared at Jessica and answered, "Now, Jessica, this is something that you just don't know about yet. You have been away for a long time. You don't know what it's like out here. I gave your brother hundreds of opportunities to stay here, but each time I gave him a chance the worse he got. He steals, lies, and heaven knows what else just to get money for drugs, and I got sick of it. First he started off asking me for money all the time, then I noticed my things coming up missing—money, jewelry, even meat from the freezer."

Her mother shook her head as she thought back. "He just started not to care anymore on how he gets it and after a while I began becoming afraid of him. When I tell him I'm not giving him any more money . . ." She looked Jessica square in the eyes and said, "I swear I think he would kill me just to get the money."

Jessica began to think about the conversations she'd had with the girls in prison and how it was exactly how they explained when a person get hooked on crack. Jessica only remained silent and continued to listen to her mother, knowing that she might be right.

"Everything was one big lie after another. Then one day I come home and opened the door and everything was gone—the televisions, electronics, clothing, everything."

Jessica looked around and for the first time noticed that there wasn't a television in the living room. Jessica shook her head, not wanting to believe any of it, but her mother continued.

"That boy even sold the refrigerator out the kitchen, Jessica, and I can't take it anymore. I'm afraid to be in my own house. Whenever I confront him about anything he yells and curses at me to mind my business. I sleep with my bedroom door locked and sleep with my money in my bra whenever I go to bed. Then one night I woke up and caught him with his hand down my bra trying to steal the money, and when I caught him he ripped my bra and took the money and ran out of the house."

Jessica put her head down, not wanting to believe what she had just heard. She became angry and rose to her feet. "So, where is he at now, Mama?"

Mrs. Jones shook her head and said, "I don't know. He comes by here from time to time asking for some money, but I tell him to go away because I'm sick of all the lies and stealing whenever I did give him a chance." She looked at her daughter and said "Jessica, that stuff that they got out there is...is bad. Promise me that you will not touch that stuff or you going to turn out just like the rest of them. You hear me?" Jessica nodded. That settled her mother down a little and she asked, "So, you going to be staying here awhile?"

Jessica looked around and said, "Yes."

Her mother nodded and stood up and said, "You can take Jordan's room. I'll change the bedding for you, ok? I also have an extra set of keys for you that I'll give to you later."

Jessica thanked her.

Her mother exhaled and told her, "I'll take something out for dinner and we'll catch up on things a little later."

As she was walking off, Jessica said "Mama . . ."

Mrs. Jones turned around to face her. Jessica eyed the floor and then lifted her head and said, "Thank you, Mama."

Her mother gave her a light smile and a nod and walked down the hall to prepare her room.

Since Jessica had to be at the parole office in the morning she turned in early so she could check in with him in midtown Manhattan. She vowed that she would do whatever it took to keep her nose clean and not go back to prison. As she lay in bed that night, all she could think of was hitting the streets the next day to search for her brother.

After she met with her parole officer, she was basically told to check in monthly, stay out of trouble, and to find a job.

"One last thing. If you violate any conditions of your parole at any time, you will be arrested and will have to finish out the six months you owe the state. Do you understand?"

Jessica nodded and was out of his office in five minutes.

When she arrived back uptown she walked aimlessly through the streets of Harlem in search of her brother Jordan. She searched for hours and finally gave up hope of finding him that day, deciding to go home and try again tomorrow. When she got to her building she saw a group of guys tossing another man around and to the ground. The closer she got the more familiar the man on the ground had become—it was Jordan. She gritted her teeth and rushed to his side and pushed the men off of her brother.

"Get the fuck off of him!" she yelled. All the boys backed off as they watched the tall pretty girl help their victim to his feet. She took him by his arm and began leading him up the stoop stairs when one of the boys blocked them from entering the building.

"Oh, hell, no," said the man as he held up his hand. "This nigga ain't going anywhere until he pays me my fuckin' money."

Jessica looked at the man, then at her brother and asked, "You owe them any money, Jordan?"

He nodded his head, too ashamed to face her.

"How much you owe him?" Jessica demanded.

"Twenty dollars," he answered shyly.

Jessica reached in her pocket and pulled out a wad of money and found a twenty-dollar bill and shoved it in the man's chest and said, "Take this shit." She looked him square in the eye. "Now you are paid, so you better leave my brother alone," Jessica said, never losing eye contact with him.

"Well, twenty dollars is not enough. I put interest on it so he owes me double."

Jessica stepped closer to the man and said point blank, "That's all the money you getting, so if you want more you are gonna have to take it."

The man was caught off guard by the challenge and didn't know what to say. Jessica knew from her experience in jail that he was just a talker and wasn't a gangster. She decided to make it clear to everyone around. "This here is mines right here. If I find out you selling him any more of your drugs or trying fuck with him y'all gonna have to fuck with me and I'm ready to die for this shit. This is the building where my mother stays and I'm staying here now, too. Tomorrow, I don't want to see none of y'all selling your shit in my building, and if I do I'm either going back to jail or you will. Make your choice."

The boys had little doubt that she was serious. Jessica looked each and every one of them in their eyes to show she meant just that. She grabbed her brother by the arm and brushed past the man and into the building.

Walking up the stairs Jordan was shaking like a leaf and started explaining to his older sister. "Jessica, I, I don't think it's such a good idea to threaten them like that. They carry guns and . . ."

Jessica stopped and turned to her brother and threw him up against the wall. "Jordan, they are the last motherfuckers you need to be worrying about! You need to be worrying about me kicking your fucking ass for doing what you did to Mama!"

With a nervous twitch he stared into his sister's eyes and lowered his head in shame. Jessica towered over her weakly and frail brother, who looked as if he hadn't eaten in month. Jessica released him and grabbed him by his collar up the remaining flights of stairs and into the apartment. She pushed him into the living room.

"Sit down, Jordan."

He looked around the bare apartment and asked in a low tone, "Is Mama home?"

"No, she is not home yet."

He looked around, still nervous and admitted, "You, know she don't want me here, right? You know she put me out?"

"Why she don't want you here, Jordan?" Jessica hissed. "Tell me why she put you out?"

Still finding it hard to control her anger, she stopped pacing and stood in front of him and yelled, "Because you robbed her fucking blind, Jordan, just to smoke that shit! You stole her televisions, radios, and food."

She looked down upon him with disgust and said, "You even went in her room and stole money from out of her bra, Jordan. Her bra?"

Jordan sat motionless and ashamed of what he had done.

"Jordan, Mama is afraid to have you around because she thinks you may hurt her. She thinks that her own son, the one who supposed to protect her, the one she raised, will one day kill her if she doesn't give you money."

Jordan looked away as his eyes became watery and reality of it all began to set in.

Jessica walked over to him and got on one knee. "Jordan, I'm telling you right now that I will not let that happen. Before I let you hurt Mama or see you hurt yourself like you doing, I'd rather see you dead. And Jordan," Jessica lifted his chin so he could see directly into her eyes, "believe me when I tell you, I will do it."

They stared into each other eyes a few seconds longer until Jordan began to break down. "I can't take this shit anymore,

Jessica, I can't take it!" he cried. "This crack shit got me fucked up and I don't know how to stop. I, I tried to stop but this shit keeps calling me back. I don't know how to stop, Jessica. I need your help, Jessica, I need your help!"

Suddenly, Jessica saw the little brother of old in him and she began to break down too. She got up and sat next to him and hugged him for dear life as they cried together like it would be their last.

"I'm going to help you, but you got to be willing to help yourself." Jessica pulled away from him. "Look at me, Jordan."

He wiped his eyes and lifted his head.

Jessica grasped her brother's hand. "You got to go away into one of those programs. That's the only way I'm willing to help you. You hear me?"

Jordan thought about it for a moment then nodded his head.

Jessica smiled and said, relieved, "Ok, all we got to do now is make a few phone calls."

Jessica stood up and went to the phone and opened up the yellow pages. She made about twelve phone calls before she finally found the right one. After they spoke for over twenty minutes and finalized everything, she hung up. She looked at Jordan and smiled.

"Well, it's done. They got a bed waiting for you in the morning where you go into detox first for about ten days. Then after that you fly to Minnesota into this thing called a Therapeutic Community which lasts for eighteen to twenty-four months."

"Minnesota, Jessica? Twenty-four months?" yelled Jordan.

"What else do you got to do, Jordan? You need to get out of Harlem anyway. These people are going to save your life. You said yourself that you need help because you don't know how to stop on your own. So either that or die on those streets." Jessica waited for a response from her little brother.

He thought about it for a long while and finally answered, "All right, I'll go."

Jessica smiled.

"Where am I gonna stay till the morning, because Mama ain't gonna want me here."

"Don't worry about Mama. I'm going to take care of that." Jessica frowned and said, "In the meantime, I want you to get in the bathroom and take a bath. You stink."

Jordan looked at the clothing he wore laughed. "You right, I haven't changed in weeks."

Jessica stood up and said, "You still got clean underwear and clothes in your room. I'll get you some."

As she was walking away Jordan called out, "Jessica."

She turned.

He continued softly, "I missed you, and I'm glad you home."

Jessica smiled and nodded. "Thanks. I missed you too."

When Mrs. Jones got home Jordan was at the kitchen table eating the dinner that Jessica had prepared for the family. Jessica met her at the door as soon as she heard her key enter the lock.

"Hey Mama," said Jessica as she opened the door for her to pass. "Let me help you with your bags." Jessica took them out of her hands.

Her mother frowned when she entered the living room and asked, "What is that smell? It smells funky in here." She walked into the kitchen and paused when she saw her son at the dinner table and turned toward Jessica. "I want him out of this house right now, Jessica."

Jessica put her hands up and pleaded with her mother. "Ma, just listen to me for a second."

"No, I don't want to hear it. I want him out."

Jordan tossed the napkin into his plate and stood up from the table to leave, but Jessica stopped him.

"Jordan, wait a minute!" Jessica screamed. She turned her attention back to her mother and said, "Mama, you said yourself that Jordan needs some help."

"You don't—" Her mother tried to finish, but Jessica cut her off.

"I am taking him to a detox program in the morning and he needs to stay here so he can at least have a chance to get there in the morning."

Her mother's face showed reservations, and she said with apprehension, "Jessica, do you know what you're getting yourself into?" She looked at her son and screamed, "He's a liar and a thief and you can't trust him!"

Jessica approached her and said softly, "Mama, I just don't want to see my only brother die on those streets without at least giving him a chance to recover."

There was a long pause. Mrs. Jones looked into her daughter's pleading eyes and said in a steady low tone, "Jessica, I gave your brother all the chances in the world and all he did was disappoint me." Mrs. Jones looked at her son with sullen eyes and continued. "I just feel sorry for you when you see for yourself how much of a liar he really is, and when he breaks your heart I pray to God that he doesn't turn you cold like he did me." She walked around

Jessica and toward her bedroom and slammed the door behind her.

Jessica looked at her brother, who had his head down shamefully.

"I'm sorry for turning her that way, Jessica. I really am. I didn't mean to."

She walked over to her brother, hugged him, and said, "I know, but, Jordan," she pulled away from him, "you got to do it this time or she's never going forgive you again. You hear me? You got to come through this time."

He exhaled deeply and agreed by nodding.

Jessica then asked him the question that was nagging her for days. "I want to ask you something."

He shrugged his frail shoulders. "Go ahead."

"How did you start getting high on that shit in the first place?"

He turned his head and spoke as if he'd told the story a million times. "After I lost you and Daddy, I had nobody. Then when we lost the house and moved to this block I was getting into fights from the day I got here. Nobody liked me because I was different. They began to pick on me and call me a retard because I rode the yellow bus. Then after being by myself for a few years, I met this dude. He let me hang out with him and his friends, partly because I always had some money, and we use to chip in to buy some weed and some wine and that was the first time I ever drank or did drugs.

"I felt accepted for the first time in my life. I didn't even like it, but I did it just so I could fit in." Jordan paused as he remembered the moment. "Then one night they was with these other dudes from the neighborhood, they was real fly and popular and they asked for money to put in for some smoke, but this time they asked for ten dollars. I thought that was way too much, but I put it in anyway because I just wanted to be accepted. When the dude came back he pulled out some the weed, some cigars, and these little bottles that I never saw before. I watched them cut the cigar open and fill it with the weed and another dude emptied the bottle and put these little white pebbles in a dollar bill and crushed it up then sprinkled it all over the weed then rolled it up all together. We stood in a circle and they lit it up and began smoking it and passing it around. I looked at each boy's face as they did it and saw their eyes light up like they went to the moon or something."

He looked at his sister. "They call that getting beamed up. Then they passed it to me and I took a pull for the first time." He closed his eyes as he thought back and smiled.

Jessica was confused.

He opened his eyes and explained, "As soon as I smoked it, sis, I felt powerful, I felt invincible. It took me outside my loneliness and had no more worries at all. For the first time in my life I felt like everyone else instead of the retard that I am."

Jessica melted as she looked at the sincerity in her brother's eyes and she knew he was serious. She again looked him in the eyes and placed both hands on his cheeks. "You are not a retard; you just learn things slower than others, and you don't need any drugs to make you fit in. You hear me, Jordan?"

He nodded.

They sat up the rest of the night and caught up on old times when the subject of their father came up. "You know, Jessica,"

Jordan said, "when you went away, Daddy was messed up over it real bad."

Jessica put her head down as she listened.

"It was like when you went away a piece of him just died. He retired early because he got real sick and just hung around the house. Then he just stayed in the bed and wouldn't eat or nothing. And that's when he had his first stroke." He shook his head, trying to fight back the tears. "When he finally was let go out of the hospital he was real small, half his size, and no longer able talk in full sentences. He would sometimes wake up in the middle of the night calling out your name over and over."

He looked up at Jessica with tears falling from his eyes. "And not long after that, he just gave up and died."

Jessica was devastated because this was the first time she'd heard any of this.

Jessica stood up quickly and changed the subject to prevent her from shedding tears and said, "We got a big day tomorrow, so you better get some sleep so we can get downtown early. You sleep in here, and I'll sleep in the living room, ok?" She smiled and exited the room and said before she left. "Jordan, I'm proud of you."

He smiled back and said, "Thanks, sis."

Jessica approached her little brother and hugged him affectionately. She pulled away and stared into his eyes and said seriously, "Jordan, I love you with all my heart and I know you love me, but before I let you live and suffer another day in hell on your knees from these drugs, I'd rather kill you myself so our mother can live in peace." Jessica never blinked her eye. "You understand, Jordan?"

He looked in her face to see if she was joking. He realized she wasn't and simply nodded.

She rubbed the back of his head and said, "Good. I'll see you in the morning." Jessica closed the door.

It was about 4 o'clock in the morning when she was startled and saw someone standing over her as she slept. Jessica adjusted her eyes and rubbed them and saw that it was her mother looking down upon her.

"Mama?" asked Jessica. "What's wrong?"

Grim-faced, her mother answered, "Are these your pants, Jessica?"

Jessica adjusted her eyes again and looked at the jeans in her hand and nodded.

"Well, I found them at the front door."

Jessica was confused for a moment when suddenly she jumped up off the sofa and ran down the hall to Jordan's room. She swung the door open and switched on the lights and looked at the bed. He was gone.

Jessica ran back to the living room and snatched the jeans from her mother's hand and quickly checked the pockets. She checked all four pockets before realizing that Jordan had in fact stolen every dime of the money Vonda had given her. Jessica looked at her mother, who simply shook her head knowingly and walked back to her bedroom and closed the door.

Chapter 13

Before Jessica exited her building that day she was fuming because she felt used by her brother. One part of her wanted to ball up and cry, and the other part of her wanted lash out and hurt somebody, and that was the reason she walked downstairs with a baseball bat sure that she would be able to release some frustration. Before she even made it downstairs to the front of the building she accosted a male and female smoking crack in the stairwell. They barely paid her any mind until she lifted the bat and banged it against the railing.

"Get the fuck out of this building right now!" yelled Jessica. She watched the two scramble down the stairs as if their lives depended on it. Jessica continued down the stairs and threatened everyone she crossed paths with until finally the dealers ran inside the building to see why everyone was running out.

The dealer, a young boy no older than nineteen, looked up at Jessica coming down the stairs palming the baseball bat in her hand and yelled, "Bitch, what the fuck are you doing? Are you crazy?"

Jessica was not fazed by his slurs and walked right up to him and swung the bat without even hesitating. The bat hit the boy in his shoulder and he backed out of the building screaming more obscenities at her. The remaining boys were caught off guard as they watched their homeboy cry out in pain.

"Bitch, do you know who you fuckin with? Do you know who I'm with?"

Jessica gritted her teeth and spewed, "Like I give a fuck! I told y'all motherfuckers yesterday if I see you in my building it was gonna be on. Now it's on, motherfucker!"

Jessica charged after him with the bat high in the air and yelled so loud she sounded like a banshee. She connected the bat to his other arm and he fell to the ground screaming in pain. She turned her attention to his partner and hit him with a brutal blow to his legs. The other boys had the sense to back far away from the bat wielding crazy woman. People from the surrounding buildings began to raise their windows and cheer loudly as Jessica warded off the local dealers.

Jessica had fire in her eyes and wasn't backing down as she challenged the boys for more. "Come on, come get some more and see what happens."

Tenants from her building began coming out one by one to show solidarity. The young boys weren't backing down and began to surround her and were ready to make their move on her until one of the tenants from her building walked out and said loud enough for all to hear, "I got your back, sister."

He then pulled out a huge pistol from his waistband and asked, "Now, which one of you want to be the first to get a bullet in their ass?"

Seeing the weapon stopped the boys in their tracks. They eyed the pistol with malice. The boys now knew they meant business.

"You got this one, but we'll be back!" they threatened.

The man behind Jessica sneered. "If you do, I'm gonna be right here to put some of these bullets in your ass, so I'll be waiting."

The four boys then backed away and walked off down the block. The man patted Jessica on the shoulders and led her back toward the building, over to the group of people that had formed on the steps. They immediately began congratulating her for her bravery.

The man stuck out his hand and introduced himself. "Hi, my name is Cleveland. I'm the building's superintendent. Pleased to meet you."

Jessica smiled. "I'm Jessica. My mother lives in 3F and I just moved in yesterday."

He smiled widely and said, "Oh, you Ms. Jones' daughter. Welcome to the building."

After things finally died down, Jessica and Cleveland sat on the stoop and spoke about the situation for nearly two hours.

"This neighborhood was a good neighborhood to live in and raise your kids. Everybody looked out for each other and respected the old folks." Cleveland pulled off his hat, exposing his graying head of hair. "But, about three or four years ago that crack shit came out and changed everything." He shook his head. "I knew all of them. I watched them all grow up right before my eyes from when they were little till now, and it changed all of them." He shook his head again. "I seen a lot of people in my time get strung out on drugs—heroin, reefer, alcohol, everything. But,

I ain't ever seen a drug change so many and so fast."

He looked Jessica in the eyes and confessed, "My own son got himself hooked on that damn drug and got his self mixed up in that game by selling it. He got his self killed just a year ago." His shoulders deflated. "You see, Jessica, that is the Devil's drug, and it will get you one way or another. It doesn't discriminate, and if the drugs don't get you, the lifestyle will. So it doesn't matter if you smoke it or sell it, it will bring you down one way or another."

Jessica listened and absorbed everything he had said.

He exhaled deeply and continued, "And now there you have it. Drugs are running rampant all over the place—on your street, in your building—and even the police can't do anything because people are so afraid to do something about it and just let them be."

Jessica became confused. "Why now? Why did you wait so long to do something about it? Why wait till now to take a stand?"

He stood to his feet and paused as if he was searching for the right words to tell her. He exhaled and admitted, "I guess it was because I was afraid." He turned away from her so she didn't see the shame on his face. "I survived the Vietnam War and saw a lot of killing, and I did plenty of it myself. If I didn't die over there, I refuse to die where I was born and raised. Like I told you earlier, it works on both sides of the fence in that crack business, and it even changes the ones that sell it for the worst. Some of these same li'l boys I used to give change to and who use to call me Mr. Cleveland are the same ones I fear the most. Now they call me 'old man' and tell me to mind my business. They disrespect me by telling me that they will sell their drugs anywhere they want and if I try to stop them they will hurt me."

He looked at Jessica, real serious, and ended it by saying, "And I believed them." He shook his head. "When they first came in the building selling their stuff I would run them out of here by calling the police, but they must have known it was me, and one day, about six of them ran up on me and beat the living daylights out of me. The people in this building didn't even come out and help; they didn't even so much as call the police." He sucked it in as he recalled the moment and said angrily, "So, I just said fuck it! If they didn't care about me, I didn't care about them and I just began to mind my own business like the rest of them. You live longer that way."

Jessica understood. "Why did you come out and help me then?"

He tossed Jessica a sheepish grin and said, "I guess I'm stupid and a glutton for punishment."

Jessica grinned back and thanked him just the same. Moments later her mother walked out the building and Jessica stood up immediately.

"Good morning, Ms. Jones," Cleveland quickly said, as he tipped his hat toward her.

Jessica tried to hide the bat behind her and stammered, "Hey, Mama, are you on your way to work already?"

Her mother eyed the bat she had behind her and nodded toward Cleveland. "Good morning, Cleveland." Ms. Jones turned around and looked back in the building and asked, "What happened? I didn't see our morning guests huddled in the building."

Cleveland gave her a faint smile. "I guess they took the day off."

She looked her daughter in the eye. "Jessica, can I have a word with you?"

Cleveland got the hint to excuse himself and said, "Well, Jessica, it was nice meeting you, and you know where I am in case you need me." He nodded to Ms. Jones again and walked into his apartment on the ground floor.

Her mother turned to face her and said shrewdly, "Jessica, I'm not stupid. I know that you are upset about your brother, and I really do know how you feel, but you cannot take your anger out on anyone just because they sell drugs. You just got home from prison and don't want to put yourself in jeopardy and go back there. These people out here are not worth risking going back to prison for."

"These boys have virtually taken this building hostage and locked people in their own homes, and I'm supposed to sit by and let them do that shit?"

"Watch your mouth, Jessica," her mother warned.

"Sorry, Mama, but from the moment I got home they were trying to push that stuff on me and called me all kinds of names when I walked in the building." Jessica paused for a moment to ensure she understood. "I was even walking up the stairs and saw a girl sucking a man's penis and they barely even moved to let me by. All I could think of was if they can do that in front of me, what do they do in front of my mother? I just can't sit by and take it."

"Well, I been doing fine all these years without you being here, so what makes you think I can't handle myself by now, Jessica?"

Jessica was unmoved. "Because, Mama, it's only going to get

worse before it gets better, and I'll be damned if I sit by and let somebody put their hands on you if I have anything to do about it!"

For the first time, Ms. Jones realized that Jessica was no longer the innocent child who went away over six years ago.

Jessica decided to give Vonda a visit because she needed a friendly ear to vent her frustration. When she arrived to her building she knocked on the door and a booming male voice answered, "Who the fuck is it?"

"It's me, Jessica. I'm here to see Vonda."

"*Who* is it?" the voice repeated as the footsteps grew louder.

"Jessica!" she said, only this time louder.

The door suddenly flew opened and Jessica looked upward into the man's face. He was a fiercely huge, dark-skinned man with a Tootsie Roll pop in the side of his mouth. She immediately recognized him as Vonda's youngest brother—Chubby.

He began to blink rapidly when suddenly his mean scowl turned into a smile. "Jessica, holy shit, is that you?"

She smiled and nodded. "Yes, Chubby, it's me."

He snatched her off her feet and swung her around the doorway like she was a rag doll. He put her down and stepped backwards to get better look at her and grabbed her tightly again. Vonda came to the door to see what the excitement was about and saw that it was her homegirl and smiled. He ushered her inside and locked the door behind him.

"Damn, Jessica, Vonda told me you got out a few days ago. What took you so long to come over and see a nigga?" He looked her up and down. "Damn, and you looking good too."

Jessica was also amazed at how much Chubby had changed. "Forget about me, Chubby. Look at you. You look like you could play in the NFL, you've gotten so big. I remember when I was able to wrap my arms around you and now look at you—all big and sexy as ever."

Chubby blushed and began rocking back and forth on his toes just as he did as a kid. "You know how it is Jesse, I got love for everybody."

Vonda intervened. She knew that Chubby had big respect for Jessica and always wanted to look good in front of her for some reason. "Don't even try playing the Mister Good Guy role, Chubby. Tell her what you really do. Tell her how you got these niggas out here shaking in their boots whenever they see you. Tell her how you take these dealers' shit and turn around and sell it back to them. Tell her."

Chubby leered at his sister for telling Jessica his business. He faced Jessica and waved his sister off. "Jesse, don't listen to what she say. I don't do that no more. I kicked the habit, and I'm not in those streets no more." He stood erect. "I'm legit now, a businessman. I own a bar."

Vonda rolled her eyes and chuckled. "Since when did you own a bar?"

"See?" Chubby said with sarcasm. "It's a lot you don't know. I was just coming to your room to tell you before Jessica knocked on the door to ask you did you want to run it for me."

Vonda observed him for a moment. She knew that her parole officer was riding her about getting a job and knew that this would be a perfect opportunity. "Don't be playing with me, Chubby, because I ain't in the mood for your bullshit."

"I ain't bullshitting you, Vonda. You know I don't play when it comes to my business. I'm on parole too, and I needed a business so my P.O. would back the fuck up off me."

Both Vonda and Jessica stared at him for a moment.

"Oh, shit, Jesse," said Vonda. "He's telling the truth because he ain't rocking." Ever since Chubby was little, whenever he would tell a lie, he would avoid eye contact and sway and rock back and forth.

"You serious, Chubby?"

He smiled, pulled out a set of keys, and held them up. "As a motherfuckin' heart attack. The Starlight Bar on 127th Street and Lenox." He turned his attention to Jessica. "Jessica, you just got out, you want a job too?"

Jessica smiled, shook her head and said, "My Chubby Wubby," and gave him a big hug.

When the three of them walked into Vonda's room Jessica looked around and immediately grew emotional. It was exactly as it was when she was last there back in the day, and most importantly, when they were still young and innocent. She walked around the room in silence as she touched the posters on the walls, then the sparkling disco ball that hung from the ceiling. She then walked over to Vonda's dresser and that's when she saw the photographs of the four of them the night of the prom at her parents' house with their dates. She suddenly thought of Kenny and thought about what could've been and put her head down.

"You ok?" asked Vonda.

Jessica nodded quickly. "I was just thinking about all the

good times we had together in this room." Jessica smiled. "Even the bad times with all the arguments and fights we had with Tiny. I wish we could go back there."

Vonda and Chubby smiled as they thought back. Vonda watched her closely. "Jessica, I know you. What's wrong?"

She looked at Vonda and then at Chubby and admitted, "It's my brother." She looked them both in the eyes and continued. "I found him yesterday and he looked real bad."

Chubby put his head down as Vonda went over to her and put her arms around her as Jessica began to break down and cry.

"I cleaned him up and even convinced him to enter one of those programs, which I was going to take him into this morning. I even convinced my mother to let him stay over even after she said he was no good and that I was fooling myself." Jessica paused and wiped her eyes. "We went to sleep and my mother woke me up in the morning and he was gone, along with all the money I had in my pocket."

Chubby quickly reached in his pocket and pulled a stack of money and offered it all to her. Jessica quickly declined the money, waving it off.

Vonda said to Chubby, "No, Chubby, she don't need your money. She got plenty." She went to her closet and pulled out a shoebox and placed it on the bed. She pulled out a thick white envelope with Jessica's name written on it and handed it to her. She started to decline and but Vonda said, "One for all and all for one. Now it's too damn hard out here to walk around Harlem with no money, so either take this or get on welfare and cash in your food stamps for seven dollars cash for every ten-dollar stamp. Your choice."

Jessica stared at Vonda's smiling face and then lowered her head. "What about Lynn and Tiny

Vonda frowned, "Them bitches got their money the first day we got out without missing a beat. Tiny already burned her cash and be hitting me up nearly every day cause she still on that shit. Lynn went back to being Lynn and all she does is buy clothes and get her hair and nails done trying to impress everybody, male *and* female, if you know what I mean. But at least she found a job and she's working at Macy's full-time now. So she's doing ok." She handed the envelope to Jessica and she accepted it. "What you need to do is find yourself an apartment like I'm about to do."

Jessica shook her head and responded, "No, not right now."

Vonda frowned and asked, "Well, why not? That building that you living in is a crack house. You'd be doing yourself a favor."

Jessica shook her head again and said, "No, I can't leave my mother there. It's too bad in there. I already got into a beef with these dudes from the building and I got to see it through."

Vonda was taken aback and asked with concern, "Beef with who, Jessica?"

Jessica shrugged her shoulders. "I beat these boys with a baseball bat and told them not to sell drugs in my building again and they threatened to come back."

Chubby came alive as his face contorted with rage. "What did you say, Jessica?"

Vonda couldn't believe what she heard and said with anger, "No, you didn't, Jessica. You could have gotten yourself hurt! What if one of them had a gun or something, what would you have done then?"

Chubby reached in his waistband and pulled out a huge gun,

cocked it, and said, "She would have gotten me to lay them niggas down!" Chubby's entire facial expression and demeanor changed in a matter of seconds. "Now, let's go Jessica so you can point them niggas out and let me handle my bidness, come on!"

Chubby was a sick man and was diagnosed as a manic depressant with homicidal tendencies as per the State of New York Mental Board. He was first arrested at the age of fourteen for nearly beating six of his former classmates to death with his bare hands after they teased him about his weight. As he grew older, things fared no better as he was put in youth detention centers throughout New York and was finally emancipated from the system when he turned eighteen. He was mandated to a indefinite parole with stipulations to take his medication and see a psychiatrist on a monthly basis. Jessica was suddenly afraid of Chubby when she realized that he was serious and wanted to kill the men for a small infraction.

"Hold up. It's no need to do that, Chubby. They are punks and if they wanted to do something they would have done it already," Jessica said, trying her best to defuse the possibly volatile situation.

Vonda wasn't buying any of it. "Naw, Jessica, you don't know how these li'l niggas are today. They would put a bullet in you just for looking at them the wrong way. You need our help on this one, so maybe you should tell Chubby who they are so he can handle them niggas for you."

"No, Vonda, I'm not going to allow you or Chubby to get mixed up in this shit if something ever goes down. I won't be able to live with myself if y'all jeopardize your parole."

"Fuck a parole, Jesse!" Chubby screamed. "If you got beef, then

I got beef ,and that's how the shit is gonna go down. So let's go, and show me where them nigga be pumping at."

"They be right in the building on 142nd Street between Lenox and 7th Ave, building 141 I think," Vonda said quickly.

Chubby smiled knowingly and said, "Yeah, I know exactly who them niggas are." Chubby was about to head out the door but Jessica stopped him.

"Chubby! Chubby! Don't go, just listen to me."

Chubby turned around. "Jessica, it's nothing you can say to stop me, so you wasting your time."

"Just listen to me a moment, Chubby. Just listen."

Chubby relaxed a minute, put his back up against the wall, and said, "I'm listening."

Jessica inhaled deeply. "Give me two days, just two days, and if I don't straighten it out by then, you can come and do what you want. Ok?"

Chubby was still boiling, but he agreed. "Just two days, Jessica, and on the third day if you ain't straighten them niggas out, I'm coming in there blazing!"

Jessica nodded and then gave him a big hug.

He pulled away and said, "I just ask that you do two things."

"What is it, Chubby?"

Chubby reached in his coat pocket and pulled out a small-caliber weapon and handed it to her. "Take this. It's a 25 automatic. It's small, but it got a bang loud enough to back a nigga up off of you. Promise me you'll use it if you need to. It's better to be judged by twelve than to be carried by six, if you know what I mean."

Chubby awaited an answer until Jessica nodded her approval.

"What about the second thing you want me to do, Chubby?"

Jessica asked inquisitively.

Chubby blushed like he did as a kid and started rocking back and forth. "Can you cook me some lima beans like you used to do for me back in the day?"

Jessica smiled. "It would be my pleasure."

Chapter 14

When Jessica arrived home that evening she was met by Cleveland, who was sitting on the stoop with what appeared to be crowd of people. Cleveland stood up and welcomed her back home.

"Hey, Jessica, how was your day?"

Jessica smiled nervously. "It was ok, but who are all these people?"

Cleveland turned around. "These are the other tenants. They heard about you standing up to those crack dealers and wanted to meet you." He smiled. "Hell, the whole block heard about what happened and wanted to meet you as well."

He saw that Jessica was uneasy about it.

"You see, Jessica, to a lot of these people all they have is their home and their neighborhood and that was taken away from them a long time ago. Like I explained to you before, since this crack epidemic came out these people had become prisoners in their own homes. When most of the tenants came out of their homes today, it was refreshing to not step over addicts or tippy-toe past the dealers and just relax on their own stoop on a nice summer afternoon like today. Look at them."

Jessica faced them and saw the people laughing and chatting amongst themselves as if they hadn't a care in the world. Cleveland let her absorb the gravity of it all.

"We all had a long discussion and came to the conclusion that our homes are worth fighting for and that if we all band together we might be able to take back our buildings again."

For the first time, Jessica smiled and knew she didn't have to take on the entire load all by herself.

"So you in?" asked Cleveland as he extended his beefy hand.

Jessica smiled and said, "Yes, I'm in."

They shook hands and he said, "Good, good." He walked her over to meet the rest of the tenants, who quickly introduced themselves and thanked her for being so brave.

Around 10PM that night, the most active time the dealers would come out and set up shop to sell their crack, to show a sign of force every single tenant stood on the stoop and did not allow a single person who didn't live in the building to enter if they weren't going to visit someone in the building. They illuminated the lights on the stoops so that their presence was known. They then set up four, four-hour shifts with at least five tenants per shift to be on duty until they were sure that they had taken back control of the building. They even repaired all locks to the building's doors and handed out new keys to all the tenants.

Within a week of constant patrols, standing up to the dealers and turning crack addicts away, the tenants of the building had taken full control of their building again. The tenants were so thankful to Jessica for coming in and risking her life that they threw a party in her honor in the building's community room in the basement.

The night of the party went off without a hitch and everyone was festive, when suddenly a teen ran into the party and said, "There was a shooting across the street and people are dead!"

Everyone stopped what they were doing and ran upstairs and out the front door. When they got outside, they saw the carnage of bodies of men sprawled on the ground in a puddle of blood. Seconds later, they heard the squeal of a mother's cry as she hugged a little girl no older than five years old on the ground.

"My baby! Someone shot my baby!" the mother cried hysterically.

"Call an ambulance!" everyone began to shout. "Call the ambulance!"

Cleveland and Jessica burst through the crowd and stared down at the mother cradling her tiny daughter as blood flowed rapidly from her shoulder and arm. Jessica recognized the three boys who laid in the gutter, now lifeless, as the ones who she'd removed from her building the morning she had the bat. Words could not describe how everyone felt at that moment as the mother's cries filled the air of the night. Three young men died and a child was in critical condition that night as the police and ambulance came and went that fateful evening.

Remnants of yellow tape and blood surrounded the area. By morning the people whispered about the incident and were sure that the shooting was drug-related. No one was even arrested for the shooting because everyone claimed not to have seen anything, so the killer got away without as much as a glance. Rumor had it, that the three young men who died that night tried to take over the building across the street and the dealers who were already occupying the building warned them earlier that day to sell their product elsewhere and they didn't heed the advice.

In light of the shooting, Jessica and Cleveland organized and set up an emergency meeting with the local precinct by posting leaflets in the every building in the block. Over one hundred people showed up that night as the captain and eight of his officers from central division command addressed the residents of the surrounding area. The locals were in an uproar as the middle-aged white officer yelled over the crowd to try to regain a call of order.

"Ladies and gentleman, please, can you calm down and let one person speak at a time? We will not get anywhere if we can't hear you address your issues at hand."

A big dark-skinned woman shouted, "How can you tell us to calm down when our children are being shot dead in the street like dogs and no one was arrested?"

The statement added fuel to the people, and the crowd yelled even louder.

"Yeah," said one elderly man, "instead of all you policemen standing up there telling us to calm down, you should be out there searching for the killer!"

The officer tried to speak, but the large crowd drowned them out.

"Please, please, people," said the captain. "Let us talk, and we can answer your questions."

The crowd slowly settled down and the captain said, "I'd like to introduce you to the lead detective on this case, Detective Harris."

Detective Harris stepped from behind all the other officers and to the podium. He was young, tall, well-built black man with a short afro and long porkchop sideburns. The crowd was totally surprised to see a Negro in such high ranking position, and it immediately got quiet as soon as he stepped in front of the podium.

He surveyed the crowd before speaking then cleared his throat. "Good evening, ladies and gentlemen, my name is Detective Dale Harris, and I have been assigned to the shooting that happened in this case. I'm not at liberty to divulge to you the particulars of the case because it is still ongoing, but what I can tell you is that we are doing the best we can with leads that we do have. Unfortunately, we do not have as many eyewitness accounts as we need, and we are hopeful that someone will still come forward to help us to bring the perpetrators to justice."

"So, what are you saying?" yelled one of the men in the crowd. "You saying that you have nothing?"

"What I'm saying," the detective continued, "is that we need more of your help to bring this case to a close."

There were many grumbles from the crowd.

"What, you want us to solve the case for you? Is that what you saying? Risk our lives so them drug dealers could come after us?" said a woman from the crowd.

"Yeah, that's your job," hollered another.

The officers looked from one face to another and saw that this was going nowhere until a woman asked, "What are you doing about the origin of the problem? The drug dealers that took over our buildings and block. What about them?"

"Yeah," said a man, "they dealing right in the open. Why aren't you doing anything about that?"

The captain stepped forth with a folder. He put on his glasses and read, "Within the last fiscal year, we made over thirty arrests, all drug-related charges, and closed down over a dozen drug houses on your block alone."

"As soon as you close one down, two others open up to replace them. What are we supposed to do about that? Point them out to you?"

"I ain't gon' risk my life to rat out none of them drug dealers. I got a family to take care of," cried another.

"Yeah!" screamed the crowd, turning it into a louder pandemonium.

Detective Harris raised both his hand up to speak. "What you can do . . ." He paused to ensure everyone heard him and repeated, "What you can do to help us is organize a tenant patrol and a tenant watch and band together as a block association and stop them before they set up these houses."

There was still a lot of grumbling from the crowd because they weren't buying any of it.

"Oh, that won't work," everyone began saying.

The officers knew there was nothing that could satisfy the crowd and began shaking their heads until Cleveland stood up.

"Hold on! Hold on, people! He's right; it can be done."

The mob suddenly turned silent as they stared at their neighbor.

Cleveland looked around at all of their faces and explained,

"I'm the superintendent for 141, and we had a big drug problem in our building no more than two weeks ago."

He turned toward Jessica and touched her shoulder. "That was, until this young lady right here said she had enough and stood up to them dealers and told them they wasn't selling no drugs in that building no more."

It was so silent that you could hear a pin drop as Cleveland continued to explain. "That next day, we organized with the rest of the building's tenants and we changed all the locks so nobody who didn't live there could get in, put brighter lights in the building, and set up 'round the clock shifts at night to let the dealers see our presence." Cleveland exhaled. "It took us only three days. Three days," he repeated, "to let them crack addicts and dealers know that we didn't want them there anymore."

The officers began to nod their approval.

"See?" said Detective Harris. "It just takes one person to make a difference. Think about the difference you can make if you had ten such persons like her. Twenty or fifty?"

Everyone began nodding.

"Now, if you organize a block patrol and association, we will work hand in hand with regular patrol to make it really happen. And, ladies and gentlemen, if we work together, I can assure you that you will have you homes and your neighborhood back to the way it used to be, maybe even better. So if you're ready to take that step, all you have to do now is pick a leader."

Everyone remained silent and shifted their eyes from one face to another until Cleveland offered, "I nominate Jessica Jones to be our leader and organizer of 142nd Street Tenants Block Association!"

Another person agreed. "I second."

And another person finalized it by saying, "I third that."

Jessica was a little stunned she'd received many pats on her back, but remained poised nonetheless.

Chapter 15

Jessica and Cleveland delved into organizing the block association with fury. They started with the worst buildings on the block and basically commandeered the building with their presence and held a sit-in to make their presence known. Every person who entered the building was asked to sign in and wait for the tenant to come down and escort them to their apartment. All broken locks were fixed and the roof and stairwell was patrolled regularly. Many minor incidents had arisen, like dealers being denied entrance to the building or someone being threatened, but they quickly followed the rules of order by Detective Harris and called the police.

Within one month time of starting the block association tenant patrol, nearly half the buildings were now free of dealing and drugs. This was also about the time that the news media took notice and did a piece on the organized tenant patrol and ran a feature story on Jessica. In addition to making the local news,

Jessica and the entire association made the *Daily News*. Jessica finally made her fifteen minute of fame in the process. She wasn't used to all the attention and stayed humble throughout her many interviews and had Cleveland, a former Vietnam Veteran, right beside her.

It was a warm summer afternoon, and Jessica had just come from midtown Manhattan from meeting with her parole officer, who was very happy that she was doing so well and had found employment by working at Chubby's bar. He told her that if she continued showing progress he would recommend early termination from the conditions of parole.

As soon as she walked in the neighborhood she was greeted by nearly everyone she passed, when suddenly she ran into a person who she hadn't seen in years. She nearly lost her breath when she saw him and stopped in her tracks, unsure whether to walk up to him and hug him or run away in the other direction. Jessica gathered her bearings and proceeded toward him.

Face to face now, Kenny smiled and said excitedly, "Hi, Jessica."

She returned the smile. "Hey, Kenny."

There was a momentary pause as they both stood in silence, unsure what to do next. Kenny finally wrapped his arms around her until she slowly embraced him back. They pulled apart and both were unsure what to do or say next.

Kenny looked around and finally asked, "Do you want to go somewhere and get something to eat and talk?"

Jessica eyed the ground and looked up and nodded. "Yes, I'd like to get something to eat."

He smiled and said, "Great. I'm parked right across the street." He led her to his black Jaguar and opened the door for her to get in.

Kenny drove off and took Jessica all the way downtown to the South Street Seaport to have some fine seafood cuisine. While they waited for their food, they made short talk and caught up on things. Kenny told her how surprised he was when he saw her in the papers and on the news and waited all day just to see her. During dinner Kenny explained to her what he'd been doing with himself over the years.

"So, you look like you been taking good care of yourself. What is it that you do?"

He wiped his mouth and placed his napkin on the table. "What did I tell you I wanted to do the first day we met?"

Jessica curled her lip and thought back for a second and smiled. "You said you wanted to get into real estate."

He smiled and said, "You got a good memory. I'm a real estate broker, slash developer."

Jessica's eyes lit up. "Really?"

"Yes, really, I own several properties in Harlem, mostly brownstones and multiple units and a couple of buildings in the Bronx."

"Oh, Kenny, I'm so happy for you. You really set out and did what you said you would do."

He shrugged his shoulders and said, "Thanks, but most of the buildings are abandoned, and I picked them up cheap from the city, but I'm just sitting on them for now and looking for some investors because Harlem is going to be booming one day, and when it is, I'll make a good return on my money."

Jessica smiled and asked, "You think so? Because the way it's going now everybody is moving out of Harlem with the drug epidemic and all."

Kenny agreed by nodding. "I know what you mean. I own a large multi-unit complex and the drug dealers have taken over the entire building, turning it into a mess. None of the tenants, the ones who are still left, are not paying me any rent, so it's costing me a fortune in taxes and mortgage just to maintain it. I just wish I knew a way of getting them out."

"Why don't you just sell it?"

He shook his head and frowned. "Like you said, the drug epidemic has taken its toll on Harlem, and everyone is moving out, so if I do sell it I would take a huge loss. Nobody wants to invest in Harlem yet, so all I can do is hold on to it until I figure something out." Kenny seemed to grow angrier the more he talked about it. He quickly changed the subject. "Enough about me and my problems, so what are you doing now?"

"Well, as you saw in the papers, I pretty much have my hands full with this block association thing, and we're just trying to make the community a better place for us to live."

Kenny smiled at her. "You know when I read the story on you it made me proud. I mean, it takes a lot of guts, even for a man, to stand up against these young kids today."

She nodded.

"How's your parents? They still live on 137th street?"

Jessica fiddled with her napkin. "My father died when I was in prison, and me and my mother live on 142nd Street now."

"Oh, I'm so sorry, Jessica. I didn't know."

She waved him off. "You had no way of knowing. He was so

heartbroken after I got arrested,; I guess he lost the will to live. Me and my father were so close, I only could imagine what was going through his head with me being in there." She exhaled. "I never forgot the look on his face when they led me out of the courtroom the day we got convicted." She closed her eyes and shook her head. "I just can't get that look out of my mind."

Kenny tried to spare her the pain by telling her she didn't have to discuss it any further, but she waved him off and said, "No, it's ok, I've made my peace with God about it." Jessica chuckled and continued. "We even lost the house after my mother couldn't keep up with the second mortgage for paying my lawyer's fee."

Kenny shook his head and frowned. "Y'all lost the house?"

Jessica nodded her head and said, "Yep. I was in that house since I was two years old, and just like that we lost everything."

Kenny inhaled deeply and tried to change the subject, "So, how is your younger brother? What's his name, Jordan, right?"

Jessica went silent again and said sadly, "He's out there smoking crack too."

"Oh, no!" said Kenny, genuinely upset.

Jessica stuck out her bottom lip and said, "Yep, my baby brother is a crack head."

Kenny put his hands behind his head and stared at the ceiling.

"That was the reason I started what I did, because that shit took my little brother from me."

They chatted and reminisced for the next two hours. When Kenny finally dropped Jessica off in front of her building, they promised each other that they would go out again the following weekend. As they stood in front of her building, Kenny held her hand as he walked her up the steps and said their goodbyes.

"So, I'll see you this Friday?"

Jessica nodded and repeated, "Yes, I'll see you Friday."

She put her key in the front door and was about to walk in when Kenny said, "Jessica?"

She turned around instantly and said, "Yes, Kenny?"

He walked directly up to her and slowly kissed her goodnight. They pulled away and stared into each other eyes and Kenny said, "I missed you, Jessica. I always did."

"I missed you too, Kenny, very much."

Kenny nodded slowly. "Friday?"

She nodded and repeated, "Friday."

Chapter 16

For the first time since Jessica had gotten out of prison, all was going so well for her. She and Kenny began dating and seeing each other on a regular basis and began rekindling the magic that they once had. Jessica told Kenny some of the things that happened since they departed, including about Officer Clooney and Officer Landry, and bits and pieces on how they had to handle the Mama situation. Kenny never flinched as she told him. He said he would have probably done the same thing if his life was on the line. Things couldn't have been better until one day, thing began to suddenly fall apart.

It was a bright and sunny afternoon when Jessica and her mother were on their way to the supermarket to do some weekly shopping. Since Jessica received the money from Vonda and was working at the bar, she was contributing to the household bills with her mother. As soon as they were about to enter the supermarket, she heard someone behind them call Jessica's name.

"Jessica Jones."

They turned and saw three grim looking men behind them, one smiling and two with frowns on their faces.

Suspicious, Jessica answered, "I don't think I know you."

The short one, the one who was smiling said, "Well, we know you."

Jessica saw where this was going and decided not to get into jail mode since her mother was present. "Listen, me and my mother are busy right now. I have to talk to you another time." She grabbed her mother by the hand to escort her into the supermarket.

"It's about your brother, Jordan."

Jessica stopped in her tracks and turned around to look at him. She turned to her mother and said, "Mama, go inside. I'll catch up with you in a minute."

Ms. Jones shook her head and said, "No, Jessica, you don't know these people. You don't know what this is about."

"Ma, I'm just going to see what they want with Jordan. I'll be only a minute. Go ahead inside. I'll only be a minute, I promise you."

Ms. Jones looked at the men and then back to her daughter and walked slowly into the supermarket looking behind her all the while.

When she was sure her mother was inside, Jessica looked at the men and approached them with her arms folded. Standing in front of them now, Jessica asked, "So where you know me from?"

The shorter man jokingly said, "I don't know, was it the papers or was it the news? I forget."

Jessica was unmoved. She shifted her weight from one leg to the other. "So, what do you want to talk to me about?"

The man stepped closer and said, "Like I said, I want to talk to you about your brother, Jordan."

Jessica was growing irritated and growled, "Well talk!"

The man was much shorter then Jessica, but his large afro made him look taller. He wore big, thick jewelry around his neck and over-sized rings on his fingers. He looked like a typical Harlem drug dealer, Jessica thought.

"No need to get hostile, baby." He smiled, revealing his gold teeth.

"I'm not your baby, so save the bullshit and tell me what you want, li'l man!"

The comment wiped the smile off his face and he snared, "All right, bitch, you want it raw? My boss ain't too fuckin' happy about your li'l protest that you doing, and that shit is gonna stop or else!" He paused to see if he hit a nerve, but Jessica showed no emotion. "Now we coming back on the block to do our business, and if any of them old motherfuckers get in the way we gonna drop 'em just like that. So go back and tell them that shit, 'cause we know where all y'all motherfuckers live. When we come, we gonna blow your fuckin' doors down and kill their whole fuckin' family. And the first person we coming after is you, your crackhead brother, and that bitch of a mother—"

Before the man could finish, Jessica unleashed a brutal elbow to the man's face and he went down in an instant. Jessica was fuming as she stood over the man and spewed, "If you even think about touching anybody in my family it will be the last time you breathe, bastard!"

The man held his now broken nose and looked up at Jessica and couldn't believe she had snuffed him. He quickly regained his balance and reached behind him in his waistband to pull out his weapon. But Jessica was quicker, and she pulled out the 25 automatic that Chubby gave her and aimed to kill.

The two men with him subdued him and warned, "Not, here man, not here."

Li'l man was in a psychotic stupor as he struggled to be released. A crowd began to gawk as they watched the tall girl aim a gun at the three men in broad daylight.

"Let that nigga go so he could squeeze that shit!" Jessica warned through gritted teeth.

The short man calmed down long enough to make a reasonable decision and realized that now wasn't the time. He wiped the blood from his nose and looked down the barrel of her gun and then at Jessica.

He smiled and shook head. "Aight, aight, you got this one, bitch, but it won't be another one, I can promise you that shit." He wiped his nose again and looked at the blood on his hand. "When you lay in your bed tonight I want you to think about your crack smoking brother. I don't know where he's at yet, but like all dirty crackheads he gonna eventually come out at night like a vampire to search for his next hit, and I'm gonna be right there to serve him."

He looked at her one final time and said calmly, "I want you to ask around about my boss. His name is Bosco. I'm giving you three days, and if you still trying be Superman, I'm gonna be right there to bring your ass down to earth. Believe that shit!"

When they finally walked away, Jessica put down the weapon and breathed for the first time.

Jessica didn't tell her mother what the boys had wanted that day only because she didn't want to worry her. Instead, she told her not to worry because they only wanted to know where Jordan was because he owed them some money. But in her heart, Jessica knew she would have to tell her eventually.

She decided to wait until she found out more about this dude named Bosco before she knew for sure what to do about the situation. She asked Cleveland to check around the neighborhood and find out about him just in case they were just some punks trying to scare her, though she doubted it. Jessica was preparing to go to bed when she heard a light knock on the door. Not taking any chances, she grabbed the weapon from her purse and crept toward the door silently and peeked out the peephole. She saw that it was Cleveland and stuck the gun in her robe and opened up the door.

Sensing that he had some bad news by the expression on his face she quickly asked, "What's wrong Cleveland?"

"Sorry for coming so late Jessica, but I couldn't wait till the morning to tell you."

Jessica placed one finger over her lips, signaling him to speak a little quieter. She looked behind her to see if her mother was around and stepped out in the hallway so they could talk.

He shook his head before he began to speak, "Jessica, I searched around neighborhood like you told me to do and asked around about your guy Bosco." He eyed the floor and then looked at Jessica with what appeared to be fear in his eyes. "From what I heard, this guy is bad news. He's one of the biggest dope peddlers on this side of Harlem, and he's Jamaican and got a strong posse." He paused briefly until he told her the real bad news. "He is also known to be very violent—a killer—and has the record to prove it. He is also known to kill off other drug rivals that try to deal in his spots. The word on the street is that he had several drug spots right here in this block and that he is pissed that he is no longer making money off of them and will be coming back real soon to reclaim them."

He stared at Jessica and admitted, "We got another problem."

Jessica could tell that Cleveland was clearly shaken because he closed his eyes and his body grew rigid.

He raised his head. "The same thing happened to you happened to some other people from the neighborhood on tenant patrol."

"Oh, my God, they went to the tenants, too?" asked Jessica.

Cleveland nodded. "And they immediately left their posts and ran to the safety of their homes."

"How many left their post?"

"All of them." Cleveland sighed. "You got to understand, Jessica, a lot of these tenants are old. They'd rather lie down and take it rather get involved with these dealers and lose their life, even if it's for a good cause."

Jessica couldn't believe all the work she had done was now in vain. She looked at Cleveland and asked, "So, what about you, Cleveland? What are you going to do?"

There was a long pause as Jessica watched him closely as he pondered the question.

"My daddy use to always tell me 'Boy, either you in for a penny or in for a pound.'" He raised his head and smiled. "Well, I never liked pennies, so I guess I'm in for the pound."

Jessica smiled and nodded her approval. They hugged and when Cleveland pulled away his face showed some concern.

"Now Jessica, you don't have to be part of this. You young and got your whole life ahead of you. I'd understand if you wanted to walk away from this."

"Not a chance. They already threatened the life of my family, and I don't know where my brother is, so I got to get to them before they get to my brother."

Cleveland agreed.

"All we got to do now is come up with a plan to get rid of them."

Cleveland suddenly had a sadistic smile on his face as his lips curled and his eyebrow raised. "Now, baby girl, you just stepped into my world. I'm a ex infantry man and a Vietnam vet. I know a thing or two about ridding an enemy, and the best defense is a good offense."

Jessica was confused and Cleveland read her face and said, "Don't worry about it. You come down to my apartment in the morning and I'll explain everything."

Jessica agreed.

Cleveland nodded and was about to walk down the stairs when he suddenly turned around and said, "Oh, Jessica. I want you to know that I play for keeps, and that some of them won't be coming back, so if you not ok with that, I suggest you back out right now."

Jessica stared in his eyes, and for the first time since she met Cleveland, she saw another side to him—she saw death in his eyes. She thought about it only for a second before she nodded her approval. "I'm with you."

He smiled. "One more thing. You need to try to get your mother to go away for a couple of weeks because they may want to get her to get to you, so think about it."

Chapter 17

Cleveland and Jessica spent the next entire morning and afternoon devising a plan to stop Bosco and his crew from not only harming them, but also ending his reign of terror and drug stranglehold on the neighborhood. Jessica found out that they would not be handling the fight alone and that Cleveland had recruited some of his Vietnam buddies from the war to help them with their problem. He also had a request for Jessica to do some recruiting of her own in order to complete the task at hand—female friends, which she had no problem getting. Jessica had a sit-down with her mother that same night and told her what she needed to hear, but not everything. Jessica was surprised that her mother took the bad news so well and agreed that she would go down south to visit her sister Cherice in Maryland. Since Ms. Jones was a schoolteacher, she didn't have to worry about taking time off from work because she was out for summer vacation.

Jessica caught up with Kenny that night, and, as usual, they went out of the neighborhood to have dinner. Since it was Friday, Jessica had gone out earlier to 34th Street and brought a nice outfit and had her hair and nails done. Since she had gotten so close to Kenny over the last few weeks, she felt it was only right to tell Kenny some of the things that were going on. If something were to go down, she didn't want him to be caught unwittingly in the crossfire. As much as she didn't want to, she decided it would be best to put the relationship on hold, before it became too serious.

She told Kenny how dangerous it would be and assured him she wouldn't be closely involved. He sat motionless and was stunned to know that she was putting her life in danger.

Kenny raised his head with sorrow in his eyes. "Jessica, I don't want you to do this."

Jessica remained silent as he continued to plead.

"I, I just don't think that it is worth the effort to put your life on the line for something you have no control of. Why do it? You should just walk away and don't look back."

Jessica shook her head. "No, it's not that simple. My brother is still out there somewhere and they can get to him and I won't be able to live with that. Besides, the people on the block need me, and I'm going to finish what I started."

Kenny shook his head again. "Jessica, those same people on your block could care less if they sold drugs or not, and they wouldn't lose a night's sleep if something happened to you. What you need to do is find your brother and I can put him and your mother up in one of the apartments I have in the Bronx, and you can stay with me."

Jessica was touched by the gesture, but knew it would not work. "No, Kenny, my mother is going down to Maryland tomorrow, plus I still don't know where my brother is, and he can't be trusted alone anyway."

"At least he'd be alive, Jessica!" Kenny snapped. He caught himself and apologized quickly. "I'm sorry, but the thought of you being put in danger got me messed up."

"I understand. You don't have to apologize."

"Then why don't you stay with me a couple of days to think about it?"

Jessica thought about it for a moment. "No, I can't do that, Kenny, as much as I'd like to. I got too much to do."

Kenny put his head down, defeated, and strained to find words to change her mind. "You got to understand, I lost you once, and I don't want to risk losing you all over again. I love you, Jessica."

Jessica was touched and took his hand into hers. "I love you too, Kenny, but I got to do what I got to do."

Kenny studied her face and knew she would not waiver. He took a deep breath then smiled. "Well, can you at least stay with me tonight?"

Jessica blushed, and with a glint in her eyes, she nodded and said, "Let's go."

Kenny and Jessica made love the entire night, then they fell into each other's arms exhausted. Kenny and Jessica held each other tightly the rest of the night, never wanting to let go. When Kenny awoke that morning Jessica was already gone.

He sat in bed and wondered what could have been.

Jessica got back to the neighborhood right on time. When she arrived at her building she met up with Cleveland, who was standing in a circle with three other middle-aged men.

When Cleveland spotted Jessica, he smiled and waved his hand. "Jessica," he yelled as she approached them. Cleveland appeared to be in an especially happy mood as he grasped his palms together and introduced her to the men.

"Jessica," said Cleveland, "I would like you to meet a few of my old buddies from 'Nam."

He put his arms on the shoulders of the man closest to him, a tall burly man with a thick cigar in his mouth. He had ugly burn marks on his face and arms.

"This here is Johnson, master of demolition and explosives."

He turned to the next man, a Puerto Rican who was small in stature. He had a no-nonsense air about him, judging from the expression on his face. "This is Shooter, expert marksman, and weapons specialist."

Shooter was still wearing his old olive green Army fatigues and tipped his black beret to Jessica.

"And this one here is Doc," Cleveland said, "and I want you to watch out for him, 'cause he's a ladies' man."

Doc smiled, revealing a perfect set of white teeth. "Don't tell her that. It ruins the excitement." He gave Jessica a light hug and a peck on the cheek."

Jessica blushed.

"He's our reconnaissance man and driver. Don't ask him why they call him Doc." Cleveland smiled and playfully punched Doc on the arm. He inhaled deeply as he looked over his men and said excitedly, "Man, this reminds me of old times. It makes me feel nineteen again."

"Hell, I'm still only twenty-five," joked Doc as he leered at Jessica.

"Oh, there he go already," joked Cleveland. "Anyway, we got a lot of planning to do and don't have much time. And by the way, Jessica, I spoke to your mother, and I'm going to drive her down to the bus station tonight to make sure she's safe and sound."

Jessica thanked him.

"Ok, we'll be in my apartment, so when you ready you can come on down we'll fill you in on the plan."

"Thank you, Cleveland. I'll be down in about an hour, ok?"

"Ok, you just take your time. We'll be here."

"Yes," flirted Doc, "We will be here waiting for your lovely presence."

Jessica arrived upstairs and was looking forward to taking a hot bath and changing out of the clothes and heels she was wearing.

When she put her key in the lock her mother was already there to meet her at the door. "Jessica, where have you been? I was up all night worrying that something had happened to you."

Jessica was caught off guard and surprised that her mother was that concerned about her.

Jessica smiled inside because in a strange way she felt a motherly love. "I'm sorry, Ma. I lost track of time and I didn't expect to stay out all night. I should have called you. I'm sorry."

"Between you and Jordan, and that incident with those men at the grocery store, my nerves have been shot lately."

Jessica remained silent, and then walked into her room.

"You know I'm leaving tonight and that Cleveland is driving me down to the bus station?"

Jessica nodded. "Yeah, I know. I saw Cleveland downstairs and he told me."

"You know, Jessica, you don't have to stay here. You can come with me. Your aunt would love to see you. You don't have anything to prove, you know."

"I know, Mama. I'm not. And besides, you know I can't go out of state without my parole officer knowing about it."

Mrs. Jones nodded. "Well, you be careful, ok?"

"Ok."

Ms. Jones glanced down at the floor then started walked out her room when Jessica called, "Mama?"

Ms. Jones turned around.

"Thanks for being concerned about me."

Her mother gave her a light smile and relented, "I think it's time we talk."

Both Jessica and her mother knew that the strain in their relationship had to be dealt with sooner or later. Both of them had unsettling questions that needed to be answered so they could move on and that time had finally come. Jessica knew how much her mother loved her father and felt guilty that she caused him so much anguish since her arrest. She also knew how much he and her mother had sacrificed financially because the lawyer fees had wiped out their entire savings. Deep down, she knew her mother blamed her for it all, and she couldn't help but admit the damage she had done and carried the burden of guilt on her small shoulders for years. When her mother lost her son to the street, Jessica knew that that must have been the final blow that left her so cold and shallow.

"Jessica, I know over the years that me and you never saw eye to eye and didn't have the best mother-daughter relationship.

But, I want to tell you that it never had anything to do with you. I guess I raised you the same way my mother raised me, and that was all that I knew. My mother told me something years ago that I never forgot. She told me that, 'A mother raises her daughters, but loves her sons.' I grew angry when she told me that because I thought she loved my brothers more than me and I resented her for that. It wasn't until I had my own family that I began to understand why she told me that." Jessica searched her mother's eyes as she awaited an answer. "When you were born, I was excited about having you, but your father . . ." She smiled as she thought back. "Your father was absolutely overjoyed when you were born. I remember how he would hold you in his arms ever so gently and sing to you every night. He loved you more than life itself, and I knew from that point on that I could not possibly give you love the way a father could." She began shaking her head as she reminisced. "That's when it hit me. I now knew why my mother told me that. My job wasn't to give you the love and affection the way your father did; my job was to raise you into a strong, self-reliant woman so you could survive and have your own family. Even though you went to prison, Jessica, I had faith in you and I was sure of one thing, and that was you would survive, because we are survivors, and you should always believe that!"

Jessica nodded her head, conveying that she understood exactly what her mother was trying to say to her. They embraced for the first time since she could remember.

Her mother stood up and said, "I've got to start packing, so I better get going."

Jessica nodded.

As her mother was walking out her room she said, "Oh, yeah, your brother left a note under the door for you. It's on your dresser."

Jessica immediately stood up, ran over to the dresser, and picked up the letter up.

Jessica,

I'm sorry for what I did to you, taking your money and all. I feel real bad about it. This crack makes you do things you never thought you would do, and I have no control. That night I really wanted to go in rehab but the crack was calling me. I couldn't help myself. The reason I'm writing you is because I saw you on the news and I'm scared for you because you're messing with the wrong people. I don't want to see nothing happen to you, so just leave it all alone. Do this for me. Daddy is gone and that hurt me in ways you can't imagine, but if I lose you, I don't think I can live no more. If you stop right now, I'll let you come get me and we can go straight down to the rehab and check me in. Meet me tonight at ten o'clock. I'm staying in an abandoned building on 144th street, building 106 on the 4th floor. I love you, Jessica.

Jordan

After Jessica finished bathing and dressing, all she could think about was the letter her brother wrote and meeting him that night. She arrived at Cleveland's apartment, and the three other men were sitting around the table, hard at work devising a plan of action. The apartment had a thick stench of cigar odor looming in the air.

"Jessica, glad you're here." Cleveland smiled, placed his arm on Jessica's shoulder, and said, "Good, let's take care of business."

He walked her over to the table and he showed her sketches and Polaroid pictures of buildings and faces of men. Jessica was amazed at how much information that Cleveland had obtained already. Cleveland smiled and knew she was impressed. He picked up a picture off the table and held it in front of her.

"This here is our boy, the infamous Bosco."

Jessica stared at the evil looking man in the picture with thick dreadlocks that fell past his shoulders. He was very dark skinned and his body was tall and lanky.

"Fellows, we got our job cut out on this one, because he is a one mean son of a bitch. He has a reputation of killing off his rivals and wouldn't hesitate killing someone without so much batting an eye."

Shooter looked confused. "Why do we have to plan anything? Just let me get on a roof and I'll take him out that way."

Cleveland shook his head. "No, Shooter, it's not that simple, what we want to do is smash his whole operation and take his drugs off the streets. You'll have your chance to put in some work, trust me."

Shooter looked disappointed, but agreed.

Cleveland continued, "Word on the street is that he likes women, plenty of women and sleeps with a minimum of two to three at a time."

"My kind of man," joked Doc. "Maybe we can have a little party before we kill him. What do you say?"

Cleveland waved him off and selected another photo. "I took this one at one of the several buildings that he sells drugs in.

Some of them from what I gather are just areas where they store or cook up the drugs."

Cleveland picked up several more pictures. "He has this building on 116th Street, this one on 118th Street. This one is right in this block across the street from where the three boys were murdered and the little girl was shot. This last one is on 144th Street right, around the corner."

Jessica took the five pictures and examined them closely one by one. Her skin began to crawl when she looked at them, especially when she looked at the picture of Bosco—which gave her chills. Jessica continued to look over the picture as Cleveland continued to explain.

"These are some of his flunkies. Do you recognize any of them Jessica?"

She looked at the pictures and nodded. "Yes, this one, this one, and this one." She pointed to one of the thugs who'd approached her at the grocery store.

"I thought so," Cleveland said excitedly. "They're the ones who are around him the most, and they might be his lieutenants." He turned to Shooter and handed him the pictures. "Ok, Shooter, these four will be our targets. If we take them out, their whole outfit will fall."

Jessica interrupted. "Do we really have to kill all of them? Can't we just find the evidence and give it to the police?"

There was a loud grumble coming from the men as they expressed their dissatisfaction.

"I told you not to have her part of this, Cleveland. She's gonna fuck everything up," Johnson said angrily.

"Yeah," interjected Shooter. "You know I'm not used to

working with outsiders in the first place, and a kid at that."

Doc joked, "She doesn't look like a kid to me."

"Shut up, Doc. I'm serious," Johnson said coldly. "This ain't no fucking game we playing here; this is real, and I'm putting my life on the line."

"He's right, Cleveland, the girl is green—she's a rookie. She might not be able to keep up," Shooter said flat out.

Cleveland looked at Jessica and was ready to defend her, but Jessica stepped forward to defend herself.

"No, it's all right, Cleveland. Let me say something." She surveyed the men eyes. "I was locked up for six and a half years for murder. When I got to prison I had to kill some more just to stay alive, and after that me and my crew ran the entire prison. A few days ago I was confronted by three of the guys in the picture, one of which I broke his nose. He tried to pull his pistol out, but I was faster and pulled mines." She showed them the gun. "My brother is on crack cocaine and these guys know who he is, who I am, who my mother is, and where I live. I could have backed out of this long ago, like Cleveland said, but I stayed around to fight this till the end. Cleveland also said, 'either you in for a penny, or in for a pound.' I'm standing before you, so I guess I'm in it for the pound. Now before you judge me and call me a rookie, I happened to have read the Art of War by Sun Tzu, and he said that when you have no other option but to go to war, strike your enemy hard and fast and totally annihilate them, but leave some alive to serve as witnesses, only to make you more powerful. Forgive me if I offered you another option, but if I got to kill, I will annihilate them." She stared at the men then said, "So, what it's going to be?"

They stared in Jessica's eyes and knew she was telling the truth. They then turned toward Johnson for his response, and he took the cigar out of his mouth and gave her a nod.

Cleveland smiled and said, "Since we got that out the way, all we got to do now is somehow provide bait, and that is going to be the hard part."

Jessica stared at the pictures again. "I know how to get them where we want them, but I need my friends with me to make it happen."

Shooter immediately said, "Oh, no, more people? Who is it now, the Girl Scouts?"

She smiled and said, "Close. My crew—the Get It Girls!"

Doc smiled widely and said, "Yes, more ladies."

"So what's your plan, Jessica?" Cleveland asked with excited interest.

She smiled. "The best way to catch rats is with some pussies."

Cleveland nodded and snapped his fingers. "That might be just the bait we need to flush him out."

"That might just work," said Johnson.

They all looked at Shooter, who reluctantly nodded and said, "I still don't know why we just don't shoot all their asses and let that be that."

"Like I said, you'll have your share," said Cleveland. He shifted his attention back to Jessica. "Anything else that might be helpful, Jessica?"

Jessica looked down at one of the photographs and then picked it up slowly. She squinted as she studied the photographs closer and said, "Oh, shit!"

Chapter 18

OH, BROTHER OF MINE

Jessica arrived in the front of building 106 on 144th Street to meet Jordan. She had already gone with Cleveland down to the Times Square bus station to see her mother off, and she felt safe for her for the very first time since all drama had begun. The block was desolate as she looked around at mountains of abandoned, boarded up buildings without a soul walking around—it looked like a ghost town.

She stared cautiously up and down the dark, empty building and saw an orange light illuminating one of the apartments on the fourth floor. She grasped the gun that she had hidden in her jacket and proceeded inside the building and up the rickety staircase slowly. It was so dark in the staircase that Jessica couldn't see two feet in front of her so she fished in her pockets and found a book of matches and struck one, giving her an instant burst of light, just enough to make it up to the third floor landing.

She looked up to the final landing above her and saw that there was a flickering amber light coming from one of the apartments. "Jordan?" She paused and awaited a response. She didn't hear anything and called out his name again. "Jordan, are you up there?"

"Jessica?"

"Yeah, it's me. Where you at?"

"I'm up here, come on up."

Jessica stepped cautiously up the remaining flight of the stairs and when she finally made to the fourth floor she saw the apartment where the light was coming from. She peered inside and repeated, "Jordan, where you at?"

"In here. Come in."

Jessica walked inside and saw several candles spaced all over the dreary apartment. She then saw Jordan sitting down on an old dirty mattress taking a hit from a crack pipe. He had his head down and blew out the thick, poisonous cloud from his mouth, avoiding eye contact with her.

"Jordan, that's enough. Put that shit down so we can get out of here."

Jordan was unresponsive and kept his head down.

"Jordan!" Jessica called louder. "Don't you hear me? Let's get out of here, now!"

He barely moved.

Jessica walked directly up to him and yelled even louder, "Jordan, look at me!"

He slowly raised his head, and it was then that she noticed tears falling from his eyes. He looked up at her with pleading eyes.

"I'm sorry, Jessica. I'm sorry," he said through cracking voice.

Jessica assured him, "Don't worry about the money, Jordan. We'll talk about that later, but we have to get out of here now."

From the corner of her eye, Jessica saw a shadow and reached for her pistol, but it was too late. Three men came from out of the kitchen with guns already drawn. They quickly disarmed her, and when they did she recognized them immediately as the men who'd threatened her at the grocery store. They held her arms behind her forcefully. The same short man with the afro, Li'l man, now had a bandage over the bridge of his nose. He smiled wickedly as he walked slowly up to her.

Jessica stared down upon him.

He said, "Your brother is sorry because he sold you out for some crack."

She turned and looked down at Jordan, not wanting to believe what she had just heard. "Jordan, you did that to me? You did that to your own sister?"

Jordan, still too ashamed to face her, shook violently as he tried to steady himself to light his crack.

"Yes he did, bitch! He's a crackhead and that's what crackheads do." Li'l man reached in his pocket and pulled out a thick cellophane bag full of crack and threw it into Jordan's lap.

Jordan scrambled to retrieve it and scooted back on the mattress and opened the bag to smoke some more.

Li'l man felt his nose and began to grow angrier. "I tried to tell you to walk away from this shit, and you thought you could play with the big boys. Now look at your bitch ass."

Jessica didn't show any fear. "Fuck you, li'l man. I see your nose didn't heal straight yet."

Li'l man looked at Jessica and laughed, then punched her viciously in the mouth.

Jordan looked up, and in a drug-induced stupor said, "Hey, y'all said y'all wasn't gonna hurt her!"

"Shut the fuck up, crackhead, 'cause you'll be dying next." Li'l man nodded to one of the men and pulled a weapon from his waistband and took aim at Jessica's head.

Jordan suddenly rose up off the mattress and let out a harrowing scream as he raced toward the man with the gun and tackled him to the floor. One of the men quickly pounced on him and began beating Jordan viciously. Jessica was horrified and tried in vain to help her little brother, but the huge man holding her made it impossible. The man picked Jordan up by his thin neck and tossed him awkwardly back onto the dirty mattress.

Jessica gritted her teeth in defiance, and once again watched the killer raise the gun toward her face. The next thing Jessica heard was a faint cracking sound coming from the window. In an instant, the man with the gun to her face let out a loud gasp and collapsed suddenly to the floor. The man holding Jessica released her as he stood confused and watch his brethren in arms gasp for air.

From the corner of Jessica's eye, she saw movement and quickly dove on the mattress by her brother and shielded his body with hers. The room came alive with gunfire and began to fill with the acrid scent of gunpowder and death. Jessica closed her eyes and protected her brother's head as she continued to hold him down.

When the gunfire ceased, Jessica lifted her head and saw Cleveland, Doc, and Johnson standing with guns in hand as thick smoke rose in the air. She stood up and saw the two lifeless bodies of the men who had tried to kill her and Li'l man cowering in the corner with his hands held over his head as he shivered.

Johnson went over to Li'l man and kicked him viscously in his side and told him to get up. Li'l man rose cautiously to his feet and they threw him up against the wall and handcuffed him.

Jessica had already prearranged to have the men cover her back. She noticed in one of the pictures that Cleveland had shown her that this was one of the buildings used by Bosco on 144th street. When she looked at the picture a little closer, she saw the building's address was 106—the same address that Jordan had written down on the note. That was then that she knew she was being set up.

Moments later, Shooter rushed in the apartment with his rifle drawn and scanned the area of the room until Cleveland waved him off.

"Good shot," Cleveland said to Shooter. "You got him in the heart."

Shooter looked down at his victim and said, "I had a close shot. I was just on the roof across the street—a five-year-old could've hit him."

Cleveland looked at Jessica. "You ready?"

Jessica looked down at her brother in disgust as he put the stem to his mouth, trying to flick the lighter as he bled heavily. She walked over to her brother in a rage and knocked the stem and the lighter from out of his hand.

"Get the fuck on your feet, Jordan!" Jessica yelled.

He searched for his bag of crack and stood to his feet.

She snatched the bag out of his hand with contempt and asked, "How could you do this to me, Jordan? How could you?" It took every ounce of strength in Jessica's body to prevent her from hitting her younger brother.

He was speechless. He never even noticed the blood leaking from his head and mouth. His shrunken and frail body was almost lost in his clothing, which looked to be three sizes too big. With all the drugs he was consuming he wasting away to nothing, but that meant nothing to him. He wobbled unsteadily as his pants suddenly fell to his knees and he fell flat on his face when he attempted to pull them back up. Everyone looked at him with pity as he tried in vain, but unsuccessfully to cover his naked behind.

The anger that Jessica once had for her brother was instantly replaced by compassion and empathy. Jessica looked at the bag of crack in her hand and then at her brother and aided him to his feet, then assisted him in pulling up his pants. She handed him back the bag of crack and looked him in his eyes and for the first time noticed that the person who stood before her was someone she no longer knew.

Jessica kissed her brother on forehead and hugged him tightly as she closed her eyes as she fought back the tears. She pulled away suddenly and then turned around to walk away not wanting to look back. As she was heading out the door, she stopped in front of Shooter and whispered in his ear and handed him her 25 automatic. He looked Jessica in the eyes to see if he had heard her correctly and she nodded slowly and walked out the apartment with Cleveland, Johnson, Doc, and Li'l man, right behind her.

"Come on, you son of a bitch," Cleveland said to Li'l man, "we got something special in store for you."

By the time Jessica reached the second landing, her body jerked when she heard the first shot. She closed her eyes and inhaled deeply and continued down the stairs as she heard three more shots.

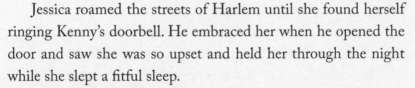

Jessica roamed the streets of Harlem until she found herself ringing Kenny's doorbell. He embraced her when he opened the door and saw she was so upset and held her through the night while she slept a fitful sleep.

She woke up the next morning, as the sun rays beamed down on her face. She looked around and realized she was at Kenny's place and he wasn't in the room. She looked at the alarm clock by his lamp and realized how long she had slept. She knew that she had to meet up with Vonda, who she told to get in contact with Lynn and Tiny so she could take care of the second phase of the plan.

She jumped out of the bed and looked around for her shoes, found them, and put them on her feet. Just then, Kenny walked into the room shirtless, with food and orange juice on a tray.

"Oh, you awoke, perfect timing," Kenny announced. "You must have been tired from staying over the other night," Kenny joked, trying to get Jessica to smile. "I cooked you some breakfast, so sit down and enjoy."

"I'm sorry Kenny, but I don't have any appetite to eat anything right now, I really have to go." Jessica put her arms through her jacket and began walking toward the door.

"Jessica, you got to eat. You are doing too much and you got to slow down."

"Kenny, right now is not the time, I got something important that I got to do."

"Like getting yourself killed!" Kenny screamed. "Can you just listen to me for a moment please?"

Jessica stopped in her tracks and knew that she had made a mistake by getting emotionally involved with him so soon. She turned on her heels to face him.

"Jessica," Kenny pleaded, "you are dealing with some bad, bad people, and I just don't want to see you get hurt."

She walked over to Kenny and placed a kiss on his lips. "I know that you love me and I love you, but I promise you that I will be ok and all of this will be over real soon."

He wrapped his arms around her one last time before she walked out the door.

Chapter 19

It was nearly 1PM when Jessica finally arrived at Vonda's house via cab service. She looked over her shoulders several times because she knew she was a marked woman at that point so she became paranoid. Jessica rang the doorbell and heard someone's footsteps approaching the door. When the door opened, it was Lynn standing in the doorway with a huge smile on her face, and she immediately began screaming for joy.

They embraced and continued to celebrate until Vonda walked up and joked, "Damn, y'all act like y'all ain't seen each other in years."

They pulled away to look at each other. "Damn, it's good to see you again, Jesse!" Lynn shouted excitedly.

"It's good to see you, and damn girl, you looking good. Macy's must be treating you well."

Lynn did a complete 360 and turned all the around, giving her a full view of her newfound fashion. "I don't work there anymore;

I resigned last week. It's too many rich-ass niggas out here that want to take care of a bitch, if you know what I mean."

"What you back to getting dick now?" asked Jessica.

Lynn smiled. "That was when we was in prison, and we only did two days in prison: the day we got in and the day we got out. Everything else don't count, remember?"

Jessica gave her five. "I hear you. We had to do what we had to do."

Lynn nodded and said, "Fuck all that other shit. I hear you got big problems?"

Jessica nodded. "Major problems."

Vonda interjected and said, "Come on. Let's go in my room and talk." They walked inside Vonda's room and for the first time in almost nine months she saw Tiny, who was sitting in the same chair as she always had.

Jessica was happy to see her also. "Tiny."

She looked up from the armchair and smiled then stood up to hug her. When they embraced, Jessica felt nothing but bones. She looked Tiny up and down and instantly knew that she was still doing drugs by the gaunt look to her face. She still dressed well, but she wore a long-sleeved sweatshirt and it was the middle of the summer. Jessica thought it was rather odd, but she overlooked it and said, "It's good to see you, Tiny."

She nodded and said the same, "It's good to see you too. When you got out?"

"About a month and a half ago."

Tiny nodded again and said to everyone, "Yo, I'm going to use the bathroom for a minute. I'll be back in a second."

They watched her exit the room and felt real sorry for her.

Jessica put her head down and asked, "She still on that shit, huh?"

Vonda nodded, and you could see in her eyes how it was affecting her.

"Yep, what's worse is that she got the monster too," Lynn said in a sad low tone.

"The monster? What is that?" Jessica looked in Vonda's eyes and saw that they were watery.

Lynn said, "AIDS. She caught the virus by shooting that heroin in her arms. That's why she wears only long sleeved shirts, 'cause her arms are fucked-up looking."

Jessica was stunned. Vonda turned away to hide her tears, and Jessica walked over to her and gave her a hug.

Jessica spent the next hour explaining to all of them everything that had gone down from the time she got home to the incident that happened last night. None of them could believe what Jessica had done to her own brother and were saddened and realized just how much trouble she was really in. After Jessica had finished explaining everything, they were all in awe and no one said a word.

"So there you have it," said Jessica.

There was a long silence until Lynn said, "So what do you do now?"

Jessica shrugged. "That's why I called y'all here today. I need your help."

Lynn nodded and said with confidence, "Well, you ain't saying nothing but a word. I'm in for whatever! That's how we motherfucking roll. What do you say, Vonda?"

"You don't even have to ask. You know I'm down."

Jessica smiled and they all looked toward Tiny, who was looking up at the ceiling as she scratched her body. "What's up Tiny? You in or what?"

She lowered her eyes. "I don't know. I know that nigga Bosco. I brought plenty drugs from that nigga, and his Jamaican ass ain't no joke. He would kill you if he even thought you was gonna cross him. And all that other shit you talkin', Jessica, it sounds like you brought it on yourself, being all in the paper and shit like that, tryna be some motherfuckin' hero or something. You are talking about kidnapping and murdering motherfuckers. If we get caught we can spend the rest of our lives in jail."

Jessica had to admit that she was right.

Lynn countered, "Damn Tiny, you know that we are crew, and if one of us has a problem, all of us got a problem. That's just how we get down."

Tiny shrugged her puny shoulders as she nodded at the same time. "I hear you, but if I'm gonna risk my life it got to be at least something in it for me."

They all knew instantly that Tiny had a motive behind her actions and that she wanted money if she was to come in with them. "You want us to give you money to get down with us, Tiny?" Lynn asked with disgust.

Tiny remained silent.

"Come on, Tiny," Vonda said. "I have been giving you money ever since you got out. I damn near been supporting you, and you going out on me like this?"

Tiny knew she was right, but held her ground anyway.

Vonda and Lynn continued to tell her how selfish she was until

Jessica said, "I'll give you five thousand dollars if you want that."

Tiny suddenly lifted her head and greed flashed across her flaming red eyes, hanging on to every word that Jessica was saying now, "I'll give you half of it now and the other half when we are done."

Vonda and Lynn looked at Jessica as if she were an alien.

"No, Jessica," Vonda said, "that's your money, and you shouldn't have to pay nobody to be in with us. We three could pull it off."

Jessica shook her head and said, "No, we are crew, and if we do something we do it together or not at all. Besides, I want her to have the money, and we need her."

Vonda and Lynn just looked at Jessica and let it go because they saw the desperation in her eyes. They then shifted their attention back to Tiny and awaited an answer until she finally said, "I'm in, too."

Jessica nodded. "Then that's it. Let's get busy."

The girls spent the rest of the evening finalizing their roles and plans for the best way to catch Bosco at his weakest. Since Tiny knew him and had had contact with Bosco on a number of occasions, they decided to build the plan around her. They knew Bosco was a big trick and that pussy would be the answer. They decided to use Lynn and Vonda as Tiny's backup to entice him into their web. To pull it off, they needed to gain entry inside his operation and get the upper hand when the assault would take place. They decided that Tiny would be best suited for that position. To make it happen, that person had to be buying a lot of drugs to gain the initial entry into the apartment. The hard part would be catching Bosco in the apartment at the right time, so they needed to put the plan in effect immediately and had no time to waste.

After they went over and everything, they went over it again till everyone knew their roles by memory. They couldn't afford to leave anything to chance. Even Tiny was alert and on point, even though she took a break every hour to go take a fix in the bathroom. When they were sure of everything, Jessica and the other girls decided to go home and get ready for the following day. Tiny hit Jessica up for a small advance. Jessica promised she'd get the rest tomorrow, but warned Tiny not to let them down. Tiny agreed and scurried out the apartment to surely get high. With Tiny and Lynn gone, Vonda said that she had something important to tell her.

"What's up, Vonda?"

Vonda was apprehensive about telling her, but knew she had to. "You remember that shooting on your block about three weeks ago when three boys was killed?"

Jessica nodded. "Yeah, how could I forget?"

Vonda eyed the floor. "Well, I think Chubby killed them."

Jessica's eyes widened as her body seemed to melt. "W-What? H-How?" Jessica stuttered.

"Yo, you know how much Chubby loves you. He loves you just like you were his big sister, and he just couldn't accept those dudes stepping to you and threatening you."

Jessica didn't want to believe it, but then she remembered. "Oh, God, did he—"

Did he shoot the little girl?" Vonda shook her head. "I don't know if it was him or one of the other guys."

Jessica still felt responsible and sighed. She wrapped her arms around herself, not wanting to believe she'd put Chubby in the mix of her troubles.

"You know this for sure, Vonda? Did he tell out of his mouth that he killed them?"

Vonda explained, "The night it had happened, Chubby came home wearing all black—black hoodie, black pants, and black boots. I didn't think nothing of it until the next day when I read in the papers about it, and they said that one witness reported seeing a very large man in all black walking away after the shooting. I went to Chubby's room and asked him if he heard about the shooting, and he began avoiding eye contact with me and started rocking."

At that moment Jessica knew without a doubt that it was Chubby who had killed those boys that night and critically injured a little girl.

Jessica knocked on Cleveland's door that night and he exhaled deeply when her saw her face, knowing that she had made it home safely. It was apparent to Jessica that he was equally paranoid because he had a large caliber weapon in his hand when he opened the door.

"You ok? I been waiting all day for you. I was getting worried about you."

Jessica nodded. "I'm ok. I was with my friends putting everything in motion."

Cleveland smiled and asked, "You talking about the Get It Girls?"

She smiled back, "Yeah, the Get It Girls. We came up with this plan that I think may get us inside with Bosco."

"Yeah, lay it on me."

Jessica spent the next two hours going over the plan with Cleveland, explaining to him his role and where he and his men should be. Cleveland thought it was a perfect plan, but Jessica wasn't sure of just one thing and decided to play things by ear.

"What do we do about your little friend from last night?" asked Cleveland.

Jessica had almost forgotten about him. "What did y'all do him?"

"Don't worry, he's not dead. We figured we keep him alive in case we can use him for something down the road."

"That's it!" Jessica said excitedly. "That was the one problem that I had." She looked at Cleveland and explained, "Remember when I told you they don't let just anybody in their drug spot and I was worried about how you and the other guys would get in without the least resistant?"

He nodded.

"Well, you bring Li'l man to the door and when they see his face they going to open it."

Cleveland finished the rest. "And that's when we bum rush the spot. I see where you going with this."

Jessica nodded.

For the first time, Cleveland noticed how withdrawn and tired Jessica looked. "Listen, you look like you could use some rest."

Jessica agreed.

He still saw something in Jessica that just wasn't right and asked, "Jessica, I know what's on your mind. Do you want me to tell you about it?"

Jessica wanted so badly to ask about her brother, but she

couldn't. All she wanted was for God to forgive her and have mercy on her soul. "No, I don't want to know, ok?"

Cleveland understood. He looked around the room. "Well, if it means anything to you and you don't want to be alone, you can stay down here for the rest of the night. I only got a couch for you to sleep on, but it's comfortable."

Jessica looked at Cleveland and smiled as she thought about how her brother used to ask her to sleep with him when he was afraid of monsters. Well, Jessica was afraid, and Bosco was the monster.

She nodded. "Thank you, Cleveland. I would like to stay for the night."

He smiled and said, "Good. When was the last time you had something to eat?"

Jessica thought about it and realized she hadn't eaten in two days.

Cleveland read her face and said, "I can cook some mean fried chicken, and I'm gonna put some on right now."

※ ※ ※

After getting up early and leaving Cleveland's house the next morning, Jessica went up to her apartment and immediately got into a long hot bath and a fresh change of clothing. She went to her closet and removed the money she promised Tiny, counted it out, and put the rest back into her stash. She found a notebook and took her time writing a letter to her mother. When she finished, she left it right on the kitchen table so that she couldn't possibly miss it. It pained her to write the letter, because it was more or less a goodbye letter letting her know exactly what had happened to her and Jordan in case she didn't make it back alive. Jessica stood up and exhaled deeply, looked around one last time, and knew that there was nothing left to be done but the mission at hand. She went to her room and cut off the light and headed toward the front door.

Since Jessica had to stay out of sight during the daylight hours, she called Vonda and had her come over to Cleveland's apartment to pick up the money. When Vonda arrived at the door Jessica introduced her to Cleveland and went over some minor details that would be vital to pulling it all off.

Vonda was ready to leave when Jessica added, "Oh, yeah, Vonda. One more thing."

Vonda turned to face her.

"You, Lynn, and Tiny may need these." She walked over to the table and showed her the guns.

Vonda only stared at them then picked one of them up.

Jessica looked her in the eyes and said, "It's better to be judged by twelve instead of carried by six." It was the same thing Chubby had told her.

Jessica reiterated to Vonda not to give Tiny any of the money until after the job was done. She knew if they did, the likelihood of Tiny showing up for the job would be nil.

Vonda left and headed back home to meet with Lynn and Tiny and to change into something more appropriate for the role she and Lynn would play that night.

Chapter 20

Jessica walked around Cleveland's apartment aimlessly, waiting for Vonda to call and say that they had spotted Bosco. The past few weeks had been a nightmare come true, and now it was taking its toll on her mentally and physically. Jessica suddenly felt sick and dizzy and ran to the bathroom to throw up. She was on her knees in front of the toilet bowl panting rapidly when Cleveland came to check on her.

"Are you ok, Jessica?"

She looked up and used her sleeve to wipe the bile off her mouth, nodded, and tried to smile. "I guess I'm not used to outside food yet."

He chuckled and left her alone.

When Jessica finally got to her feet and washed off, the phone rang and she rushed out of the bathroom to see who it was.

Cleveland picked up the phone and said, "Hello?" He listened intently, then looked at Jessica and handed her the phone.

She listened intently. "In an hour . . . ok . . . ok," she repeated before she hung up the phone. She looked at Cleveland and said, "They located Bosco at the spot on 116th Street, and we gonna meet them in an hour right around the corner on 117th Street to follow them."

Cleveland picked up the Polaroid picture of the building and examined it.

"Yes," Cleveland said excitedly, "this building is perfect for our thing. Lots of empty surrounding buildings so we can enter the building from an adjacent roof without being seen." He then flipped through his notes and said, "Jackpot! This is also his main location that he uses cook up and bag his drugs up. Now, let me make a couple of phone calls and then get on the road to pick up our package from the Bronx."

The sun had just gone down when the two cars filled with Jessica and the four men pulled up behind Vonda, Lynn, and Tiny. They were sure not to make any contact with each other, and when they saw them pull up in the car, that was the three girls' cue to begin the mission and meet Bosco, who was standing in front of his building with several of his associates.

Jessica saw that Vonda and Lynn were dressed to kill in their tight fitting jeans and heels. The plan was to get the attention of Bosco so they could get not only get inside the building, but the apartment as well. The girls would use Tiny to introduce Vonda and Lynn to Bosco and tell him that they wanted to buy a large amount of cocaine to sell.

Normally, Bosco would have to have done business with you

in the past to sell you that much weight, but he knew Tiny very well, and the two girls she was with would secure the deal. They were betting their lives that his sexual tendencies would cloud his judgment that night. Jessica and Cleveland were parked at an angle that they would not be seen, but in a good enough spot that they could also watch the girls' every move.

The closer Vonda and Lynn got to the men in front of the building, the more they found it harder to breathe. Tiny showed no emotion as she coolly smoked on a Newport cigarette and swaggered with an air of confidence in every stride. Standing before all the men now, Tiny walked directly up to Bosco and balled her fist and gave him a pound. Bosco barely looked at Tiny, as his eyes were stuck on the two other girls standing no more than two feet in front of him.

"Yo, Bosco," said Tiny. "Can I holla at you for a second?"

He finally took a gander at Tiny. "Yeah, mon, we talk in de building," said Bosco in his thick Jamaican accent.

Tiny followed him inside the building and the stopped at the stairwell.

"Out there are my girls and they wanted to get a little something from you."

He frowned and asked quickly, "Dem girls smoke?"

"Naw, man, do they look like they smoke? They sell it."

He hesitated for a second then asked, "Why you come ta me? Why you don't get from de other spot?"

"I did! I took them to the other spot and they told me they ain't holding that much powder on them and that I had to see you if I wanted so much weight."

Dollar signs flashed before Bosco's eyes and Tiny knew it.

"How much you talkin' 'bout?"

Tiny shrugged her shoulders and said, "We was hoping you could give us a half of key for seven thousand."

He frowned again then sucked his teeth. "Blood clot, me nay sell half o' key for no seven. Me could get nine easy," he complained.

"Come on, Bosco. You know me. I do a lot of business with you, and we all just starting out tryna get on our feet."

"Where you know girls from?" he asked suspiciously

"They my homegirls I grew up with. I knew them my whole life."

Bosco rubbed his chin and peered at the men trying to rap to the girls outside. "Ya, tink dem two want to have a party wit me upstairs for de two thousand dollars off de product?"

Tiny knew that she had him and shrugged her shoulders. "I, don't know. You want me to ask them?"

He smiled. "Ya, you ask em for me, will ya?"

Tiny nodded and walked out the building and consulted with the girls. Moments later, Tiny walked up to Bosco and nodded.

Bosco didn't hide his pleasure and whispered to Tiny, "Bring dem up."

Tiny walked back over to where Vonda and Lynn stood and gestured for to them to follow her. They did.

"They on the move!" said Cleveland to Jessica as they watched their every move through a pair of binoculars. He waved to the car behind him to follow him as he drove around the corner on 115th Street so they could enter a building through the alleyway and get to the roof without being seen.

By the time the girls arrived to the apartment on the fifth

floor, Vonda and Lynn had unzipped their purses to have easy access to their pistols. Bosco knocked twice on the door, then three more times. Vonda knew at that moment that it was their signal and cursed under her breath for not considering that into their plan. They heard the peephole latch slide and then multitude of locks being unlocked.

When the door finally opened up, a huge, grim-faced man was on the other side with a black pump-action shotgun dangling from his shoulder, held by a strap. The man was so large that they all had to squeeze past him to get the narrow door and hallway to get by.

As the girls walked into the living room they heard the door slam, then relock. Vonda surveyed the sparse living room, which had only one sofa, two chairs, and a plain kitchen table with a triple beam scale on it. She was at least happy that the two men were the only ones in the apartment.

Bosco stared at Lynn's huge breasts and buttocks and then at Vonda's long, lean body and wanted to put the carriage before the horse. "Let's go in de bedroom."

Lynn was the first to speak. "Slow down, baby. I like to take care of what we came here for before I fuck a nigga to death. You know what I mean?"

Bosco smiled knowingly at Lynn's sexually charged comment and knew that he was in for a freaky night. "Ok, girl. We take care of business first. Show me de money."

Vonda was about to reach in her purse, but she heard the huge man grumble, "Wait a minute!"

He walked over to Vonda and said, "Let me see inside your purse."

Vonda went numb, but remained cool.

He walked over and snatched her purse and opened it and searched inside. He paused when he saw the gun and pulled it out and showed it to Bosco.

He stared at the small gun for a moment then asked suspiciously, "What do ya have de gun for? You planning to rob me or somet'ing?"

Vonda didn't miss a beat. "Yeah, I'm trying to rob you with that big-ass gun." She smirked.

He examined the weapon for a moment and asked, "Why you do carry a gun?"

She walked directly up to him, looked him right in the eye, and retorted, "Because I'm a gangster, and I do gangster shit."

Bosco looked at the man with the shotgun and chuckled. "She say, she gangsta. Bwoy I like dat, I like de women who got heart." He smiled at Vonda and repeated, "And you got heart." He looked over at Lynn and asked, "You got heart too, you got weapon?"

Lynn stared at him coldly and reached into her purse and pulled out her gun.

The man with the shotgun walked over to her and collected her gun as well. He then looked at Tiny and asked menacingly, "Do you have a weapon?" he growled.

Tiny raised her hand and said, "Nope, I don't carry a gun." Tiny lifted up her shirt to prove it.

The grim-faced man turned his attention back at Vonda and Lynn and stated, "You'll get this back when you leave!"

"Ok, let's get down to business. Let me see de money."

Vonda reached cautiously inside her purse, with the gunman

eyeing her every move. She pulled out the thick white envelope and attempted to hand it to him.

"No, hand 'im de money." He gestured toward his gunman.

Vonda followed his order.

The gunman placed his weapon against the wall and proceeded to count it out. While they waited for him to finish, Bosco questioned the girls. "What cha gon do wit so much drugs? Where you got such business? I know every spot in Harlem, I never saw ya."

Vonda cleared her throat and knew he was growing suspicious. "We don't clock in Harlem; we clock upstate."

"Where?" he asked quickly, trying to catch her in a lie.

"Binghamton, New York. We get a lot more than what you get here. Ten dollar pieces here go for fifty dollars up there."

He nodded. The gunman finally finished counting out all the money, and Vonda was thankful because it was only a matter of time before he caught her in a lie. The only way she knew about Binghamton was because she'd heard her brother Chubby talk about it all the time.

Bosco gestured to the gunman to come over to him and whispered something in his ear. He immediately walked back down the hall and inside the bedroom closest to the front door. Seconds later, the gunman came right back out empty-handed. All the girls grew perplexed as they stood around without a word being said as the gunman gripped his gun tighter.

Suddenly, they were all surprised to hear movement coming from the room he had just come out of, but what they saw next stopped their hearts. A woman appeared from the room with a brown paper bag in her right hand. When they looked in her face it was none other than Cookie, the girl who'd caused them all to be arrested nearly seven years ago. They were ready to panic when Cookie walked past without acknowledging or seemingly even noticing any of them.

The girls watched her place the brown bag on top of the table in front of Bosco and turn around and walk back off as her dilated eyes stared straight ahead like a zombie. Her clothing was worn and she looked much, much thinner than they last remembered. It was obvious to them all that she was on some form of drugs by the way she now looked. Vonda and Lynn finally let out a breath and forced themselves to maintain their smiles, but Tiny could not help but sneer at Cookie as she passed her by.

"Dat's, my scientist. She cook up de best crack in Harlem. She bag up all de product for me and don't steal a dime because I pay her wit all de crack she need," Bosco said with a wide smile on his face. He nodded to the girls, and Tiny took her cue and opened up the brown bag and pulled a thick brick of cocaine in cellophane.

Tiny put the brick on the triple beam scale on the table to weigh it. After they were all was satisfied that it was in fact a half a key, Tiny smiled and said, "Yep, 500 grams exactly." She then made a small incision in the bag with a knife that was also on the table and used the point of the knife to scoop out a small amount and put it to her nose and snort.

She closed her eyes and started sniffing loudly and scooped out some more and put it on the back of her hand and into her mouth, then used her tongue to mix the cocaine around her gums. They stared at Tiny closely as they awaited her approval.

She finally opened her eyes and turned toward Vonda and Lynn and nodded.

"Yes, me dear, my product is de best." Bosco looked toward the two girls and said with lust in his eyes, "I did me part, let's go in me room now."

Vonda knew Tiny still had her gun on her and quickly spoke up and said, "Ok, but I want my girl Tiny to wait here till we finish."

"Tiny can stay. Solomon, ya keep an eye on her and give her fifty dollar of cook-up and have her sit on de couch."

Tiny smiled widely and thanked him.

"No problem, mon, ya did me good." He examined the two girls' backsides again and closed the door behind him as they walked into his bedroom.

Solomon told Tiny to have a seat on the couch and walked down the hall into the room where Cookie was. Tiny waited until he went into the room, then stood up quickly and reached inside her pants to pull out her gun. She placed it in her waistband and quickly sat back down before he came back. When he came out he had a huge piece of crack rock in a sheet of aluminum foil and handed it to Tiny.

"You mind if I smoke here?"

Solomon shrugged. "Do you. I don't care."

Tiny went into her sock and pulled out a pack of Newports and opened it, pulling out her glass stem and a lighter that she had stored inside. She broke off a little piece and began smoking it. Tiny's entire demeanor began to change as she started twitching and geeking. Solomon knew from experience of crackheads' behaviors and simply ignored her. Tiny started rocking back and forth as she kept gazing at the bedroom door where the person who'd ruined her whole life was at, and she began to grow angrier.

Inside the room, Vonda and Lynn had already stripped Bosco out of his clothing and had him totally naked lying on the bed. He told the girls to do the same, but they chose to tease him first to kill some of the much needed time and began to rub his erected penis and kiss him all over his body. Bosco wanted more and demanded them to remove their clothes as well. Vonda stole a quick look at her watch, knowing they had five minutes left till all hell would break loose. So, she and Lynn would have to do the ultimate and actually engage in a sex act with him to dwindle the time even further. They took turns giving him head, and when he could no longer take their hot mouths, he ordered Lynn to get on top of him.

"Come on, ride me pony."

Lynn, needing to burn some time quickly responded, "You got any condoms?"

"What ya say?"

"Condoms. Before we can do this you have to use a condom," Lynn repeated.

In frustration he quickly rose to his feet and walked over to the dresser to find one. Without any luck, he slammed the drawer closed and went to the door and yelled, "Solomon, go to Cookie room and get me condom, mon, fast!"

Solomon quickly followed his boss's orders and went to Cookie's room to retrieve one. Just hearing her name again made Tiny angrier as she smoked some more crack to prevent herself from running in the room blasting.

There was a knock on the door as soon as Solomon exited

the room. He gripped his shotgun and walked toward the door and looked through the peephole to see who it was and said in a loud, booming voice enough for the people on the other side of the door could hear.

"Who the fuck is it?"

"It's me, Shorty."

At ease as he stared at his familiar face, Solomon smiled and asked, "Where the fuck you been?" He began unlocking the door as he continued. "We been looking all over for you." That was the last thing he would ever say as he received a bullet wound right between his eyes, delivered by Shooter.

Hearing the gunshot, Bosco panicked and got into battle mode and quickly pushed Lynn off of him and ran to the closets. The girls knew he was going for a weapon and reacted equally fast and jumped on him from behind before he could open the closet door.

Vonda screamed as she fought with him, "Don't let him open the door, Lynn. Don't let him open the door!"

They fought violently as Bosco flipped Vonda off his back and down to the floor. He was much too strong for them, and he kicked Lynn in the chest, causing her to fly backwards.

Free, he began cursing in his native tongue. "Fuckin bumbaclot, want to fuck with real dred, I will show ya some'ting!" He opened his closet and reached inside and pulled out a Samurai sword and said, "Ya done fuck with de wrong dred!"

Vonda raised her hands in terror, staring back into Bosco's flaming red eyes as he raised the weapon high in the air to cut her in half, when suddenly the bedroom door flew open and Tiny came in blasting.

"Die you motherfucker! Die!" she yelled as she hit him up with bullets all over his body until he fell back on the bed.

Vonda turned around, still in panic, and looked hysterically at Tiny, who was still pulling the trigger of the revolver. Jessica and Cleveland ran into the bedroom seconds later with their guns drawn ready to shoot anything that moved.

Jessica looked at Bosco's lifeless, nude body on the bed and yelled out, "Vonda! Lynn! Are you all right?"

They stood on their feet and said they were ok. They quickly retrieved their clothing and began to dress.

Cleveland returned down the hall and stealthily crept toward the bedroom door and signaled to his men with his hand as they got in place and drop-kicked in the door, ready to shoot anything that moved. When they entered, they all pointed their weapons at the lone woman sitting on the edge of the bed almost in a catatonic state watching television. They knew she wasn't a threat and lowered their weapons. Suddenly, the girls entered the room one by one. When Jessica entered, she fell in momentary shock to see the one person in the world that had caused her so much heartache and pain—she could not believe it. They stared at Cookie for a long while, and she barely looked away from the television as if none of them were even there.

Jessica had thought about this moment for nearly seven years, wondering what she would do if she ran into Cookie on the street. All of them had—they wanted to kill her. But, looking at her now, so helpless and so weak, and for reasons that Jessica didn't know, she suddenly felt sorry for her and didn't want to do her any harm.

Jessica thought back to what her friend told her in prison

when she said she wouldn't wish crack on her worst enemy. She realized at that moment that she understood what the girl had meant. She wasn't going to kill Cookie, because she was already doing it to herself.

The men looked around the room and found the mother lode. They found over nearly ten kilos of cocaine and assorted bags filled up with crack rocks. They searched Bosco's room and found stacks and stacks of cash and hauled it all out into the living room. Jessica and Vonda saw Tiny staring at all the cash and drugs, and she started twitching. They blocked her from exiting the bedroom and Vonda said, "No, Tiny. I want you to stay in the other room."

Tiny's eyes widened and said, "Stay in there for what?"

"To keep an eye on Cookie, that's what," Jessica stated.

"Why do I have to watch her? Her brain is fried. She is no threat to us," Tiny said in frustration.

"Because we want you to," responded Vonda. "And besides, you're getting paid for the job, remember?"

Tiny reluctantly agreed. "Ok, but let me know what y'all gonna do with the drugs and money. Make sure I get my cut."

"I'm telling you right now, Tiny, we ain't keeping no drugs," said Jessica. "We'll decide later what's going to happen with the money, and then we'll tell you."

Tiny nodded. "Ok, but hurry up, I'm ready to go."

They nodded, and Tiny quickly added, "Oh, yeah. Leave me a gun; I ran out of bullets."

"Why you need a gun, Tiny?" Jessica questioned. "She ain't gonna do nothing. Her mind is fried."

"Shit, I don't know that. She could snap out of that at any second and try to kill me. I ain't taking no chances."

They looked at Tiny with apprehension until Jessica gave her a gun.

"Don't do anything stupid, now, like shooting her. We got enough bodies on our hands, and there's no need to kill her 'cause she already gone." Jessica gave Tiny a stern glare. "Don't shoot her, Tiny. I mean it."

They closed the door and went into the living room with the rest them of the men. When they were gone, Tiny went into her pocket and pulled out her stem once again. She opened up the aluminum foil and broke off a large piece of crack and began smoking it. She blew out the dense smoke and it instantly raced through her bloodstream as she began to leer back at Cookie.

Tiny mumbled under her breath, "Six years, six long motherfucking years, bitch!"

She looked at Cookie once again and then toward the door and sneered wickedly. "Don't shoot her, Tiny. I mean it."

When Jessica and Vonda got to the living room, they already had Li'l man tied up in a chair with his hands tied behind his back.

Cleveland approached Jessica. "You ready to do it? I got that thing you told me to get."

Li'l man's eyes widened when he heard them talking about him. "Please, please . . . don't kill me! I, I did everything you asked me to, so please don't kill me. I won't say nothing, I promise!"

Everyone looked at Jessica for a decision. She contemplated what she wanted to do with him.

Shooter reminded her, "He saw our faces, so we got to kill him."

Li'l man started crying and pleading for his life again. "I

promise you, I won't tell a soul. I'll leave town and never come back, I promise you. Please, please, just don't kill me!"

Jessica smiled. "We not gonna kill you, you gonna kill yourself."

She nodded to Cleveland and he pulled out a glass stem and a lighter. He passed the glass stem over to Doc and opened up a baggy of crack and pinched off tiny pieces of crack and loaded it till he couldn't load it any more.

Li'l man began to sweat profusely. "Hey, what are y'all doing?"

Jessica said to him, "So, you hate crackheads, huh? Well I got a little deal for you. Smoke all of that crack . . ." she pointed to hundreds of bags of crack, "or let us put a bullet in your head right now. Your choice."

Shooter began to snicker. "Oh, I love this."

Li'l man looked at Jessica as if she was insane. "Wh-what?" he stuttered.

Johnson made him nearly shit his pants when he got in his face and yelled, "You heard her, motherfucker, either smoke the crack or lose your life. Answer her right now." He put a handgun to Li'l man's head. "Which one, motherfucker? Pick one right now!"

"I'll smoke the crack, I'll smoke the crack!" he cried reluctantly.

Doc put the stem to his mouth and Johnson flicked the lighter. "And take a deep, long pull and swallow it or I'm gonna blow your fuckin' brains out!"

He took a long pull from the stem.

"Hold it in, motherfucker," Johnson warned.

He did and then blew it out, causing a huge cloud of smoke to loom in the air. Li'l man's eyes widened like a cartoon character and his whole body began to twitch. Slobber fell from his mouth. He tried to speak, but he was unable to form any tangible words. Doc put the stem back into his mouth and repeated the process again and again.

Cleveland informed the girls that they could leave and that the men would clean the place up. "Come by my apartment later and I'll split the money with the men and give you your share."

Jessica wanted to decline, but she looked at Vonda and Lynn's eyes and knew they wanted it and agreed.

"What about the drugs?" Jessica asked.

"We'll leave it for the police so they can make this a drug-related killing, that way it would be justified," Cleveland offered. "But what about the girl up front?" Cleveland asked.

They'd almost forgotten about her, and the four of them walked back to the room and opened the door. They saw Tiny sitting in the same place where Cookie had sat, but didn't see Cookie. They looked around the room for Cookie, and when they didn't see her, they asked Tiny. "Where she go?"

Tiny used her head and gestured toward the bed.

The four of them slowly walked over toward the bed and saw Cookie's lifeless body on the floor. Cleveland bent down to check her pulse, and there was none. He shook his head at the girls.

Jessica looked at Tiny and screamed, "Tiny, I fucking told you not to kill her!"

Tiny shrugged her shoulders as if she didn't have a care in the world. "No, your exact words was 'Don't shoot her,' and I didn't shoot her. I choked the bitch!"

Chapter 21

The next day, Jessica was in an especially upbeat mood because she was no longer on someone's hit list and she could now breathe freely and get closer to Kenny.

She went down to Cleveland's apartment and he explained to her everything that had gone down after they left. He told her to not worry too much about the killings because they left all the drugs and some money behind to set it up and made it looked like the gunman was Li'l man. They made it look like he was one of the robbers and that Cookie got caught in the crossfire. He looked at Jessica and said sadly, "We had to put a bullet in her to make it look consistent."

Jessica agreed that it was the right thing to do. "What happened to Li'l man?"

Cleveland smirked and said, "He got it worse than them all—we turned him into a crackhead! And it's no turning back for him now because we made him smoke at least twenty grams of crack in one sitting before his heart exploded. We also took out an insurance policy and put his prints on all the guns and left them inside the apartment just in case."

"Cleveland, how you get so much information on Bosco, his location, and everything in the first place? You never told me."

With a sly smile, Cleveland answered, "I never told you what my occupation in the military was?"

She shook her head.

"I was counter intelligence."

She looked at Cleveland with surprise. "You were a spy, Cleveland?"

He tilted his head. "If I tell ya, I have to kill ya."

They both laughed.

"Oh," Cleveland remembered, "this is you guys' share of the money. We split it fifty-fifty, between the four of you and the four of us. That's over ten thousand dollars for each of you."

Jessica was dumbfounded when he said how much their take was. He handed her their share of the money.

"I want you to know, Jessica, I wasn't in it for the money. I did it because it was the right thing to do."

Jessica nodded and truly believed him. "I know you were, Cleveland. So was I. And that reminds me, I never got a chance to thank you or the other guys."

He waved her off. "You don't have to thank us. I would have did it any old way because you like a daughter to me now. As far as the other men are concerned, they'd do it just to do it because they are patriots."

Jessica nodded and gave him a hug and a kiss on his cheek.

※ ※ ※

Jessica arrived at Kenny's apartment later that night and knocked on his door. Kenny opened the front door and simply stared at her. Jessica eyed the floor like a little girl trying to make up with her best friend.

"Are you ok?" asked Kenny in an emotionless tone.

Jessica folded her arms. "Yes, I'm ok, now."

Kenny continued to lean on his door. "So, what do you want now, a place to lay your head for the night and leave as soon as you wake up again?"

Jessica knew that Kenny was taking the short end of it all and wanted to make up with him.

"No, Kenny, I came to spend some quality time with you."

Kenny nodded and opened the door for her to enter. Jessica walked into his apartment and sat on his sofa and let out a loud sigh of relief.

Kenny stared down upon her and asked, "Long night?"

Jessica remained silent.

"What's the matter, Jessica? Don't you think I have the right to know what I'm involved in?"

Jessica simply stood up and gave him a long passionate kiss and then led him into the bedroom.

Jessica stayed with Kenny for nearly a week and they made love the whole time she was with him. They grew even closer as they talked for nights on end. She told him everything about Cleveland and his crew, getting back with her crew of Vonda, Tiny, and Lynn, and even Bosco and Cookie. She held nothing back, and he was glad that she came out of it alive and they could now build a life together.

It was almost fall, and three months had passed since the Bosco incident. Everything was going well for Jessica. Her relationship with Kenny was as strong as ever, and she was spending her time between her mother's house and Kenny's. Her mother was back home and back at work, and their relationship couldn't have been better—but, just when things couldn't have been better, something would come up to rock Jessica's world. She was pregnant.

Jessica had been throwing up and feeling nauseous for weeks, refusing to believe that she was in fact pregnant. But when she missed her third menstrual cycle she began getting worried and asked Vonda to come with her to the local health clinic at Harlem Hospital. The doctor later told her that she was around three months into her pregnancy. Jessica went numb and wasn't sure what to do, and most of all, how Kenny would take it. Jessica knew that she wasn't going to have an abortion under any circumstances and had no other choice but to tell the father—Kenny.

Jessica decided to break the news to Kenny in public, so she invited him out to dinner at a popular restaurant on the Upper East Side called One Fish Two Fish.

They were enjoying their dinner and having a good conversation and company when Jessica came out and said, "Kenny, there's something I got to tell you."

Kenny smiled and said, "What is it, babe?"

Jessica couldn't keep eye contact with him and hung her head down low. "Kenny, I'm pregnant."

Kenny continued to smile. "What?"

She finally raised her head to face him and repeated, "I'm pregnant, Kenny."

Kenny was momentarily at a loss for words but continued to smile at her. The pause was excruciating to Jessica.

She lowered her head again and asked, "Kenny, could you say something?"

He regained his equilibrium and gathered his thoughts. "Are you sure?"

Jessica nodded. "Yes, I got the results back from the clinic yesterday."

He nodded, but still remained silent.

"Can you say something, Kenny? Anything?"

He suddenly shook his head and asked, "So are you going to keep it?"

"Yes, Kenny. I'm going to keep it."

He looked away from her for a moment, then stood up and sat down next to her on the other side of the table and hugged her. "So you mean, I'm going to be a father?"

Jessica smiled and nodded her head rapidly. She couldn't fight back her tears because she was so happy.

"It's ok, baby. It's ok," said Kenny as he stared off in a distance while softly rubbing her back.

Chapter 22

Jessica eventually told her mother, but Ms. Jones wasn't too excited about hearing the news. She felt that Jessica wasn't ready to have any children because she wasn't financially stable, and above all, she should be married first. Jessica knew her mother was right, but she didn't have much of a choice.

Kenny had been asking her for weeks to move in with him, but each time she declined and said that she didn't want to leave her mother alone. She argued that she still didn't feel safe with her mother being in that block all alone even though it was now drug-free. Kenny said that he understood and would accept it for now, but when the baby came she would have to make some concessions for a better environment for the baby.

Jessica and her mother began looking for a bigger apartment but found nothing that looked good in their price range. The apartments that they liked were always in a drug infested area, and that was not an option for them anymore.

One Saturday Kenny drove Jessica and her mother around to look at an apartment. Since Kenny was already in the real estate business, he called up one of his business associates and asked for a favor. On this day, he turned his vehicle into a neighborhood that they both were familiar with: 139th Street between 7th and 8th Avenue.

Ms. Jones looked at her daughter and asked excitedly, "Jessica, you found us an apartment in our old block?"

Jessica looked at her mother and smiled slyly. "Something like that."

They found a parking space and got out of the car and began walking up the block together, admiring the perfect row homes and reminiscing on their formidable years growing up in the neighborhood. When Jessica and her mother came to their former place of residence they stood and looked over their old home with nostalgic sadness and pride. Jessica put an arm around her mother's shoulder because she knew her mother was thinking about the good years she'd had in the building with her, her brother Jordan, and especially her father.

Her mother exhaled deeply and said, "Let's go," and waited for her daughter to take the lead and show her what building they would be living in, but Jessica stood there and smiled. What Jessica did next almost caused Ms. Jones to lose her breath—she extended her hand and presented her mother with a new a set of keys.

Her eyes widened, and Ms. Jones placed her hands toward her mouth. "Jessica, what is this?"

She smiled and said proudly, "It's a set of keys to your new home."

Mrs. Jones let out a cry. "Jessica, what are you saying?"

"I'm saying, this is our new home. I bought the building for you, Mama."

Ms. Jones let out a huge scream and jumped excitedly in her arms and hugged her with all her might and kissed her and Kenny.

"Mama, Kenny found out that the bank still owned the mortgage and it was still up for sale. I had some money put away and made a down payment and took over the mortgage."

Jessica stared at her mother looking over the building again and she seemed to sadden. "What's the matter, Mama? Aren't you excited about us having our home back?"

She nodded and said, "Yes, but I can't move in here with y'all. I would feel out of place. I just wouldn't feel right coming between the two of you."

"Ms. Jones, I will be living at my own building. Jessica put the building in your name so this is actually your home and you are the owner."

Ms. Jones looked at her daughter and was speechless.

Jessica confirmed it. "That's right, Mama. I put enough money down that the mortgage is only six hundred and twenty four dollars a month. That's if you don't mind having your child and your grandchild as roommates for a while?"Jessica waited with anticipation for a final response.

Her mother suddenly smiled and nodded. "Yes, yes, I would love you and the baby as roommates."

They were excited and ready to enter their old home until Kenny said, "Hold on, just one more thing."

Mother and daughter turned around and looked at Kenny. He approached Jessica and took her by the hand and bended to one knee and showed her a ring. Jessica couldn't believe what was happening and put her hand over her mouth and then looked at her mother.

He looked her in the eyes and spoke in French. After he was finished he said, "That means, Jessica Jones, would you do me the honor of marrying me and being my wife forever?"

Jessica nodded her head rapidly. "Yes, Kenny, I would love to marry you."

Kenny stood up and gave her a long kiss and swooped her off her feet and carried her into her new home. Jessica beamed with elation. She promised herself at that moment to love him forever. She decided right then and there that she would start brushing up on the French that she'd learned in prison and surprise him on their wedding day as she said her vows to him in French. She dreamed about that moment for years when she was in prison and thought it would only be just that—a dream. But now it was becoming a reality. She made a mental note to go downtown and purchase some tapes to aid her in speaking French fluently even if it killed her.

※ ○ ○ ○ ※

Jessica and her mother moved into their new home immediately. Since Jessica's mother still had all their furniture placed in storage, they were able to put everything back into place as they'd once had it with help of Cleveland and some of his friends from the neighborhood. Cleveland ensured Ms. Jones and Jessica that they didn't have to lift a finger as he allowed them enough time decorating their home on every floor.

When they finally completed the move, everything looked exactly as they last remembered it.

※ ※ ※

Everything couldn't have been better as life went on, as they once knew it. Ms. Jones was the happiest that she'd ever had been as her relationship with her daughter grew by leaps and bounds. Jessica even noticed her mother had started wearing makeup again when she knew Cleveland who still was coming around, doing minor and major repairs around the house and boiler room. She was happy to know her mother had a close friend and had come out of the hardened shell she'd worn since her father died.

Jessica still spent many nights with Kenny at his home in the Bronx, and he treated her like a queen, waiting on her hand and foot, not allowing her to do anything for herself. Even though she wasn't showing much, Kenny would rub and talk to her stomach at night and ensure his unborn child knew that their father loved them very much. That brought so much joy to Jessica that she'd cry. She finally felt that all the drama in her life was well in her past, and she looked toward a new future with her child and Kenny being one happy family, just like the one she once knew.

Everything was going perfect, until one day out of the blue, Jessica saw a letter with her name on it under her door. She took the letter upstairs and opened it when she got to her room.

Dear Jessica,
We have to meet up immediately because something went wrong. I don't want to say too much, but somehow somebody found out what the four of us did. Do not

use the phone to call me. Me, you, Lynn, and Tiny will meet at Burger King on 125th tonight at 6 o'clock on the dot to discuss it. Don't mention this to anybody until we find out what's happening.

Peace,

Vonda

Jessica read the typed letter and immediately felt a sharp pain in her stomach. She thought about calling Vonda up, but remembered what the letter said. It was already three o'clock and figure she had only three hours to find out everything that was going on, so she decided to wait it out.

✺ ○ ✺

When Jessica arrived at the restaurant, it was already ten minutes to six, and she saw that Lynn was already there sitting at one of the tables in the rear. They greeted each other with a hug and sat down.

Lynn appeared nervous and asked, "So, what is this all about? I mean, you think something is wrong? Vonda just told me to show up and that we're all to meet up. She wouldn't tell me anything else."

"Calm down, Lynn. Let's not get ahead of ourselves. It could be nothing."

"You think so?" Lynn said.

"Maybe, but let's wait for Vonda to tell us what's up."

Lynn nodded and looked at her watch. A few minutes later, Vonda and Tiny walked in together and Jessica waved to them to let them know where they sat. Lynn scooted over in the booth and Vonda sat next to her. Tiny did the same and sat right next to Jessica. Tiny began coughing loudly and looked very sickly. She looked as if she shouldn't even be there but in a hospital, Jessica thought. As they all settled in, everyone looked from one face to another until Vonda finally asked, "So, what's up, Jess?"

"What's up?" Jessica responded back.

There was a momentary pause until Lynn asked in frustration, "Come on, Vonda. You were the one who called us here. Tell us what's up."

Vonda frowned. "No, I didn't. Jessica told me to meet here."

Jessica shook her head. "No, I didn't. I received this note from you telling me I should meet you here." She pulled out the letter to prove her point.

Vonda frowned as she read the letter and chuckled. "I didn't write that!" Vonda pulled out a letter of her own and said, "This is the letter you left under my door telling me to contact Tiny and Lynn and meet you here."

Jessica snatched the letter and read it quickly and saw her name at the bottom. "Vonda, I didn't write this either."

They were all stunned.

"If y'all didn't write the letters who the fuck did?" Lynn said quickly, growing more agitated by the second.

Just then, a bike messenger wearing black spandex pants and a helmet came in through the front door and paused. He opened the bag he had over his shoulder and pulled out a package. "Is there a Jessica Jones in here?" he yelled as he looked around the restaurant.

The four girls turned to face him, and Jessica reluctantly waved her arm. "That's me, right here."

He walked his bike over to where the four girls sat and pulled out a clipboard. "Can you sign here?"

Jessica looked at the clipboard and asked, "What is this about?"

He rolled his eyes and said sarcastically, "It's a clipboard. You sign it, and I give you a package."

Jessica disregarded his smart comment and said, "I know what it is. What I want to know is, who sent it?"

"I just deliver packages, ma'am, that's all. You gonna sign for your package, or what?"

Jessica looked at Vonda, who nodded, and Jessica signed for the package. He handed it to her and left. The four girls looked at the package in Jessica's hand in silence, unsure what to do next. Jessica took a breath and ripped open the thick yellow envelope. They watched nervously as Jessica pulled the contents out of the envelope. It was filled with newspaper clippings and articles pertaining to recent murders throughout Harlem. As they sorted through each article they recognized the murder scenes they had participated in, including the bodies on 142nd Street, 144th Street and the bodies on 116th Street. None of them could believe their eyes as they sifted through mounds of clippings from various newspapers.

"What the fuck?" Vonda cursed.

"Oh, shit!" said Lynn as she put her hands over her eyes, not wanting to believe what she was seeing.

"Hold up," said Jessica. "Here's a note."

Everyone looked at Jessica with anticipation as she began to read the typed letter.

I pray that by now that I have your undivided attention. Believe me when I say that this is very real and very serious, and I hope you see that your life depends on it. I know everything that you did— EVERYTHING, including the killings that you done to an old friend of yours from prison, the now deceased Eartha Lee Jenkins, better known as Dear Mama and her sidekick Precious, that you all slaughtered like a pig. I have in my possession direct evidence linking you to at least eight other murders, which will almost guarantee you the death penalty. However, I do have compassion in my heart to give you four an option out of this life-changing event with something on the side that can prove very lucrative for all parties involved with no further repercussions. If you are interested, go back to Jessica's house and wait for another package that will arrive at 8PM this evening, and you will receive further instructions thereafter. You are being watched at all times, and if I see any of you deviate from each other or try to leave town, the other three will be arrested for all the murders I've mentioned.

When Jessica finished reading the letter, the girls seemed too overwhelmed to even speak.

"So, what do y'all think?" Jessica finally asked.

"What we think? What we think?" Lynn repeated in exasperation. "We going back to jail! That's what I think!"

Vonda exhaled deeply. "I don't know, this motherfucker seems to know everything about us, down to the shit we did in prison."

Tiny looked at each of them and snarled. "Somebody been running their mouth, that's what the fuck is happening."

They began staring at each other as if they were waiting for someone to tell them it was just a joke, but it never happened.

"Let's just wait and see if we get a package and take it from there," Jessica offered.

Lynn began to grow hysterical, "Fuck that! I don't know about y'all, but I ain't waiting around to find out what happens. I'm gonna get the fuck outta here before anything goes down."

"No, Lynn," Vonda snapped. "You heard what this motherfucker said; if one of us leave the rest of us get arrested. I ain't taking that chance. Let's just go to Jessica's house and wait for the package and find out what he wants us to do. He might want some money or shit and is only trying to extort us."

Tiny casually purposed, "What make you think it's a he?"

Again, they looked at each other for an answer. Vonda repeated that they should just go to Jessica's house again.

Jessica looked at her watch and announced, "We still got an hour, so let's leave now so we can be there when the package arrives. They all nodded and exited the booth and headed to Jessica's house.

The package arrived exactly when the mysterious person said that it would via another messenger. They followed Jessica to her room and eagerly waited for her to open the box. The first thing Jessica pulled out was another folder with several 8x10 black and white photos of a single Hispanic male. Jessica continued and removed another letter and read it.

If you are reading this letter, you successfully completed the second phase on your way to freedom. The man you're looking at name is Carlos Sosa. He is one of the biggest drug distributors in New York City. He is the mastermind from Columbia that introduced the first wave of cocoa leaf paste, a highly addictive form of cocaine which would become known as crack to the ghettos of New York City and Los Angeles.

Your mission is very simple: kill him and anyone else associated with him and shut down his headquarters.

The building is a one-stop drug haven that produces and manufactures all the drugs in-house, and the tenants in the building are virtual hostages. It is infamously known within the neighborhood as The Castle of Greyskull and is located on 129th Street between Lenox and 5th Avenue.

Just like in the television show Mission Impossible, if you decide to take the job, you will be rewarded handsomely upwards of a half million dollars from the cash that Mr. Sosa keeps in the building on any given Sunday that is to be picked up on Monday.

If you do this, all records and evidence will be destroyed and you will live your life and spend the money as you see fit. Inside is a schematic of the entire building down to the smallest detail. The number of armed lookouts, the location of staircases and exits, and the best time to enter and exit.

You have 72 hours to come up with a plan before Monday and make a collective decision to complete your mission. I will monitor your every move, and if one of the rules is deviated from, all of you will spend a lifetime regretting it. This will be your last contact.

P.S. Get the job done by any means necessary. You can also recruit outside help, such as your Vietnam buddies. Ha, ha. Yes, I know about them also.

None of the girls could conjure any words to say at that moment. The only sound that could be heard was Tiny's dry and rough cough. Jessica felt dizzy as she tossed the letter on the bed and put her head to her knees and began crying as she thought about her unborn baby. Lynn followed suit and began to cry also. All Vonda could do was watch them all in silence, knowing there was nothing she could say to make them feel better.

"Something about this shit ain't right. It ain't right," Tiny said. "If you ask me, it sounds like somebody we know is setting us up for a fall."

"What are you saying, Tiny?" snapped Lynn

"I'm saying that it's got to be somebody that knows a lot about us. It could even be one of us for that matter."

Vonda frowned. "How the fuck could it be one of us, Tiny, and all our lives are at stake?"

"Well, how the fuck would somebody know about Dear Mama and Precious then?" Tiny posed a good question. "Unless one of y'all told somebody?" Tiny coughed and looked from face to face suspiciously.

"I probably told a couple of my brothers in passing conversation, but I never explained no specifics," Vonda admitted.

Lynn raised her head and admitted also, "I probably told one or two of my girlfriends in prison about it, but, hell, who in there didn't know we offed them bitches?"

"She got a point, because everybody knew about it and they could have easily seen me on the news or in the paper and put two and two together," explained Jessica.

"That's bullshit!" snapped Tiny, "I'm not buying that shit because they know too much."

"She's right," said Vonda. "It could be anybody, so all we can do is concentrate on what we going to do about this shit or we all going to be locked back up." Vonda shook her head and continued. "Like Lynn said, I ain't going back to jail."

Tiny smirked and shook her head sadly. "Either y'all in denial or this shit got you all stuck on stupid!"

The girls tossed Tiny a venomous gaze. "Who but us would know about Mama, Precious, Cookie, Bosco, and all those Vietnam motherfuckers? What's the chance an outsider would know all that?"

The girls simply put their heads down because they knew she was right. For the first time, distrust came across each girl's mind as they looked at each other warily.

Jessica finally raised her head. "So what are we going to do?"

Nobody said a word until Tiny coughed harshly and said, "Yo, read that part about the money again."

Jessica picked up the letter and cleared her eyes and reread it.

"If you decide to take the job, you will be rewarded handsomely upwards of a half million dollars from the cash that Mr. Sosa keeps in the building on any given Sunday right before it is to be picked up on Monday."

Tiny nodded and said, "Now, that's what's up. I wouldn't mind getting my hands on that type of loot even if one of y'all is using me."

"Fuck that shit, Tiny. We talking about our lives here," cried Lynn. "And stop saying it's one of us, because no one here would do that shit to each other."

"Yeah, whatever Lynn," Tiny said vaguely. "If we got a way to get that type of money, why not?"

Jessica looked at Tiny as if she were insane and screamed, "Tiny, we can get ourselves killed!"

Tiny stood up quickly and yelled, "What the fuck you think we were doing when we got in the mix for you with Bosco, Jessica?" Tiny challenged. "It was ok for us to put our life on the line for you, right?"

Jessica knew Tiny was blinded by greed, but knew she had a point.

Vonda added, "But, this is different, Tiny. Bosco was unorganized, he was—"

Enraged, Tiny cut Vonda off before she could finish. "Bosco was what, Vonda? Unorganized? He was so unorganized the he was about to cut your fucking head off if I wasn't there to pop his ass and save your life! Remember?"

Vonda didn't have a response.

"If somebody telling us where the money is, why don't we take it? Shit, I say they doing us a favor."

Vonda, Jessica and Lynn only stared at Tiny, realizing she was too far gone to reason with her.

Tiny felt the heat from their stares and asked them all, "What, y'all looking at me like I'm crazy, like I don't know what y'all thinking about me. 'Oh, Tiny got the virus and she don't care because she going to die anyway.' Well, guess what? You damn skippy, I don't give a fuck no more. If I'm gonna die I might as well try to get all the shit I can before I do. Doctors told me that I can die from this shit in ten days or ten years. Do any of y'all know how it feels to know you can die at any moment and it's nothing nobody can do about it?" Tiny stared at them as she awaited and answer, but she received none. "So either I'm gonna get rich or I'm gonna die trying and live every day as if it was my last. So you better find a reason to want to survive, because I did already."

The girls understood her pain and just sat around the room in silence until Jessica offered, "What we got to do is vote on it like we always did."

Vonda shrugged her shoulders and agreed with Jessica.

"Don't you think we should think things over first?" Lynn asked nervously. "Shouldn't we wait to see what happens first?"

Tiny was at wit's end. "Lynn, did you not hear what the fucking letter said? He or she or whoever it is got us over a barrel. We fucked either way. Either we are going to get this money and have a little chance, or we can go back to jail and have no chance at all."

At that moment all the girls knew they had little choice.

A full five minutes passed without a word being said when Vonda said, "So, whoever in it to do the damn thing, raise your hand."

Tiny was the first to raise her hand. "Fuck that shit, yo. I don't give a fuck. I'm in."

Vonda was next and raised her hand.

Lynn looked around and knew she didn't have a choice and raised her hand also.

All eyes shifted toward Jessica.

"So what's up, Jesse? It's either all of us or none of us, remember?"

Jessica did remember the pact, but all she could think of was her unborn child inside of her. But before she knew it she had her hand raised also. Tiny coughed harshly then stuck out her fist and smiled. "Get it girls?"

One by one, they touched fists and repeated in unison, "Get It Girls."

Jessica's whole body was numb as she walked around Harlem for hours thinking about the challenges ahead of her. She knew that she couldn't go to Kenny for support and tell him about her dangerous predicament because he would not allow anything to happen to her nor his unborn child inside of her. She needed to talk to someone or she would go crazy, so she went to the only person she knew who would be able to help her—Cleveland.

When she got to Cleveland's apartment, she knocked on the door but no one answered. She waited around for another hour, but he still hadn't shown up so she headed home. Just as she arrived home and was about to stick the key in door, the door opened and she stood face to face with her mother and Cleveland. Her mother had on her house gown and blushed when she saw her daughter stare at them knowingly.

Her mother stammered, "Oh, Jessica, you're home. Cleveland had just stopped by to move around some furniture that I needed to be moved, and he was just leaving."

Jessica looked at Cleveland, who was avoiding eye contact with her. Jessica decided not to embarrass them more than they already were and played it down and said, "Thank you, Cleveland for helping my mother out. We need a man like you around more often because this place isn't easy to maintain."

Cleveland and her mother smiled widely, appreciating that they were given an out. Cleveland tipped his hat to them and bade them both a good night.

Just as he was proceeding down stairs, Jessica said, "Oh, Cleveland, I came from your apartment just now to ask you is it possible you can stop by tomorrow. I need you to help me take my air-conditioner out my room window. It's too heavy for me to lift by myself. I asked Bosco to do it, but he was too busy."

Cleveland knew immediately she had a problem when she mentioned Bosco's name, but he kept his smile. "Sure, Jessica. I'll be over by ten. Don't you worry about a thing, because I hear you loud and clear." Cleveland knew to come after nine in the morning to ensure that Ms. Jones would already be at work.

They nodded and Cleveland walked off down the block.

As mother and daughter closed the door behind them and headed upstairs, Ms. Jones inquired, "Who is Bosco?"

The strain of it all kept Jessica awake the entire night. Jessica eagerly awaited his arrival, and when he finally arrived and rang the doorbell, she immediately threw her arms around him and began to cry. Cleveland was perplexed, and his suspicion that something was terribly wrong was confirmed.

They sat in the dining room, and Jessica explained to

Cleveland everything that had transpired over the last twenty-four hours. Cleveland listened intently and didn't say a word until Jessica finally finished and admitted that she was also pregnant.

Cleveland removed his hat and began scratching his head before he looked into her eyes. "This just doesn't sound right, Jessica. It sounds to me like one of those girls is running a number on you, because it's nobody else that would know all that information."

Jessica thought long and hard about his words and dismissed it. "No, Cleveland, I don't think so. I think I would know if one of them did."

Still not convinced Cleveland gave her a knowing look and asked, "Well, how else would someone know that much information about you all if it wasn't someone who was present with you for the past seven years?"

Jessica didn't have an answer that would make any sense. So, she just told her how she felt. "I see your, point Cleveland, and it don't make any sense to me either, but I been around these girls for over eleven years, over six of which we were around each other every day. We knew more about each other than anybody on the planet. I would know if one of them was gaming me, but that's not the case here. I looked in every one of their eyes when this happened and I saw the same thing—fear."

Cleveland looked into her eyes, and that's was exactly what Jessica still had in hers. He scratched his head once again and asked to see the letters again. He removed his glasses from his shirt pocket and placed them on his face and began reading each of them slowly. When he finally finished reading them he still wasn't fully convinced.

"Jessica, this sounds like a set up, plain and simple, but I see how you don't have much of a choice in the matter. Either you do it and risk your life in the process, or you dismiss the letters and risk going back to jail."

They both sat in place for a long time without a word being said until Cleveland folded his burly arms and exhaled deeply and said, "Well, like I said, 'if you in this thing for a penny, you got to be in for a pound.'" He smiled at Jessica and she suddenly began to smile again.

She stood up and hugged him again. As she pulled away from him, he observed her closely.

"Jessica, I know you have been noticing me and your mother have be getting very friendly lately, and if I know one thing about you, I know that you are smart enough to see what's going on."

Jessica only smiled and let him continue.

"Well, I respect you enough to tell you that I have strong feelings for your mother, I always have, but she ain't never showed me no interest until recently. She always seemed so sad and unhappy before you came home, and I've noticed a change in her. It's like she's finally allowing sunshine back in her life." He put his head down for a moment as he searched for the right words to say to her. "The reason I'm telling you all this is because she told me she is going to be a grandmother already." Cleveland finally lifted his head to face her. "Jessica, when she told me that, I swear that was the happiest that I've ever seen her in the four years I've known her, and it was then I realized that you and your baby have given her back her life."

He paused for a moment. "I'm ready to do what I have to do to take care of your problem, but I can't allow you to risk getting hurt in the process for the sake of your mother."

Jessica was floored that a man outside her father could be concerned about her mother so deeply that he would risk his life just so she wouldn't experience another day of unhappiness.

Jessica took Cleveland's hand into hers and said to him softly, "I couldn't imagine a better person to be with my mother than you, Cleveland. You been with me through thick and thin and risked your own life when you didn't have to, but you did. But, I have to be part of this because me and the other girls made our own pact years ago that no matter what the situation was, we would have each other's back even if it meant dying together. I know what we are up against isn't going to be easy. In fact, it's a chance somebody might die, but I'm willing to take that chance because I have no other options."

Jessica rubbed her growing stomach. "Just like you said, 'if you in for a penny, you in for a pound.'"

At that moment, he knew she was a warrior and could never change her mind. He acknowledged her by shaking his head.

"Let me get a look at those layouts of the building they sent you."

Chapter 23

hey had only three days to devise a plan to overtake the building and come out of it with the least amount of casualties possible. Jessica and Cleveland called an emergency meeting to have everybody show up that that night at his apartment. By eight o'clock that evening everyone had arrived except Lynn and Tiny. Vonda explained to Jessica that she hadn't heard from Lynn since they'd had their first meeting.

Tiny finally arrived moments later and looked worse than they had ever seen her. She limped in and immediately sought refuge in an unoccupied chair and sat down. Breathing heavily, she looked as though she had just run a marathon—trying to catch a breath. It was obvious to all present, that small, frail girl was dying a slow death, and nobody dared to question her either out of pity or shame. By nine o'clock they decided to start the meeting despite Lynn not being there.

Cleveland took the lead since he had called the meeting and

formally introduced everyone to each other again; Cleveland thanked everyone for showing up on such short notice and briefly explained to them why they were there. After he explained the short version to his men, he asked Jessica to stand up and explain to them the rest.

Jessica was nervous, but she had no choice but to tell them the complete account of everything that had transpired in the last twenty-four hours. When she finished, all the men were poker faced and silent. Seeing the men's skepticism, Cleveland joined in and tried to make light of the bad situation.

"The good part about this is that we can shut down the biggest drug house in Harlem and get paid a lot of money to do the job."

The men seemed to not be buying into it.

Johnson spoke up for the first time. "First of all, this ain't no drug house, Cleveland. It's an entire building. Secondly, this whole shit stinks. It doesn't sound right."

Shooter agreed. "Johnson is right. This shit sounds like something out of a movie. Plus, in order for someone to have that much information about you it got to be somebody you all know."

Johnson then added, "It can be one of you, for that matter."

Cleveland felt their tension and opposition and decided to interject reason. "Look, bottom line is that we all can go down on this because we already got our hands dirty. This person knows about the job we did on 116th Street, so we got just as much to lose as them."

Nobody said a word about that, so Cleveland continued. "All we got to do is figure out a plan to shut down that building permanently and we are home free. It's probably a bunch of untrained junkies that are guarding a post or two and we can overtake the whole building just like that."

Shooter still wasn't buying into it and played the devil's advocate. "We can't afford to assume anything, Cleveland. You most of all should know that. We need positive I.D. on the locations, how many people we are dealing with, and most importantly, the kind of weapons they'll be holding."

Johnson spoke up. "Yeah, and the only way we can know that is if we have someone on the inside. If we don't, we could be walking into an ambush and get slaughtered."

Cleveland knew he was right and didn't have a good answer to tell them.

All seemed impossible from the start until Tiny managed to speak up though her rough, crude voice. "I can get that information for you."

Everyone turned their attention toward the sickly girl with reservations.

Skeptical, Johnson questioned her, "And how are you going to do that, little lady?"

Tiny stared at the man and was offended by him calling her little. Tiny countered back coldly, "Because, I'm a motherfucking dope fiend, and I get high in that spot all the time and everybody knows me, old man."

Johnson stared at her grimly, until Doc broke the tension by laughing out loud.

Cleveland nodded his approval and quickly inquired, "Do you think you can get us information on their security, their locations, and where they hold the drugs and the money at?"

They looked at Tiny with anticipating eyes and she simply answered, "Yeah, I can do that, but that's the least of your problems."

Everyone's smiles turned into frowns as they awaited an answer. Impatient, Johnson spewed, "Ok, spit it out."

Tiny didn't like the huge man much and snarled at him before she answered. "Getting into the building is going to be the problem. If you ain't no smoker or a tenant they ain't letting you get in the building. And even if you do get in to cop the drugs, if they don't remember you are going to raise suspicion and they will test you by making you smoke crack right in front of them to be sure. And trust me; none of y'all want to hit that glass dick."

They all thought about her words then Cleveland asked, "So what about other entrances?"

"They have every entrance—the roof, the side entrance, and even the first and second floor windows booby trapped," Tiny answered. "They got low explosives for the windows, and you might just lose a finger or two, but its primary function is to warn them in case someone tries to get in. But on the roof I hear they got that big shit, that C-4. Even if we make it in there, it's going to be a problem getting out without getting blown up."

Being that he was an expert at explosives, Johnson grew alarmed by her vast knowledge about explosives and challenged her again. "How do you know so much about the locations of the explosives? Better yet, how do you know about explosives period?"

Everyone was still skeptical about the job from the beginning, and this seemed like a question they all needed to know. Tiny scanned the room at everyone waiting eagerly for her response. She turned her attention back to her questioner and said, "Because me and some other people was going to rob the place about six months ago."

Johnson, still not convinced said, "Cleveland, that's too much of a fucking coincidence for this li'l girl to be so close to this shit. Before I go further she got to tell us everything and convince me she ain't trying to use us to do the robbery for her. She got to provide some names or something."

Tiny jumped, enraged, and said, "Motherfucker, I don't need to convince you to do shit for me. You free to do whatever the fuck you want to do because I don't have to answer to your old ass or nobody else."

Johnson had enough and stood up to leave. "Cleveland, you my man and all that, but this whole shit smells like a damn setup if you ask me. I suggest you stay out of it too."

Cleveland tried to stop him, but Johnson had already made up his mind and continued to walk toward the door. As he opened the door to leave, there was a large box in front of the door with a mysterious note attached to the top of it.

To the people inside this room

Cleveland and Johnson looked at each other in silence. Johnson bent down and shook the box gently before he picked it up and handed it off to Cleveland. The small group of people inside the room were surprised to see both men reenter the room carrying a box. Cleveland brought it into the living room and placed it on the table and then passed around the note. When everyone read the note they eagerly awaited Cleveland's next move.

Cleveland reached in his pocket and pulled out a folding knife that was attached to a valley of keys and opened it. Everyone stood and walked closer to the box as Cleveland made an incision to the stripping. He looked around at everyone before he opened, and when he did all they saw was balled-up newspapers. He slowly began removing the contents, and that's when they all saw it—the severed head of their homegirl Lynn.

Jessica and Vonda immediately backed away from the box and began to cry hysterically. Tiny fell back into the chair and began to shake uncontrollably as she lifted her knee to her chin. Cleveland and Doc ran over to Jessica and Vonda, who were both on the floor crying their hearts out, and tried to console them. Johnson even approached Tiny and put his hand on her frail shoulders and offered her his condolences. Shooter stared down into the box and removed another letter that was inside.

When everyone finally gained their composure, Jessica and Vonda sat on the couch in a daze. Shooter handed Cleveland the letter and he read it quickly. He looked at the three girls, dumbfounded, and didn't know whether they could handle any more bad news. He decided it was best that they know and cleared his throat.

"Uh, um, ladies, I think you should hear this."

He stared at the letter again proceeded to read it aloud.

I guess most of you didn't take my warning serious enough, and as a result, one of you paid for it with their life. I warned you that I will be watching, but your friend had other plans and had her clothes packed to leave town. BIG MISTAKE! You have four days to fulfill our contract and hopefully you now realize that I'm serious.

Nobody said a word and realized that this mysterious person was playing for keeps. The men also knew that they were now involved just as deep as the girls since the package was delivered to Cleveland's apartment. They knew they were all being watched.

Humbled now, Johnson was the first one to speak. "I'm sorry about your friend, ladies, and I don't want to sound insensitive, but we got to come up with a plan and soon, because whoever this person is, he is deadly serious and we don't have much time to waste."

Doc finally spoke up and for the first time he was all business. "He's right; if we have any chance of pulling this off, we are going to need all the information that we can get from all of you."

He looked at Tiny, who was still sulking in the chair.

Doc bent down and spoke to her softly, "Now, we are going to need that information to help you three live. So you got to tell us everything you know, starting with the robbery you were to be involved in."

Tiny closed her eyes and nodded. She took a deep breath and said, "About six months ago I was approached by a friend of mine that I've known for years. He told me that he had plans to rob this stash house that had a lot of money and drugs stored inside and needed some people in on the job with him. He had a dude that worked on the inside who provided him with all the information that I told you, down to the rooms that had all the money and where the drugs were stashed at. It would have been perfect, but none of us knew anything about explosives and had no way how to get around it, so I guess they gave up and didn't want to risk getting blown up."

Doc smiled at Tiny and said, "Good, real good, but I'm going to need something else from you."

He paused to give her a moment; he didn't want to press her too hard.

Tiny nodded.

Doc gave her an assuring smile again and asked, "Do you think that person still has that information and does he have a name? Because this could make the difference if we live or die, so you got to tell us."

There was total silence as they awaited an answer. Tiny knew he was right and looked at Vonda and Jessica and answered, "Yeah, it was my friend Chubby, Vonda's baby brother."

Everyone turned and looked in Vonda's direction.

They asked Vonda to see if she could contact her brother and see if he could come over and fill them in on what he knew. Vonda called her house throughout the night and was told by her mother that Chubby had yet to arrive home. Vonda finally told her mother that when he arrived to come over to where she was at and gave her the address and apartment.

For the remainder of the night and till nearly dawn, they slaved over coming up with a feasible plan. They were happy with the plan that they devised but still needed the vital information from their missing link—Chubby.

It was nearly six in the morning when they heard a loud crash at the door, catching them all by surprise. A huge man in a ski mask wielding a 12 gauge shotgun ordered everyone to the floor. Shooter was the first to react and reach for a weapon, but the gunman proved to be faster and pointed his weapon in his direction and warned him, "One more move, motherfucker, and I'm putting your brains on top of the ceiling."

Shooter slowly removed his hand from behind him, where he had his weapon concealed.

Vonda jumped up and screamed, "Chubby, put that weapon down, we are ok!"

Chubby stared around and saw that they were in fact safe,

lowered his weapon, and removed his mask. Everyone began to breathe easier knowing that their lives was no longer in danger.

Vonda scolded him. "Why the fuck would you come busting in here like the police, Chubby?"

Chubby suddenly began to sway back and forth. "Mama told me you were calling all night looking for me. She said that you sounded like you were crying, so I thought you were in trouble and wasn't taking any chances."

"But still, Chubby, tell me why did you have to kick this man's whole door off?"

Chubby eyed the floor like a child who was caught stealing cookies out of the cookie jar and had to tell the truth. "Because I rather shoot first and ask questions later."

His cavalier answer sent chills down everyone's spine, especially Jessica's, and she knew at that moment Chubby was far from the loveable little boy she once knew—he was a killer.

Doc relieved the tension and joked, "I like this young man's style. I never saw anyone get the jump on Shooter before."

Vonda grabbed him by his arm and led him over to Cleveland and introduced him, "Chubby, this is Cleveland; it's his door that you kicked down."

They shook hands cautiously, and Chubby humbly apologized. "I'm sorry about your door, man."

Cleveland was surprised with his sudden change of character. Just a moment ago he was a monster, and now he was shaking hands with the gentleness of a lamb.

"Don't worry about it. I'll get another one."

Chubby said, "Naw man, it was my bad, I'll take care of it." Chubby reached inside his pocket and pulled out a large wad of cash and peeled off two crisp one-hundred-dollar bills and handed it to Cleveland. He peeled off an additional hundred dollars and added, "And this one is for your troubles."

Vonda introduced Chubby to everyone as he acknowledged them with a nod. He smiled when he saw Jessica and Tiny and gave them both a hug. After a momentary period of silence Chubby noticed that all the girls had their heads hung low and knew something wasn't right.

"So what's wrong?"

Vonda suddenly burst into tears, followed by Jessica who did the same thing. Both girls were crying so hard that he could not make out a word that they were saying, until finally, Cleveland gestured for Chubby to follow him into the back.

Cleveland took Chubby to the bedroom where he had taken Lynn's severed head. Cleveland told him that he should brace himself before he opened the box to show him. Chubby stared down at it long and hard while Cleveland informed him, "This is their friend Lynn, I think you know her."

He nodded slowly and showed no outward emotions. Chubby finally looked up from the box and into Cleveland's eyes and asked through gritted teeth, "Who did this shit to her?"

It was then Cleveland noticed that the huge man eyes were now bloodshot and watery. Cleveland patted him on his wide shoulder and said, "I think it would be best if we explain everything from the beginning."

When Jessica watched the two men enter back into the living room, it was clear by looking at Chubby that it had affected him deeply because his jaw was clenching wildly and he had the look of revenge in his eyes. Jessica knew that Chubby had loved Lynn as much as her, and knew someone had hell to pay.

Vonda asked her little brother, "You ok, Chubby?"

Chubby looked his sister in the eye and needn't say a word and she got the message.

It was a momentary stillness until Cleveland broke the ominous silence and offered, "Jessica, I think it would be best if you explain to him everything that led up to this."

Already exhausted, Jessica found enough strength to tell Chubby everything that went on since the beginning. Chubby never even flinched. They gave Chubby a moment to process everything that he had just heard.

He suddenly looked up and asked, "How can I be part of this?"

Cleveland looked around at all the men to see if he could be a part of their group, more out of courtesy, and one by one, each man nodded their approval. Even Johnson was happy to have him aboard and smiled widely. They knew from experience that the huge man-child that stood before them was a natural born killer and were happy to have him on their team instead of against them.

Cleveland smiled. "You're in, young man." Cleveland wasted no time as he looked at Chubby and requested, "First things first, we need to ask you some important questions that can help us."

Cleveland gestured toward Doc, and he didn't hesitate to ask him the one question that would help them the most: "The person you had on the inside, does he still work for them there?"

Chubby, still grim-faced, answered, "Yeah, he still there, but like Tiny told you, I was gonna hit them before, but it was no way around those booby traps."

Cleveland gave him a cunning smile and said, "Young man, I don't think that's going to be a problem anymore."

Chapter 24

It was Friday, and no one had left Cleveland's apartment for the past two days. Johnson did leave the house only out of respect for the girls, and took their best friend's body part far away from them and stored it in a freezer. Tiny and Chubby proved to be a vital part of the operation, and it would've been impossible to pull off without them. Tiny was given the first assignment to go to the intended building and simply get high all day and do an early assessment of the inner workings of the building. She was given five hundred dollars cash to stay as long as it took to gather as much information as she could. Since Chubby's inside man worked a full twelve-hour shift, seven days a week, he knew exactly where he would be at that time.

Chubby and Johnson pulled up in front of an old and decrepit tenement building on 126th Street between St. Nicholas and Morningside that appeared to be abandoned. Chubby nodded to Johnson and cut off his ignition, then they exited the car. Even though the building was officially abandoned by its owner, it still had electricity on inside. They entered the makeshift door and proceeded up to the top floor. The well-worn rickety staircase creaked loudly as they made their way up the stairs.

They were almost at the final level when a tall, medium-built, brown skinned man, who appeared to be in his late twenties, opened a door and yelled, "You better have a good reason to be here, motherfucka," as he wielded a wooden bat.

Chubby didn't even bother to answer the man and continued up the stairs as if he wasn't even there. When the man recognized who it was he nearly panicked and began apologizing immediately. "Oh, shit, Chubby, I . . . I didn't know that was you," he stammered.

The man backed away as Chubby approached him. Chubby only stared down upon the man with his dark, sullen eyes until he began to tremble. Chubby simply walked past the man and into his apartment without as much as an invitation. Johnson followed suit as Chubby scanned the sparse and unkempt empty apartment and saw drug paraphernalia littered all around the room. Chubby knew the man was a crack addict and all his pay went toward drugs.

Chubby asked, "Anybody else here, Sweets?"

"Yeah, Chubby, just my old lady. I think she went into the bathroom."

"Tell her to come out," Chubby said simply.

Sweets didn't hesitate and walked over to the bathroom and opened it. "Come on out, baby. It's ok, it's just some friends of mines."

It was obvious that the woman was just as scared as her man by the way she eyed the floor as she slowly exited the bathroom.

The woman was light-skinned and very small, no bigger than Tiny. She couldn't have been older than twenty years old, but could've passed as younger if it weren't for her stress-marked face caused by lack of sleep and everyday drug use. As they got closer, Chubby and Johnson immediately knew she was pregnant from the hard, round bump on her stomach that she desperately tried to hide.

Sweets tried to smile and introduced her to Chubby and his scary looking friend behind him. "Chubby, this here is Katie."

She acknowledged them with a slight nod, still avoiding eye contact. Chubby turned his attention back to Sweets, who also was avoiding Chubby's penetrating stare. He knew Chubby wasn't a fool, and he wasn't too happy that he had his girl still smoking crack while she was pregnant. "Ok, you go over there and sit down now."

She scurried off immediately.

Chubby looked around the apartment and saw the kitchen was on the left and entered it. Old dirty bowls and dishes were stacked all over the counter and inside the sink as roaches ran freely over them. He proceeded to the refrigerator and opened it and saw that it was bare, just as he thought. He closed the refrigerator to face Sweets, who was already preparing for the worst and immediately began explaining.

"Yo, Chubby, we eat out every day, so it's no need to buy any food. I brought her some Chinese food before I left to go to work yesterday."

Not used to being anyone's fool, Chubby tilted his head to let Sweets know he knew he was lying. Sweets put his head down and decided to remain silent instead of risking being caught in a lie again. Chubby reached in his pocket, pulled out his money roll, and removed two twenty-dollar bills. He handed them to Sweets.

Chubby said in a low tone, "Tell your people to go around the corner and buy some food from M&G's."

M&G's was a soul food restaurant that was part of the community for years.

"Tell her to buy enough for tomorrow too and to also buy some milk."

He quickly followed Chubby's orders and almost ran to Katie and explained to her what to do. She obeyed, put on a sweater, and was out the door.

When Chubby was sure she was gone, without warning, he slapped Sweets viciously across the room and he fell hard to the floor. The man cowered on the floor as Chubby approached him.

"Motherfucka, what kind of nigga are you to let your girl still smoke that shit while she pregnant with your baby?"

Sweets pleaded with his eyes for forgiveness. Chubby only looked down at the man with disgust and told him to stand up. Sweets rose to his feet with caution, and he once again stood before Chubby's fierce and no nonsense eye's.

"Here's what you going to do," said Chubby, in the most chilling tone, "By tomorrow, that li'l girl is going to be in some kind of hospital or one of those drug program so y'all can give that baby chance to live. You understand me?"

Sweets nodded his head rapidly to let Chubby know he got his point.

Chubby continued, "And, Sweets, if I find out she didn't go in and you are playing me, I swear to God, you will never get a chance to see if you had a boy or a girl."

Sweets nearly lost control of his bowels because he knew Chubby's reputation and that it wasn't an idle threat but a guaranteed promise that he would kill him.

"You ain't gonna have to worry; we wanted to do that anyway for the baby's sake. But first thing tomorrow when I get off in the morning, I'm gonna take her straight to Harlem Hospital. I promise you, Chubby. I promise!"

Chubby seemed convinced, so he changed the subject. "Ok, now me and my man here," Chubby gestured behind him with his head, "we got some business to talk to you about. You remember the job we were going to do a while back?"

Sweets nodded his head and Chubby continued. "Well, it's on again. Are you still down to be part of it?"

Again, the man nodded his head quickly.

Chubby knew he would say yes because he had no choice but to do so. "You still got all that information you gave me last time about the location of them explosives them niggas got hidden in the building?"

Sweets finally smiled and ran to the kitchen and removed a folded brown shopping bag and handed it to Chubby. "It's right here, Chubby, and I got everything. I even know what kind of explosives they have set up, I know the best time to hit the place, how many people gonna be there on a given day, and what they will be packin'."

Chubby handed the bag to Johnson and said, "What you gonna do now is sit down and answer any question my man ask you."

Sweets nodded.

Jessica's head was still spinning after the events that transpired over the last 48 hours. She hadn't slept or eaten the entire time she was there and still couldn't believe that one of her best friends was really dead. Now that reality had set in, she knew she'd have to go home and face her mother and eventually Kenny. She hadn't called or spoken to either in the past two days, and she knew both would be worried sick about her. The last thing in the world Jessica wanted was to have to explain to her mother where she had been. She wanted so badly to simply take a hot shower to wash away the shame and guilt she was experiencing at that moment and go to sleep.

Jessica finally made it home and hadn't even made it halfway up the stairs to her building when the door flew open and there her mother and fiancée stood.

"Jessica," her mother scolded, "where in the world were you?"

Jessica closed her eyes and put her head down, wondering what lie she could possibly tell them. She felt horrible as Kenny stood silent with a discerning look on his face. Ms. Jones continued to inquire the reason she hadn't bothered to call, and Jessica knew that it wasn't the time or the place to tell them what had gone on and simply walked right past them and up to her room. Over her shoulder, Jessica heard her mother yell more bad news, "Your parole officer was here yesterday. He said you haven't reported into him in two months. He said that if you don't report in today you will be arrested again."

Jessica sat at the side of her bed pondering how much more could she actually take. The last 48 hours had physically and mentally drained her and pushed her to her limits. She suddenly broke down from all the stress and fell to her knees and asked

God to help her.

"God, please help me through this. Please, God, help me by giving me the strength to overcome this. If not for me, just let me survive long enough to ensure the safety of my baby."

Jessica took a deep breath and stood up and wiped the tears from her eyes. She gathered her thoughts and realized that she'd totally forgotten about reporting to her parole officer. With so much going on over the last few months it totally slipped her mind. She decided she would go see her parole officer first thing tomorrow morning, because she knew he could remand her back to prison for six months if she didn't. Jessica was in dire need of a shower and sleep, so she began to get undressed to do both.

Moments later, and just as she expected, there was a knock on the door and it was Kenny. There was a brief silence until Kenny broke the ice.

"So, are you ok, Jessica?"

Jessica shook her head and continued to undress out of the stale clothes she had worn for the past two days. Kenny was growing angrier by the minute as she continued without so much as an explanation to why she was gone for so long.

"Jessica, can you at least stop and look at me?" Kenny finally asked.

She stopped and turned around to face him, but remained silent.

"What's going on with you, Jessica? You disappeared for days without so much as a phone call and then you finally show up and don't have anything to say?"

Jessica smoothed her hair out of her face, unsure how to answer him and only whispered, "I'm sorry."

Her cavalier response only aggravated him more. "Is that all you have to say, Jessica? I'm sorry?"

"What do you want me to tell you, Kenny? Me, Vonda, and the rest of us had to take care of some business and we got caught up and lost track of time."

"Jessica, you were gone for over two days! What's so important that you couldn't take time out and contact me or your mother to let us know you were ok?"

Jessica didn't know how to answer. She knew she could not under any circumstance tell him the truth because it would cause a whole lot more problems for the both of them. She knew she was already knee-deep in conspiracy to commit robbery and murder and didn't want him in involved in any way if something should go wrong.

Her silence constituted an admission of guilt to him because he painstakingly asked, "Jessica, are you seeing someone else?"

Jessica never expected that question and gave him a smile. "No, Kenny, it's nothing like that. It's just that we got caught up into something and we just lost track of time."

"Jessica, please tell me the truth. I don't know what I'm going to do if I lose you and the baby."

For the first time she looked into his eyes and saw that he was actually hurt and concerned about possibly losing her. She approached him and took him by the hand and said softly, "Kenny, you are the first and only man I have ever been with and ever will want. You and the baby mean the world to me, and I would never do anything to put that in jeopardy. Right now I got something very, very, important that I have to take care of, but give me a few days and it will be all over with, I promise you. I can't tell you everything, but I just need you to trust me on this, Kenny."

Jessica could see through his eyes that he had a million questions to ask her and was fighting asking her.

"Jessica, it's not about you or your friends anymore. You have your child in you—our child—and whatever you're doing you'll be jeopardizing its safety, and I can't have that."

His words stung because she knew that he was right, but she had no other choice and had come too far to turn back.

Jessica forced herself to smile then lied, "No, Kenny, it's nothing like that. I wouldn't do anything to put our baby in jeopardy."

Kenny stared at her with conjecture, unsure, yet wanting to believe her.

Jessica said with forced excitement, "I tell you what, remember when you said you wanted to go away the Poconos Mountains and stay there, just the two of us, for the weekend?"

Kenny nodded.

"Well, after this is over I'm taking you there and I'm treating." Jessica seductively wrapped her arms around his neck and gave him a passionate kiss. When they pulled away Jessica mimed with her lips, "I love you."

He blushed and repeated, "I love you too."

Just like that, all was forgiven. She wrapped her arms around him to squeeze him closer and felt something bulky in his jacket pocket and asked, "What is that, Kenny?"

He pulled away and pulled the item in question out of his jacket pocket. "Oh, this, I wanted to surprise you. This is what they call a mobile phone."

He held it up to show her. It was huge with a long antenna protruding from it.

Jessica looked at it oddly and chuckled. "What you need with a walkie-talkie, Kenny?"

Kenny smiled and said, "It's not a walkie-talkie, it's a real live phone. These are new on the market, only those rich Wall Street dudes have one of these. Since you having the baby and I be working outside all the time, I decided to get one of these so if you do go into labor and I'm not there you can call me wherever I'm at so I won't miss the baby being born."

Jessica was smitten by that fact that he was so concerned in the birth of his unborn child's life at that moment and grew to love him even more. He handed it to her and it weighed a ton, she thought.

"You carry this around with you all day? It's so heavy."

"I usually keep it charging in the car, but I was waiting for a call from my uncle; he's coming into New York up from Miami today and I have to pick him up from the airport."

Jessica smiled and then thought for a moment and asked, "Kenny, is that the same uncle you told me sold drugs?"

Kenny tilted his head. "How did you know that?"

Jessica chuckled and reminded him, "You told me that years ago when we first met at Stevo's party that you used to stay with him. Don't you remember?"

Kenny thought about it for a moment and shrugged it off. "Yeah, that's him, but he gave that shit up years ago and moved to Florida." Kenny's smile grew wider and said, "Damn, you got a good memory, I didn't remember telling you that about him. He moved to Florida and got rich by buying condos and undeveloped land down there."

Jessica nodded and said, "So, you going to introduce me to him? Because he would be the first person in your family I've met."

✺ ✺ ✺

Jessica was awakened by her mother and was told that she had a phone call and that it was Vonda. She adjusted her weary eyes and looked over at her alarm clock and saw that it was only 7:36 in the evening. "Ok, Ma, tell her I'll be there in a minute."

Her mother nodded and closed the door behind her. She looked beside her and saw that Kenny was still laying right next to her in a deep sleep and smiled. He told her that he, too, was up for the past two days worrying about her and hadn't slept.

She scooted out of the bed, not wanting to wake him, and searched for her slippers and house gown. She went down to the kitchen and saw the phone dangling off the hook and picked it up.

"Hello?"

"Yo, Jess, it's me, Vonda."

"Yeah, what's up?" Jessica asked, sensing something was wrong.

"Yo, Tiny is in the hospital."

"In the hospital?" Jessica repeated.

"Yeah, they say she got walking pneumonia. And she's fucked up real bad," Vonda admitted.

"For real? How'd you find out?"

"Because the hospital called me and told me I should come down because they don't think she's going to make it."

Jessica nearly dropped the phone. "Vonda, are you serious?"

"I'm not going to lie to you. They say it got something to do with that virus she got."

Jessica remained speechless, unable to believe what she was hearing.

"Jessica? You still there?"

Jessica suddenly snapped out her trance and answered, "Yeah, I'm still here."

"Are you ok?" Vonda asked with concern.

"Yeah, I'm ok. Which hospital are you at?"

"I'm at Harlem Hospital."

"Ok, I'll be there in a minute."

Jessica hung up. She ran upstairs and woke Kenny and explained to him what was happening. Kenny didn't blink and told her he was coming with her. As they both got dressed her mother, again, knocked on the door.

"Come in, Mama," Jessica said, as she was putting on her sweater.

"What's going on?" Ms. Jones inquired with genuine concern.

"Tiny's in the hospital, Mama, and she's real sick . . . they say she might not make it."

Ms. Jones' hand flew to her mouth and she shuddered. "Oh, my goodness, no."

"I'm meeting Vonda right now, so I may be there for a while."

Her mother nodded and asked her to give her a call and let her know what was happening. Jessica nodded and she and Kenny were out the door.

When they arrived at Harlem Hospital, they rushed into the emergency room, looking frantically around for their friend. The place was packed with ailing patients who moaned on beds and gurneys as the sickening combination of antiseptic and death loomed in the air. Over her shoulder, Jessica heard a familiar voice and turned around and saw that it was Vonda waving for them to come over to where she was at.

They ran over, and when she got to the bed and saw her friend Tiny, Jessica gasped at the sight of her. Tiny's shrunken and skinny body was beyond anything they would have imagined. Her skeletal, torn body was hooked intravenously to bags that hovered above her in into her tiny arms. She wore a flimsy hospital gown that exposed her body, and it was the first time that any of them saw her without the double and triple layers of clothing that she normally wore. She had an oxygen mask over her face, and her chest heaved heavily for each breath of air.

Vonda gestured for Jessica to come over and talk to her and backed out of the small section to give her some space. Tiny's sunken eyes batted rapidly when she saw her friend Jessica approach, and she outreached her trembling hands as if she was asking her to save her. Jessica quickly took her hands in to hers and tried to smile, but could not manage one.

No words needed to be said and both of them knew her time was near. As if all the weight of the world had come down upon her, Jessica suddenly collapsed to her knees and cried as if there was no tomorrow. Kenny reacted and attempted to assist his fallen woman, but Vonda stopped him because she knew this was two friends' final moment together and they needed to be alone. Vonda closed the curtain for their privacy and she and Kenny walked away to let them have their final moments together.

Jessica cried uncontrollably as she continued to grasp Tiny's hand at her bedside.

Through glassy eyes, Tiny managed a tremulous smile and removed the oxygen mask on her face and whispered, "Jessica . . ."

Jessica looked up and wiped the tears and hair out of her eyes and regained her bearings. She rose from the floor, feeling ashamed for breaking down in front of Tiny when she needed her to be strong. "Yes, Tiny?"

Tiny seemed to fight for every breath as her frail chest and lungs siphoned enough air to continue speaking in short bursts. "I'm . . . I'm sorry . . . I . . . I let you down. I messed you over my . . . my whole life."

Jessica was crushed to think she was more concerned about her situation then her own and quickly refuted her, "Oh, Tiny, you didn't let me down."

Tiny shook her head, "No, Jessica, I did a lot of evil things to you because I was jealous of you. And . . . and if it wasn't . . . for me . . . we would never had went to jail . . . in the first place."

Jessica rubbed Tiny's face affectionately and smiled. "Don't worry about that, Tiny; I never blamed you for anything. You came through more times for us than anybody, and I love you for that. We are going to take care of you until you get better and . . ."

Tiny closed her eyes and shook head. "No, Jessica . . . no . . . I'm gonna die, so . . . don't do that to yourself."

Jessica was taken aback by her bluntness and hadn't a word to say. She put her hand to her mouth and began to break down again.

Fighting past the pain, Tiny gritted her teeth and said, "Jessica! Look at me!"

Jessica focused her eyes on Tiny again, but her tears refused to let up.

Tiny put the oxygen mask to her mouth to get some fresh air into her lungs and continued, "You . . . got to be strong or you ain't gonna make it."

At that point, Jessica's world was a haze, and she could no longer keep it together. "I'm scared, Tiny, I'm just so fucking scared. Too much is happening too fast, and I just can't take it anymore. First Lynn, and now you . . . shit!"

Tiny only stared at her because she'd never seen Jessica fall to pieces like that. "It's ok to be afraid, Jessica, and every . . . everything . . . is gonna work out."

Jessica caught herself and apologized, "I'm sorry, Tiny. I'm supposed to be here for you, and here you are comforting me." Jessica wiped the tears from her puffy eyes and chuckled as she rubbed her growing stomach. Jessica gazed up toward the ceiling and admitted more to herself, "I got a strange feeling I'm not going to come out of this alive. I just wish I could've given my baby a chance."

For the first time Tiny noticed that Jessica's stomach was round and hard and realized all at once that she was pregnant.

Jessica chuckled and said, "It don't matter none because I missed my appointment with my P.O. and he probably already issued the warrant for my arrest by now."

Tiny suddenly began to wheeze violently, unable to get air into her lungs. Jessica snapped out of her trance and immediately asked her what was wrong. Tiny began to gasp louder as her eyes began to roll to the back of her head. Jessica didn't know what to do and screamed for help. Within seconds a squadron of doctors and nursing staff swarmed around Tiny's bed to resuscitate her convulsing body.

After they stabilized Tiny, they moved her upstairs to the I.C.U. Since she was inside the intensive care unit, commonly called 'death watch' by the staff, she was allowed to have visitors 24 hours a day until she would expire. Tiny was now unconscious and hooked up to a ventilating machine to breathe for her. Jessica couldn't help but feel responsible because Tiny took off her oxygen mask to talk to her.

They spent the next ten hours standing vigil. Jessica, Kenny, and Vonda was all saddened to see their friend so helpless and vulnerable and didn't want her to die alone, but they knew that time was running out and they had to leave because their lives depended on it. Vonda signaled to Jessica by tapping on her watch. She acknowledged her with a nod. Jessica asked Kenny could she speak to him and they proceeded out the room.

"Kenny, me and Vonda have to take care of something real important, and we need your help."

"Anything, baby, you know that."

"We don't want to leave Tiny here by herself and want to know if you could stay with her for a couple of hours in case she . . . you know . . ."

Kenny saved her the angst and quickly told her he would. She thanked him with a hug and a kiss.

He held on to her longer than usual and said, "Whatever it is you doing, I want you to be careful."

Jessica knew Kenny wasn't a fool and decided not to lie to him and simply nodded. They pulled away and Jessica went back in the room to get Vonda. They both stared down at Tiny with sadness and each gave her a kiss on her forehead and cheek and walked away.

Just as they were about to leave, Jessica remembered, "Oh, Kenny, I forgot to call my mother, do you think you can find a payphone and tell her about Tiny?"

Kenny smiled, reached inside his pocket, and pulled out his mobile phone. "Why would I need a find a payphone when I got my own right here?"

Jessica had forgotten all about the portable phone he showed her earlier and thanked him again and walked toward the elevator.

Kenny watched them leave and then dialed the number to her mother's house and explained to her Ms. Jones Tiny's grave condition. When Kenny finished speaking to Ms. Jones he went back into the room and walked over to Tiny. He stared at her and shook his head, still not believing how much damage she'd done to herself. He continued to stare at her until he dozed off for a while.

His mobile phone suddenly rang and he pulled it out his pocket and answered it.

"Hello?" He listened intently into the phone and then frowned once he heard the voice. "Oh, hey, Uncle . . ." Kenny had totally forgotten that his uncle was coming into town that day and that he was supposed to be picking him up from the airport. Kenny took a seat in a chair that was by Tiny's bed and he spoke to his uncle. Kenny talked business to his uncle for several minutes and hung up. He stood up to stretch and then looked at his watch and then at Tiny, who was in the same condition that she'd been in an hour ago. Kenny made one more phone call and decided that he had to leave and exited the room.

Seconds later, Tiny miraculously opened up her eyes and immediately ripped the oxygen tube from her throat and gagged loudly. The pain was excruciating as she held her throat and rubbed it. She then looked at her arms that had been riddled with I.V.'s and took a deep breath and removed each one from her arms.

She slowly got out of bed and limped over to the closet to search for her clothes. Since the machines that she was on were monitored with activating alarms, a nurse rushed in her room to check on her. When nurse saw Tiny out of the bed she was highly surprised because most patients in her unit never walked out of there alive. She quickly tried to assist her in case she was delusional and warned, "Ma'am, you can't be out of bed. You are extremely ill and have to get back into bed."

Tiny didn't even turn around to acknowledge her as she found her clothes and began to dress slowly. The nurse approached her and gave her a sterner warning.

"Ma'am, if you don't get back in bed I will be forced to put you back in myself."

Tiny turned toward the nurse and with her deep, dead eyes said, "Get the fuck out of my face, bitch!"

The nurse knew to heed the small, but frightening girl's warning and ran out to get help, but it would be too late. Tiny was already out the door and stepping into the elevator. When Tiny got outside, the first thing she did was bum a cigarette from a man passing by and then fished inside her pocket and found a lighter and lit it. She looked around and spotted a payphone and walked over to it and placed a call.

"Hello, yeah, is this the Division of Parole Office? Listen. I got information about a fugitive who has a warrant out for their arrest and I'm looking at her right now. Yeah, her name is Jessica Jones, a convicted murderer and she's inside building 141 West 142nd Street. All you have to do is wait for her to come out."

Tiny hung up the phone and took another toke from the cigarette and tossed it aside. She coughed harshly then smiled and made her way downtown to her next stop.

❄ ❄ ❄

Jessica and Vonda arrived at the scheduled meeting just as everyone else began to arrive. Johnson and Doc had just pulled up in a battered old Ford. Shooter pulled up shortly after in a blue van and parked right behind them. Chubby, ever so paranoid, parked his car two blocks away and had just walked up wearing all black everything. They greeted each other and stepped inside the building and knocked on Cleveland's door and he let them in.

Cleveland greeted everyone and looked at his watch and said, "Ok, glad that everyone is here on time. We ain't got too much time left, so we got go over everything to pull this off."

It suddenly occurred to Cleveland that somebody was missing. "Where's your other friend?"

Jessica and Vonda put their heads down and began to explain. "I'm sorry to tell all of you, but Tiny's not going to be working with us because she's in the hospital," Vonda said sadly.

"Well, is she going to be ok?" asked Cleveland.

Vonda shook her head. "No. The doctors say she doesn't have much time left."

All the men were genuinely saddened by the news. No words were exchanged until Chubby broke the silence.

"Let's do this for Lynn and Tiny."

They all nodded and Cleveland instantly took lead. "Now Chubby, where do we stand with man on the inside?"

Chubby, who seemed to always have a permanent grim mask on his face, gave a rare smile. "We got everything arranged on the inside. I gave him some guns and weapons he stashed for when we get on the inside. We got detailed maps of every important room we need to concern ourselves about." Chubby pulled out the map and unfolded it for all to see. "Right here is the entrance to the building, and they have three armed dudes positioned right here, here, and here. They have another one posted by the staircase on the second floor one flight up, whose job is to warn the people on the third floor of something like a bust and then release a bunch of attack dogs to buy them time to make it to the safe apartments upstairs. They have over eighty-six apartments in the entire building, so they would never get caught because the police can't obtain warrants for every apartment."

"What about the explosives?" asked Cleveland.

Chubby looked over at Johnson, who explained, "Chubby's man gave me some good details of the locations and kind of explosives that we dealing with. The ones they have rigged on the first and second floor apartment windows, back and side doors in the lobby are lightweight stuff. I already met him and gave him instructions on how to neutralize the explosives in the lobby and back door so we can slip in easy. We have nothing to worry about, as far as the windows go so as long as we don't go messing with them. But, I have yet to figure out one problem." Johnson rubbed his beard. "From what he told me, the explosives that are supposed to be on the roof are some heavy stuff. When he described to me how it looked, it was pretty consistent with C-4."

"So, why should we be worried about the roof if we don't have to go there?" asked Cleveland.

Chubby spoke next. "Because that will be our safest exit out."

Cleveland seemed confused. "How is a roof exit filled with high explosive the safest way out the building?"

Chubby and Johnson looked at each other and Johnson explained, "Thanks to Chubby's inside man and what we didn't know, was that they have men scattered all over that block whose sole purpose is to shoot and kill anyone who comes out of the building in case they are robbed. They have men with AK-47's and two-way radios set up in assorted apartments across the street from the building's entrance to cut down anyone as they come out. We would've been slaughtered."

Cleveland was at loss for words and didn't have any answers.

"Like I said," Johnson continued, "the safest way out would be through the roof. If I had enough time I could deactivate the detonator on it. It's not too hard to do; you just need to know what it looks like, but it could be rigged anywhere, on the steps, the door, or even a line wire. I just don't know how many they may have scattered around up there, so I may need some time because it's a slow process."

"How much time you talking about?" asked Cleveland.

Johnson shrugged and said, "I don't know, at least twenty to twenty-five minutes."

Doc finally reminded them, "That's impossible because we have to be in and out of that building in less than ten minutes, fifteen at the most, before half the police precinct shows up."

"He's right," added Shooter. "If we got any chance of making it out that building safely we got to be out of there quickly. Shit, we still didn't figure out a way how we all can get in the building in the first place."

There was a momentary period of silence, and everyone knew he was right.

Vonda finally suggested, "I know a way to get you in the building."

They turned their attention toward Vonda.

"Tiny said before that the only people they let in the buildings are tenants and smokers. Well, since Tiny's not here that means we got to have someone inside before we do anything, right? If I get there early and dress like a crackhead and cop some drugs, can't you get your friend to sneak me upstairs, Chubby?"

Chubby nodded and said, "Naw, it shouldn't be a problem because they have rooms upstairs where they take them crackhead girls and freak off on them while they smoke."

"Exactly," answered Vonda. "So, if he can get me upstairs I can make it to the roof and dismantle the bombs myself and let you all in from the roof."

Everyone was speechless as they waited for Vonda to tell them she was kidding, but the look on her face showed them she wasn't.

Chubby frowned. "Vonda, are you crazy? I'm not letting you risk your life trying to play a superhero."

Vonda snapped, "What other choice do we have, Chubby? My fucking life is on the line, and I got to try something. These motherfuckers is playing for keeps, Chubby. They killed one of my best friends and cut her fucking head off just to prove a point!"

She turned toward Johnson and challenged him, "Johnson, you said yourself that it was a simple process and you only needed to know what the detonator looked like to defuse it, right?"

Johnson shrugged his shoulders. "Yeah, basically, the hard part is to locate them, and after that you won't have any problem."

Vonda quickly offered, "Can't you give me a quick lesson and then test me and if I pass would you consider it?"

Johnson nodded again.

She looked at her concerned brother also and said, "Chubby, I promise you, if I didn't think I could pull it off I wouldn't do it, but right now time is running out and we got to make a decision."

Chubby knew his sister had the heart of a lion and she was in it for all the way, so he looked at Johnson and said, "I'm putting my sister's life in your hands, bro. Make sure you teach her all you can, ok?"

Johnson nodded. "Young lady, come with me."

Vonda stood up immediately as Johnson announced, "I'm taking you back to my shop in the Bronx and teaching you everything you need to know."

He nodded to Chubby and they both were out the door.

For the next five hours Cleveland, Doc, Shooter, Chubby, and Jessica devised plan after plan until they all agreed to the one they felt offered the least collateral damage. Their plan would be simple: take out anyone that was a threat, get in, and get out. Just as they were about finished, Vonda and Johnson had arrived back. They all awaited Johnson's answer.

He took out the cigar in his mouth and said, "She's ready."

Everyone patted her on the back except Chubby, who still

had reservations about his sister being in harm's way.

They presented the final plan to both Vonda and Johnson and explained to them their roles, the time and location they should be there. Jessica's role would be fairly minor; she would pose as a crackhead with Vonda to gain entry into the building and wait in one of the crack dens and simply serve as Vonda's eyes while she disassembled the explosives.

Cleveland, Doc, Johnson, and Chubby would be on the roof waiting for Vonda to complete her task and open the roof door when so they could enter and raid the designated apartments where the money and drugs were located. Shooter, as always, would serve as their eyes and ears on an adjoining roof with his snipers rifle.

When they were sure they were ready, Cleveland suggested they all hold hands for a moment of prayer. They got in a circle, held hands, and bowed their heads as Cleveland said a heartfelt prayer. When he finished they all packed up their things and got ready to head out the door when Cleveland suggested that they keep all the weapons stored in the house until they were ready for the mission that night.

"It makes no sense risking getting stopped, so better we be safe."

Shooter and Chubby were apprehensive, but complied anyway. When they exited the building, out of nowhere, a half-dozen plainclothes policemen jumped out of nearby parked cars and adjoining buildings pointing weapons at the group.

Seconds later, they heard, "We got her!"

The cops had Jessica on the ground as they cuffed and arrested her.

Chapter 25

Vonda walked aimlessly around Harlem trying to settle her nerves before the giant task in front of her. No more than three hours ago, she transformed into a modern day vampire—a crackhead. She put on the most raggedy looking clothing she could find; a well-worn pair of jeans, a sweatshirt, and a funky pair of sneakers. To top things off, she wore the street girls' headgear if choice—a blue bandana—over her head. After she was dressed, Chubby took his sister over to Sweets apartment ensure he knew exactly what she looked like and the rest of the plan. Chubby told him that it was important to get her upstairs into one of the crack rooms, and then come back and sneak up to the roof so she could do her job. The very last thing Chubby told him was to look out for her with his life. Afterwards, Chubby tried his best to explain to her the ropes, the mentality of a crackhead so she could be passable. She still had two hours to waste and asked Chubby to let her out on 116th Street and 8th so she could clear her mind.

Vonda tried her best to put everything out her mind as she thought about Jessica, Tiny, and Lynn. She shuddered at how things were falling apart so quickly. As she walked down Lenox Avenue, she kept a close eye on every female crack addict she came across, which was quite a few. She watched how they walked, their body mannerisms, and if she was close enough, she listened to their form of conversation. Within the hour or so that she'd roamed street, many men and cars vied for her attention, either with a charming proposition of having a good time or blatant disrespect for her to suck their dicks for a hit. One thing she knew for sure and that was she altered herself into a believable addict and she felt the bitter coldness of their world.

Vonda finally arrived on the corner of 129th Street and Lenox Avenue at exactly 1 AM that morning. She looked around the block and it was swirling with activity, especially in front of and around the notorious Castle of Greyskull. A large group of addicts waited in line for the entry inside the building to purchase their drugs. The outside lookouts, teenage boys, would curse and bark orders at any addict who didn't follow their instructions.

"Now, get the fuck in line and stay there. Have your money out and we ain't taking no shorts, no change or singles! So if you have that get the fuck off the line!"

Most of these addicts were old enough to be the boys' parents, or grandparents. They were slave to an addiction, and at that moment those boys were their masters and they would take any form of humiliation, so long as they got their fix. Vonda checked her watch and realized it was time and joined the amassed line ready for her performance. When she got in line she wrapped her arms around herself and began to rock side to side as if she had to pee real badly. That seemed to be what everyone else was doing, so she followed suit.

They allowed only five addicts in the building to be served at a time, so Vonda had been waiting over fifteen minutes at that point. Her stomach began to churn out of control as she got closer to the building's entrance. Suddenly, the one of the young boys walked up to her and looked her up and down then asked, "Are you Sweets' people?"

Vonda nodded and wiped her nose with her forearm, still trying to remain in character. He gestured with his head to follow him, and she did. He walked her to the front of the line and tapped on the door. When it opened, a huge, dark man holding an automatic pistol appeared. His distrustful, cold eyes zoomed directly at the outside worker who said, "Yo, this is Sweets' people, let her in."

The huge man never gave Vonda a second glance as he ushered her in and barked over his shoulders, "Somebody get Sweets and tell him his people is here."

Once inside, the first thing Vonda did was survey the entire lobby and count the number of armed workers and where they were positioned. She counted five, including the man at the door. She stood off in a distance as she awaited Sweets and watched the full operation take place.

One man sat a table with a triple beam scale atop of it. The customers would tell him how much they wanted in grams—one gram was going for thirty dollars, half a gram was fifteen—which they weighed and wrapped in aluminum foil. The reason that customers patronized The Castle of Greyskull by the hundreds was because it was the cheapest and the crack was the most potent. It was a quick and simple operation, Vonda thought as she watched addicts buy their drugs and rush out in less than a minute.

Sweets finally came down from upstairs and greeted her and took her to the head of the line. You could hear a few grumbles of resentment coming from the addicts behind them, but they dared not go further than that and risk not being served. As she stood in front of the table, an older Dominican, in his forties, stared at the girl who stood before him with one of his workers. Vonda tried her best to avoid eye contact with him and simply gazed at a spot on the ground.

Suspicious, the Dominican man asked Sweets, "Who is this?"

Sweets stuttered and answered, "Oh, this is my friend, she going to buy something and then I'm gonna take her up and we gonna do our thing, you know what I mean, Tony?"

Sweets tried to keep his composure too, but was failing badly. Tony stared at her closely and questioned Sweets, "She smoke?"

Sweets chuckled and said, "Hell, yeah, she smokes. We smoke all the time."

There was a long pause until Tony stood up from his chair to get a closer look at her. He looked her up and down slowly then finally asked one of his men who was behind him something in Spanish that neither Vonda nor Sweets understood. Vonda's heart skipped a beat when she realized what he had asked him for—it was a crack pipe! When Sweets realized what he had in store for Chubby's sister, he nearly panicked and stammered, "Tony, man, she don't like smoking in front of all these people, she ain't been smoking but about a month now."

Tony paid no mind to what his underling had to say and clipped off a small piece of crack and pressed it into the stem. He added one more piece to ensure that she would smoke every bit of it and extended it out to her.

Vonda thought back to the chilling words Tiny had said just days earlier, "If you ain't a smoker or a tenant they ain't letting you get into the building. And even if you do get in to cop the drugs, if they don't remember you and become suspicious they make you hit the pipe right in front of them to be sure. And trust me; none of y'all want to hit that glass dick."

Vonda stared at his outstretched arm and saw the plan falling apart. She had to make a decision quickly, so she took the glass pipe from him and put on a false smile. Sweets attempted to make a final plea but was quickly cut off by Tony.

"Shut the fuck up and go back to you post!"

Sweets reluctantly followed his orders and walked away slowly.

Tony turned his attention back to Vonda and extended her a lighter. Tension began to mount as all eyes were glued to her.

Tony reminded her, "Now, take a deep, long pull, my dear."

She never saw anyone smoke crack before, so she decided to follow his instructions to the letter in order to convince him. She put the stem in her mouth and flicked the lighter and inhaled deeply. It took but seconds for Vonda to feel the powerful effect of the potent drug as it raced through her bloodstream and register in her brain.

Tony smiled when he saw Vonda eyes light up like a Christmas tree and said, "Yes, my dear, I got more where that comes from."

Tony spoke to one of his workers to take over serving the customers and gave him a devilish smile and said, "This one here is still fresh, and I want some of this black pussy."

Vonda could no longer hear or feel a thing as she stood stuck in place, unable to move as the drug took over her being. Sweets stood by petrified, unsure what to do next as he watched Vonda be led away by his boss and up the stairs to one of the rooms. He cursed himself for not being man enough to stop it, but he knew he had to do something to protect Chubby's sister if he wanted to live to see another day.

❋◉❋◉❋

The four men crouched patiently on the dark roof, eagerly awaiting the door to be opened so they could take action. As time ticked away, doubt was becoming a factor with each fleeting second as they kept in close communication with Shooter, who was on another roof eyeballing the front of the building.

Vonda took unsettling steps up the stairs with Tony's assistance as he held her closely in his arms. It went right back to business as usual as the addicts were relieved and waited long enough to get served. Suddenly, from the bottom staircase, Tiny, who was watching the entire episode go down, emerged.

Sweets could no longer stand still. He realized it was now or never and had to make a life changing decision, so he ran up stairs to retrieve the guns that Chubby had given him. Sweets entered the empty apartment where he'd stashed the bag of guns and checked them to see if they were loaded—they were. Sweating profusely, he quickly put two guns in his pockets and one behind his waist and was about to stand up and run out the door when he turned and saw Tiny standing behind him. He nearly lost his bowels as he collapsed backwards and fell into a wall.

Tiny put her finger to her lips. "Be quiet, it's me."

He adjusted his eyes and when he saw who it was he was relieved. Tiny looked over her shoulder at the entrance door.

"We got to stop that motherfucker from raping my girl!"

Sweets nodded and whispered back, "I know, that's why I came up here to get some guns to try to stop him." He showed Tiny the guns.

Tiny quickly snatched one of them. "We can't shoot him because if we do, they going to hear it and we are fucked!"

He agreed and asked, "So what we gonna do?"

Tiny looked around the room for a moment and said, "Got it."

Inside the room, Vonda was still in a zombie-like state as trails of saliva leaked from the side of her mouth. Tony smiled wickedly as his penis hardened at the thought of being in total sexual control. He felt Vonda's breast and then lifted her sweatshirt over her head. She offered him no resistance because the drug he gave her was too powerful for a first-time user. He marveled at the size and perkiness of her breasts, and he stood up to unbuckle his pant. Just as he was coming out of his shoes Tony heard a knock on the door and immediately yelled, "Go away, I'm busy!"

"But, it's me Tony, Sweets."

Tony frowned and yelled again, "I told you that I'm busy." Tony thought that was the end of it, but Sweets persisted.

"I know, Tony, but it's a matter of life and death what I got to tell you, man."

Tony reluctantly zipped up his pants and walked toward the door in a huff and opened it. "Now what the fuck is so important? And it better be quick."

Sweets quickly looked inside the room and saw that Vonda still had her pants on and thanked God silently. He turned his attention back to his boss. "Yeah, I got somebody you need to talk to before you touch her."

Tony was suddenly confused and asked, "What are you talking about?"

Sweets edged closer and spoke in a whisper, "This girl came up to me after she saw you take her upstairs and told me that she knew her."

"Knows her how?" Tony asked.

"She said that girl gave her the virus ."

Tony turned around and looked at Vonda. Not wanting to believe it he asked Sweets, "What girl told you this?"

Sweets stepped back and waved to Tiny, who approached the door. Tiny looked inside the room and angrily said, "Yeah, that's that bitch!" and charged inside the room wielding a bat that she had hidden behind her.

Tony grabbed her before the small, wiry girl could get close to his guest. Sweets looked down the hall to ensure they didn't attract anyone's attention and stepped in the room and locked the door behind him.

Tiny struggled to be released and cursed, "Let me go, Tony, I'm gonna beat this bitch ass!"

Tony overpowered her and snatched the bat out of Tiny's hand and tossed it on the floor. "Now, calm down and tell me what happened," Tony said as he released her.

"This bitch is the one who gave me H.I.V. when she let me eat her pussy last year. And I been looking for this bitch ever since," Tiny said convincingly.

He looked over at Sweets and asked, "Sweets, did you know this bitch was burning?"

Sweets expressed a surprised look and answered, "Hell, no, Tony, I'm scared to death now because I fucked her before."

Tony waved him off and walked over to where Vonda still sat frozen on the bed. Tony looked down on her in disgust and spat on her. Just as he was about to turn around, Tony was hit with a vicious blow to the side of his face with the bat by Sweets. It knocked him out instantly.

Tiny and Sweets quickly began working on Vonda, trying to get her to snap out her drug-induced stupor by slapping her face.

"Yo, Tiny," Sweets said in near hysteria, "we got to get her straight because she's the one who supposed to take care of those explosives on the roof and open the door for them niggas to get in here."

"She supposed to do what?" Tiny asked, in total surprise.

Sweets nodded as he wiped the sweat that was pouring from his forehead on his sleeve.

"Yeah, Chubby told me they taught her how to remove them without getting blown up and I was supposed to watch her back."

Tiny shook her head and knew Vonda wasn't in any condition to walk, much less disengage some explosives. Tiny thought quickly and said to Sweets, "Yo, go in the bathroom and run some cold water and find a bucket and fill it up and bring it back!"

Sweets had no choice but to follow her orders and ran to the bathroom and turned on the cold water in the tub and looked around for something to fill it in. Moments later, Sweets returned with a bucket full of water and Tiny laid Vonda back on the bed and ordered Sweets to empty the entire bucket on her face. Tiny moved out of his way and Sweets walked up to her and followed her instructions and poured it all on her face. In an instant, Vonda sat upright and began to gasp for air.

Fifteen minutes had passed and Tiny had Vonda on her feet walking around the room to clear her head. Sweets had taken the time to tear up the bed sheets to tie Tony's arms and legs together and gag his mouth. When the cobwebs finally cleared, Vonda returned to her normal self.

"Tiny, I thought you were supposed to be in the hospital?"

"Yeah, I'm supposed to, but I had to get out of there and . . ."

Sweets interrupted them said sternly, "Yo, we ain't got time for a discussion. Tony gonna be coming out of it soon, and you still got to take care of that shit on the roof!"

It suddenly occurred to Vonda that too much time had elapsed and she still had a job to do. She panicked. "Oh, shit, we got to go!"

The three of them rushed toward the door and Sweets opened it slightly and peered out. It was clear and he waved the girls out and they headed up the seven flights of stairs as quickly as they could. When Vonda turned around, Tiny was winded and on her knees, gasping for a breath.

"Tiny? Vonda asked. "Are you ok?"

Tiny nodded and waved her hand forward and said, "Don't . . . don't worry about me. Take care of what you got to. I'll be up in a minute."

Vonda was reluctant to leave her, but Sweets' reminded her of the time and she raced to the roof. The roof landing was dimly lit, and Sweets was already prepared and handed her a flashlight from his back pocket. Vonda closed her eyes to remember what Johnson had taught her and proceeded up the landing slowly as she scanned every inch of the area that might be booby trapped.

After five minutes, Vonda spotted five of them and whispered to Sweets, "Listen, I found them, now go back downstairs and get Tiny while I clear them out."

Sweets nodded and quickly ran back down the stairs to get Tiny.

Vonda slowly and methodically began dismantling the explosives one by one by removing the blasting caps. It was just like Johnson had told her, and when she finished she pulled off her bandana and placed them inside it and laid it carefully off to the side. She began to breathe easier and rushed to the roof door to open it, but the latch would not budge—it was rusted shut.

Sweets ran up to Tiny, who was still on the stairs gasping for a breath. Sweets was in a near panic when he saw that she hadn't moved an inch since he left her. "Tiny, what are you doing? Why you still on the ground? We got to get out of here!"

Tiny simply could not answer him and waved for him to come closer. He kneeled down beside her and she handed him an envelope and managed to say, "Give this to Vonda."

He took the envelope and stuffed it into his pocket just before she began to convulse and tremble. Sweets could not believe what he was seeing. She shook violently. Unsure what to do, Sweets was aroused out of his daze when he heard several banging sounds coming from the roof and picked Tiny up and carried her back upstairs with him.

When Vonda saw Sweets carrying Tiny's body in his arms she screamed, "Is she ok?"

Sweet s shook his head and laid her on the ground and into Vonda's arms. Vonda tried to get to answer her, but there was no response.

Sweets looked downstairs and wiped the pouring sweat from

his brow. "Why didn't you open the door yet?"

Through tears, Vonda answered, "It's rusted, and it won't open."

Sweets was livid as he examined the door and attempted to open it. But it would not budge for him either. He had come too far, he thought, to let a mere door come between him and his safety, so he backed up and with all the strength he could conjure, ran toward the door. With one thunderous kick, he broke the door open. As soon at the door was opened, the door was ripped opened wider and the four awaiting men rushed inside. Sweets nearly collapsed in tears from the sight of them and knew he would live to see his unborn child.

Chubby rushed over to his sister and asked, "Vonda, are you ok?"

Still in tears as she cradled Tiny in her arms, Vonda answered, "No, I think she is dying!"

Chubby quickly yelled for Sweets to come over. "Carry Tiny and take my sister across to the other roof, the door is open and get in a cab and take them to the hospital and don't leave them till I get there. You hear me?"

Sweets was more than ready to comply with his orders and exited the roof landing as he carried Tiny in his arms with Vonda right behind him. Sweets suddenly turned back around and said, "Yo, Chubby, it's a dude who tried to rape your sister. I got him tied up in apartment 23. She'll tell you about it later, but I don't need nobody walking around who is going to recognize me."

Chubby nodded and waved him on. After Chubby knew his sister was out of harm's way, the four heavily armed men nodded to each other and stealthily headed down the stairs to complete the final phase of their bloody mission. As they crept down the steps, Cleveland pointed to the door that was supposedly the money room. He put his back toward the wall and nodded to the three men to proceed with their mission. Doc took lead and became the point man, and crouched down lower as her proceeded down the steps that led to the lobby. From his vantage point, Doc saw a total of four armed men in plain sight, with high caliber handguns. He signaled to his men above with his fingers, directing their location as well.

Doc accessed the best time to strike was when the last addict was served. He would signal them to blind side them at their weakest moment. Cleveland's job was to blast the door lock with his shotgun as soon as he heard the first shot fired, and the three remaining men were to kill anything that moved or offered any resistance.

Doc watched the last addict leave and counted down with his fingers. *3, 2, 1.* . . The fury of hell was released as the three men blasted everything in sight. The hapless victims never saw it coming. Their bodies twisted and turned from a volley of automatic weapons that pierced through them. It was over in an instant, and the three men surveyed the wreckage, ensuring no one was a threat any longer. As quickly as they appeared, the three men ascended back up the stairs and accessed the money room where Cleveland was.

To their surprise, when they entered the room Cleveland was standing before them with a wicked and almost sadistic smile on his face. What the men saw next made their jaws drop to the floor. Four green duffle bags, filled to the hilt with money. All the men smiled and shouted in jubilation except Chubby, who only frowned and seemed uninterested.

He had other things on his mind and told the men, "I'll meet you on the roof," and proceeded down the hall in search of a room.

The men soon realized that it wasn't the proper moment to celebrate and each grabbed a duffle bag and left the room and made their exit, but they refused to leave a man behind and followed Chubby to watch his back as he settled a score. Chubby eyed each apartment door with fury until he finally came across the door with the number 23 on it. He slowly opened the door and entered it as if he hadn't a care in the world. He saw his victim was still on the floor, tied up, yet conscious.

Chubby circled the man as his 45 automatic dangled loosely from his hand. Chubby stopped suddenly and squatted beside him then removed the gag from out of his mouth. "So, you like to take the pussy, huh, mother fucker?"

Tony screamed as loud as he could for help, but his cries would go unanswered. Tony quickly began to make a plea for his life. "Go to apartment 15, that's where all the money at. And, right next door, in apartment 17, that's where we stash the drugs. You can have it all. I got the keys in my pocket."

Chubby showed no interest. "Oh, this ain't about no money, amigo, this is about revenge!"

Chubby pressed the cannon to Tony's forehead and pulled the trigger. His head exploded on impact. Chubby stood up and stared at for a moment longer and smiled. Over his shoulder, Chubby heard Cleveland's voice.

"Ok, Chubby, we got to go."

Chubby acknowledged him with a nod and said, "Yeah, ok, but, we forgot something."

Chubby reached inside the dead man's pockets and retrieved

the keys and proceeded to apartment 17, but this time the door had a pad lock on it. Chubby put the key in the lock and opened the door. He stared inside the room for a moment then turned toward his three cohorts in amazement. The three men sensed something wrong and slowly edged forward to look in the room.

To their surprise, they saw four young black and Spanish girls tied up and gagged. The girls squirmed and cried in fear at the sight of the heavily armed men, not knowing if they were friends or foes. Cleveland slowly approached them with his hands up in the air to prove he meant them no harm. He slowly untied them one by one and jumped into his arms for being their savior. While the men untied the women, he began to search the apartment for other survivors and saw none until he came across a room and opened it. Mounds and mounds of kilos of what appeared to be cocaine sat in open view on a table. He whistled and Chubby and Johnson quickly responded and stood in awe of the quantity and amount of expensive, yet deadly drug.

It proved impossible to take any of the drugs, but Chubby could not resist several kilos because it was in his nature. The men led the women to the roof and across to the next building and to their freedom. They piled the women inside their cars and duffel bags in their trunks and drove away far enough until they were satisfied that all would be clear and let the women out to their safety.

No words needed to be exchange as the women hugged each and every one of their saviors before walking away. Cleveland looked at them with sorrow, never truly knowing what they really endured and impulsively called for them to come back. Cleveland went to his trunk and pulled out one of the duffel bags and handed each girl stacks of money.

The girls could not believe their eyes and humbly thanked him again before going their separate ways and into the night. All the men knew it was the right thing to do. Feeling content, they walked to their cars without a word being said.

When Chubby arrived at Harlem Hospital's emergency room, he could already tell by looking at his sister, who was crying uncontrollably as several nurses and Sweets tried to console her. When Vonda spotted her brother, she collapsed in his arms and buried her face in his chest.

"Chubby, Tiny is dead."

Chubby gripped his sister tighter.

After they received all the information from the hospital about obtaining Tiny's body, they were ready to leave to put the trying day behind them. Chubby turned to Sweets, who had just came back from checking on his girlfriend who was already a patient in detoxification unit.

"Yo, thank you for looking after my sister. You saved her life, man. You really came through."

Sweets blushed and said, "Man, anything for you, Chubby, you know that."

Chubby nodded and said, "I'm gonna come see you with your split of the money in a couple of days." Chubby reached inside his pants pocket and peeled off five hundred dollars. "In the meantime, take this. It should hold you down till then."

Sweets looked at the money and shook his head. "No, Chubby, I'm not going to be needing that right now." Sweets saw that Chubby was confused and continued, "I just signed myself in to the Harlem Hospital drug program, and I'm going in right now. Like you said, I should give my unborn child a chance in this world."

A huge smile came over Chubby's face as he nodded and put his hand on Sweets' shoulder.

"Just do me a favor, Chubby."

Chubby nodded.

"After we leave here me and my girl going away to a six-month treatment program and we ain't gonna have a place to stay after that with the baby. You think you can find us an apartment by then?"

Chubby shrugged and said, "You ain't got nothing to worry about. I got you covered and don't worry about your share of the money either because I'm gonna hold it for you till you get out."

Sweets smiled and thanked him one last time and headed upstairs and into a new life.

Chapter 26

The papers dubbed it the worst drug-related massacre in Harlem's history, but the people in the neighborhood called it a blessing in disguise. Because of infamy the building received in the news and press, the New York City mayor made a crackdown on drug spots and dealers who lorded over tenant buildings. The mayor received a slap in the face when news teams began interviewing tenants of the building who questioned his leadership ability. How could he allow an open drug market right under his nose without one single arrest or raid after tenants had been complaining for years about it?

To ensure that the building never returned to its former state again, the mayor ordered police presence in front of the building and a team of inspectors from various agencies to write up and fine the building's owner of any defects in the building and have them fixed. Since it was drug-related homicides, the detectives did not consider it a high priority case, and after two months the case would never see the light of day again.

It took nearly two days to count up all the money, and when they finally did, it was a grand total of nine hundred fifty seven thousand dollars. Each player involved, Chubby, Vonda, Jessica, Doc, Shooter, Johnson, Cleveland, Sweets, and Tiny, would receive one hundred thousand dollars.

The remaining fifty seven thousand was endowed toward Lynn's funeral and the remaining share to her family. They knew from the beginning that there was nothing they could do to bring Lynn's killer to justice without complicating matters, so they mailed her head with Lynn's full name and address to city coroner's office, who'd already found an unknown black female headless body floating in the East River. That was the only way they could possibly give Lynn a proper burial.

Since most of Tiny's family was still on drugs, Vonda would hold onto Tiny's share of the money until someone in her family became responsible enough for them to take it. Vonda offered to pay for their stay at a rehab, but no one was ready at that point so she simply put it a bank and waited. They threw Tiny a warm and beautiful funeral that was attended by many of her former schoolmates and neighbors alike. Vonda and Chubby vowed to sponsor a yearly memorial in their old block in memory of Tiny and Lynn and have free food, drinks, a D.J. playing music, and games for the kids in which they'd win prizes.

Chubby even had a change of heart when Vonda told him what it was like when she walked the streets of Harlem posing as a crackhead and how horrible it must be on the women who were caught in the cycle of addiction to get abused on a daily basis. And when she told him how she felt when she had to smoke the pipe, it nearly brought him to tears.

That same night, Chubby sat by the river on west side of Harlem till the sun came up. After sitting and thinking for six hours about his sister, his brothers who were all strung out on the poison, and finally Tiny. Chubby came to a decision and went to the trunk of his car and removed the four kilos of cocaine that he took from the night of the robbery. One by one, he tossed each package of drugs into the river. Chubby never looked back as he drove off in the sunset a new man with new principles.

The following day, Chubby went to the pediatric wing of Harlem Hospital to visit a little girl who had recently made the papers from getting shot in her tiny arm during a drug war in 142nd Street. He stood at the entrance to the hospital room with a teddy bear and brown shopping bag in his arms. The little girl's mother smiled when she saw him and welcomed him inside.

He eyed the floor as he approached them and said in an almost whisper as her rocked back and forth. "How are you ma'am? But I read about your daughter in the paper and I just wanted to bring her something that might make her feel better."

The woman smiled brightly and thanked him. She led him over to her daughter's bed and her arm was in a long cast that reached her little shoulders. "Monet, this kind gentleman came by to give you a little gift."

Chubby finally got the nerve to look her in her eyes and handed her the large fluffy teddy bear. She reached for it with her good arm and quickly smiled and hugged her gift tightly. Her mother watched her daughter with glee. It was the first time she'd seen her daughter smile in the time since her tragic incident.

The woman thanked him and said, "Now, Monet, tell the kind gentleman thank you."

She turned toward Chubby. "Oh, I didn't catch your name."

Chubby only stared at the floor and simply said, "Just say it's from a Harlem boy that was lost." He then handed the woman the brown shopping bag and said, "Maybe this will help y'all out with everything y'all been through."

As quick as he'd entered, Chubby exited even quicker. The woman found the visit rather odd. She opened up the bag and looked inside and became weak in her knees and sat down to prevent herself from falling. She looked toward the doorway before she looked inside the bag again, only this time she reached in and pulled out stacks and stacks of hundred-dollar bills.

Vonda was so moved by her brief, yet powerful experience as crack addict that she decided to go back to school and pursue a career in drug prevention and social work. She thought about the Get It Girls every day and it only added strength and motivation to her when times got too rough. She became a model student and hoped someday to receive her Masters Degree in Sociology.

6 MONTHS LATER

Jessica had to complete six months in prison for violating her parole. The timing, she thought, couldn't have been worse. She felt she'd let everyone down and was powerless to do anything about it. What pained her the most was knowing she would have her baby born under the supervision of the prison system. She was relieved to know that Kenny and her mother understood enough to stand by her during one of the darkest moments of her life.

When Vonda came to visit her, she was also relieved that they'd pulled off their mission and that they were now free from fearing about their future. But when she told her about Tiny, she was surprised and sad. They hadn't a clue why Tiny would show up in her condition, but Vonda told Jessica that if wasn't for her she would not had come out of it alive. Jessica felt bad about not being able to attend her two best friends' funerals, but Vonda explained that she was there with the in spirit. Vonda held Jessica down the entire six months she was away with visits and commissary.

Kenny came every visit to see her to see her through it and to see the baby grow. They talked mostly about their wedding, the baby, and their future together as a family. Kenny told her that his real estate worries were over and that he could now began receiving rent again from his tenants. Jessica was pleased everything was finally going well for the both of them.

Jessica spent most of her time brushing up and perfecting her French, which she began speaking nearly fluently compliments of her cellmate, who was also pregnant and a Haitian named Gwendolyn Corde. Jessica made it a point that she and Gwendolyn only spoke French around each other so she would get better. Jessica dreamed of her wedding day when she'd be ask to say her vows, and when she read them, it would be in French to prove to her husband she cared enough to learn his native language.

It was exactly 5:46 in the morning when Jessica felt the first sharp pain, then another. She clutched her stomach and immediately knew the baby was coming and woke up her cellmate.

"Gwen, I think I'm having the baby."

Gwen awoke instantly to press a panic button that was installed in the maternity wing of all expecting mothers' rooms. The C.O.'s and medical staff arrived immediately and took Jessica to the infirmary. After the doctor examined her and was sure she was in fact in labor, a call was placed to the local hospital for her to be picked up and admitted in the hospital to give birth.

Three hours later, Jessica was ready to deliver, and the nurses prepped her for birth. As she endured that labor pain, she hoped that her mother and especially Kenny were there to watch her give birth, but state regulations would not permit it. Moments later, Jessica delivered a healthy baby girl. She was excited as well as relieved when she finally gave birth.

After they cleaned up and checked the baby thoroughly, a nurse carried the newborn to Jessica and cooed. "Why she is such a beautiful child, you should be very proud."

Jessica smiled, and said, "I am, I'm very proud of her."

As the nurse cuddled her in her arms she said with amazement, "Look at her, she's opening up her eyes for the first time." She quickly handed her to Jessica and they both stared into her eyes.

"Wow," said the nurse, "she has amazing eyes, they're beautiful. They almost look silver."

Jessica stared at her daughter and realized she had her father's eyes.

"So, what is her name?" asked the nurse. Jessica never really thought about it, so she looked at her daughter again and answered, "Silver."

Two days later, baby Silver was given to Jessica's mother. Kenny was there also, but since they weren't married yet and he wasn't established as the father, state regulations only permitted the maternal parent to take custody at that time. Needless to say, Jessica was heartbroken and felt like a failure.

Though she only had a month left on her sentence it didn't make her feel any better. Most of the inmates were mothers themselves and rallied behind Jessica and comforted her, making it easier on her to get by. Jessica and her mother opted not to bring the baby to see her because it was winter and extremely cold that time of the year. They didn't want to risk the baby getting a cold.

Kenny showed up for nearly every visit to make her time go by quicker. On visits, Kenny brought Polaroid pictures so she could see their daughter and talk for hours about her. Kenny admitted that he didn't know how precious it was to have a child and wanted only the best for her. He even got choked up when he talked about the safety of his child to having to grow up in Harlem. Jessica understood his concern, because of what happened to her despite being raised as well as she did with both her parents.

"I talked to my mother," said Kenny, "and she feels the same way as I do, and she's willing to let her stay there with her and my family till I can buy a house out there in New Jersey near them."

Jessica was taken aback for a moment and asked, "Kenny, I never even met your mother, and what's wrong with us staying at my mother's house until we can find somewhere to live?"

"Because, she'd be better off in New Jersey with my family to be raised. I'm not saying your mother is a bad person, but—"

"But, what, Kenny?" Jessica challenged.

Kenny stared at her for a moment and came out and told her

how he really felt.

"Jessica, have you forgotten about your brother? Not for nothing, but look what happened to you. Jessica, I love you, but I have a daughter to think about now."

Jessica could not believe he said that and turned away so he wouldn't see the tears forming in her eyes. Kenny knew immediately he had made a mistake.

"I'm sorry. I'm so sorry I said that, and I didn't mean it." Kenny threw his hands up, stood up, and continued. "Jessica, it's just that this is my first time having a child, a girl at that, and I'm scared."

Jessica turned and looked at Kenny who seemed actually afraid and worried. "When I hold Silver in my arms, a feeling that I never felt before overcomes me and I get so overwhelmed with fear and happiness at the same time, I can't explain it. One thing I do know is that I have to protect her at all costs, and if I'm wrong for wanting to do that then I'm guilty, Jessica. I just want what's best for her, that's all."

Jessica did understand, because that was exactly how her own father had felt about her. She couldn't fault him, but she knew he was acting on emotions and would allow him his right to feel that way.

"Kenny, I love you even more to know how you feel about our child, but understand equally that I love her the same way, even more. But, I will not let anyone raise my child if I have anything to do with it. We can talk about moving out of Harlem one day, but until that happens, we're both going to be sure she's ok."

Kenny gazed at her, finally relented, and smiled. "I'm sorry, baby, I don't know what I was thinking." He recouped quickly and said excitedly, "Once you get out and get settled, you promised to take me up to the Poconos, remember?"

Jessica smiled. "You don't forget anything do you?"

"No, I don't. I need my time with my baby because I miss you that much. When you come home and settle in, I'm booking us a cottage up there for a weekend, ok?"

Jessica smiled. "Ok."

Ten days later, Jessica was finally released from prison and she could hardly wait to be processed out of prison for good. She was met by Vonda in a brand new Honda Accord, who greeted her at the front gate with a wide smile. They embraced as if they hadn't seen each other in years and hurriedly hopped inside the car and headed off to her first day of freedom. They talked and caught up on everything as they made their way home to Harlem. Jessica had to pinch herself to remember that she would finally be able to hold her daughter again. Vonda bragged how beautiful her god-daughter was and couldn't wait to see them all together as well.

"You, know Chubby was so excited to know that you named him Silver's god-father that he furnished her entire room. He bought her everything, the crib, bassinette, clothes, diapers, toys, everything. Silver don't need for nothing."

Jessica smiled excitedly and knew Chubby would have been the perfect god-father.

"Guess what?" Vonda said with excitement to Jessica.

"What?" answered Jessica?

"I don't know if you met Sweets before, but he was Chubby's inside man in the building that we took off, but he and his girl named Chubby their son's god-father too. They had their baby like a month before you."

Jessica nodded her approval and enjoyed the rest of ride home.

Over the next two months, Jessica and baby Silver bonded as if they never were apart. Kenny stayed with Jessica and the baby from the day they got out and decided that they could now go away on the much needed trip alone together in the Poconos.

Kenny arranged everything, and they were scheduled to leave that Thursday for a three-day excursion to catch up on the time that they desperately needed together. Before they left, Jessica, ever so cautious, left her mother all the information that she would need in case an emergency should arise. Jessica gave her mother the location, directions, and which cottage they'd be staying in. Kenny and Jessica were all packed and kissed their daughter goodbye and were off to the Poconos.

Vonda was on her way to school when she opened her front door and was surprised to see Sweets, his girlfriend, and their newborn baby standing there. It was Vonda's first time seeing Sweets since the night of the robbery and she was happy to see him. Sweets and his girlfriend had just gotten out of their programs recently and came to see Chubby to thank him for setting them up with a nice apartment as he promised.

Vonda smiled widely and embraced the couple as they introduced her to their newborn son. Vonda peered inside the stroller and said, "Oh, Sweets, he's gorgeous, what's his name?"

Sweets beamed proudly and answered, "His name is Chancellor. We name him Chance for short."

Vonda nodded, and said, "Oh, that's a beautiful name. How'd

you come up with it?"

Sweets looked at his girlfriend and admitted sadly, "When your brother came by to see me before we did that job, he saw that my girl was still smoking crack while she was pregnant."

They both put their heads down as he continued. "Well, your brother was pretty disgusted and basically threatened my life and told me to put her in a rehab so our child would at least have a chance at life. I never forgot those words. So when he was born healthy, we decided to name him Chancellor, short for chance at life. If it wasn't for you brother, he wouldn't have made it. We wouldn't have made it."

Vonda was smitten and invited them in. She called out for Chubby who was in his room.

"Chubby, your god-son is here."

Chubby came out his room smiling widely and shook Sweets' hand and hugged his girlfriend. He went to the stroller and picked up his god-son Chance and began playing with him.

Sweets suddenly remembered, "Oh, yeah, Vonda, I forgot to give this to you." He reached in his coat pocket and handed her a letter. "Your friend, the one who died, gave this to me to give to you the night of, you know, the night all that went down. I forgot I had it until I was released from the program a week ago and they gave me everything I came in with."

Vonda looked at the letter and ran to her room and ripped it open. She read it quickly and dropped the letter as her hands flew to her mouth. She ran out of the room and yelled, "Chubby!"

Kenny and Jessica arrived at the Cottage Inn four hours later.

They got there just as snow began to fall heavier and checked in the main office to get their keys. They didn't worry about getting their things out of the truck; they just hurried inside to see their living space. Just as they'd seen in the brochures it was spectacular. An indoor fireplace, an oversized plush bed, a Jacuzzi, and a stock of alcohol and snacks.

Jessica noticed that there wasn't a phone in the cottage and was disappointed because she wanted to call her mother to tell her they got there safely. She said, "It's nice, Kenny, but you didn't tell me they didn't have a phone in the room."

Kenny picked up Jessica and swept her off her feet and kissed her deeply and while carrying her toward the bed. He laid her down gently while they began removing their clothes never missing a beat. Caught up in the moment, they soon were totally nude and made love to each other for the next four hours and slept the night away in each other's arms.

When Jessica awoke, she was surprised to see that Kenny had brought in all their luggage. She called out for Kenny but he didn't answer. She went to her luggage and found her house gown and put it on and searched the bathroom and kitchen for Kenny, but he was gone.

She looked out the window and saw that the car was also gone and figured he went out to get breakfast. She decided to go take a shower first and unpack her things later. She smiled when she entered the bathroom because it was as big as her living room with every amenity she could think of—bubble bath oils, in every scent, body lotions, bath crystals, and scented candles. She thought back to just a couple of months ago how she'd had to shower with other women on a regular basis in prison and smiled when she realized how far she'd come.

The bathtub was huge. It was pure white marble and large enough to fit five people. It took her nearly twenty minutes to fill it up fully, and she added her favorite oils and crystals in it. When she entered she closed her eyes and savored the moment, enjoying her quiet time alone. She stayed in the soothing tub for nearly an hour when the door opened and Kenny's smiling face peeked in.

"So, you going to take a bath without me?" he joked.

Jessica smiled. "No, I saved the Jacuzzi for us tonight, babe."

Kenny smiled and said, "Good point. Listen, come on out 'cause I got us breakfast. I don't want it to go cold."

Jessica nodded and lifted herself out of the tub. Kenny stared at her glistening, well oiled body and said lustfully, "Well, maybe breakfast can wait."

Jessica blushed and grabbed a nearby towel and said, "Boy, we going to eat breakfast, I'm hungry and sore after the way you wore me out last night."

He laughed and exited the bathroom. When Jessica exited the bathroom, Kenny had all the food and beverages set out on the table and he was on his mobile phone talking to someone in French. Jessica smiled because she now could understand what he was saying. From what she gathered, he was talking about one of his buildings that were costing him a small fortune to repair and how costly the fines were becoming. When he finished, he pressed the phone off and sat down at the table with Jessica.

As a joke, Jessica asked, "What was that about?"

He waved her off and answered, "Oh that was nothing, just some business, that's all."

"Is everything ok?" she asked.

Kenny smiled and said, "Nothing I can't handle."

They ate breakfast and talked the rest of the morning. Kenny told her that he'd even set them up to take some skiing lessons later that afternoon.

"Skiing lessons, Kenny? I can't ski."

"That's the reason we going to take some lessons. It'll be fun."

Still not convinced, Jessica frowned. "I don't know. Kenny. People be breaking their legs and falling off of cliffs skiing."

Kenny chuckled. "You be watching too many movies. I checked out the resort already and the hills are not steep at all. We came up here to have fun and do things we never did before, so trust me, I'm not going to let anything happen to my baby."

Kenny always knew the right words to say, she thought, and when she looked in his eyes she could never resist him. "Ok, but if I fall and bust my butt, don't be laughing at me."

"I'll try not to laugh too hard, I promise."

After they finished breakfast, Kenny took a quick shower as Jessica unpacked their clothing and began to get dressed for their fun filled excursion. While Jessica was unpacking their things, a small bottle fell out of one of Kenny's bags and she picked it up and read it. Jessica shrugged and put the bottle back in his bag and continued unpacking.

When they both were finally dressed, they headed out the door and noticed it was snowing again. They got in the car and drove about two miles north to the ski lodge. When they arrived, it was mandatory for all new skiers to take an hour lesson in skiing before they could get on the slopes. After an hour, Jessica, to her surprise, was quite good her first time out and was enjoying herself. She couldn't wait to actually go skiing at that point. But, to their disappointment, the sudden downpour of snow caused hazardous conditions and they shut down the slopes and everyone was notified that it would be closed until further notice. Jessica couldn't believe their luck, but Kenny assured her that they would return the next day.

They were ready to leave when Kenny spotted a ski shop and told Jessica he wanted to check it out. Kenny looked around the store and saw a salesman and asked, "Excuse me, sir; I'm looking for some good skis for my wife."

"Yes, over here, sir."

Jessica looked at Kenny and asked, "Why would you buy me a pair of skis when we can rent them?"

"Because, I saw their skis and they looked cheap."

"But, Kenny, we only going to use it one time. Why spend all that money on a new pair of skis?"

Kenny shook his head. "I'm not going to have my baby get hurt with some cheap ski's. You're worth it."

Jessica smiled and let him have his way.

They found a nice sturdy pair of ski for Jessica, and Kenny purchased them and headed back to the car. Since it was getting late, they decided to go to a local restaurant and have dinner. They ate and enjoyed each other's company when Jessica began to think about her daughter. "Kenny, call my mother and check and see how Silver is doing."

"Now Jessica, this is supposed to be our weekend. Your mother is taking good care of her, and she is fine." He took her by the hand and said in French, "This is me and the love of my life's time to be alone."

Jessica understood every word and smiled. She wanted so badly break her cover, but she wanted to wait until their wedding day to surprise him. "That sounded so beautiful, what did you say?"

He repeated every word in English and reached over and kissed her. When they finally arrived back at the cottage Kenny said excitedly, "I'm going to light up the fireplace and then heat up the Jacuzzi and we are going to have some drinks and continue what we did last night."

Jessica smiled and said, "That sounds romantic to me, but Kenny, you know I don't drink. I haven't had a drink since the night of the prom, and you know what happened to me after that."

Kenny walked over to her and said, "That was a long time ago. You got to learn to leave your past in the past if you're ever going to move forward. We are together now, having our moment. We're just going to have a drink to relax and enjoy ourselves, that's all."

"Ok, only for you, but I'm just having one drink. I don't want you taking advantage of me," she joked.

Kenny bent down and kissed her and then went to the fireplace and began to light it to set the mood. After he had the fire going and the Jacuzzi heating, they sat at the table and Kenny prepared their drinks.

"Baby, do you want vodka or rum?"

Jessica shrugged and answered, "It doesn't make a difference. I never tasted them before, pick one for me."

He nodded, and unscrewed a fresh bottle of vodka. "What do you want to chase it with? Orange juice or cranberry juice?"

"Orange juice is good."

Kenny finished preparing the drinks and placed one in front of Jessica and another one beside him when suddenly his phone rang. He quickly ran to retrieve it out of his coat pocket and pressed talk. Kenny once again spoke in French apparently to the same person he was talking to earlier that day.

Jessica was just about to try her drink when her heart skipped a beat. She immediately put her drink down and stared at Kenny, who smiled back at her and continued talking for next five minutes. He hung up the phone and quickly returned to the table and lifted his drink for a toast.

"I dedicate this night to the two ladies of my life, my soon to be wife, Jessica, and my beautiful daughter, Silver."

Jessica smiled and lifted her drink and tapped his glass.

Kenny smiled and suggested, "Let's drink it all down. The Jacuzzi is about ready for us to get in."

Jessica nodded and they both drank it down quickly until it was all gone. Kenny smiled at Jessica widely. Jessica fanned her mouth and said, "Wow that was strong. How much liquor did you put in there, Kenny?"

Kenny only smiled and remained silent. In an instant, Jessica suddenly began to get light-headed. "Kenny, I don't feel so good. My throat feels like its burning."

Kenny walked over to Jessica slowly and kneeled down beside her. "Just relax, baby, it won't be long."

Jessica's eyes began to blink rapidly. Kenny, did you put something in my drink?"

Kenny stood up and answered coldly, "Yep, you caught me."

"Why?"

It was if Kenny was irritated by the question and said, "Why?

You really want to know why, Jessica?"

She nodded.

"You think I was going to allow a person like you to raise my daughter? What do you think I am? Stupid?"

"So, you are doing this because you don't want me to raise my daughter, Kenny?"

Kenny shrugged and answered, "Well, partly. Jessica, I been using you and your friends from the very beginning. I happened to have a problem with my building on 129th Street." Kenny paused and smiled, "You might know it as the Castle of Greyskull. Since you told me all about you and your buddies in prison, and how you were so good at handling things, I simply put two and two together and decided to use you to my advantage and clean up my problem buildings in Harlem."

Jessica couldn't believe her ears. "So, why'd you have to kill Lynn? She wouldn't have caused you any harm; she was just trying to get away because she was scared."

Kenny chuckled and said, "Oh, she never tried to run away, I just needed something to get your full attention. So I tracked her down and killed her. You all were expendable to me, damaged goods. Do you really think I would want to marry a fucking convicted murderer?"

"If you didn't want me Kenny, why did have a baby with me?"

Kenny grew irritated and cursed her. "You think I wanted to get you pregnant, Jessica? That shit was a mistake. I was going to kill you after you finished the job for me, but your stupid ass got arrested and had the baby in jail. But I'm glad you did have her, because I really do love her."

"You're not going to get away with this, Kenny. Everyone knows

I'm with you up here."

Kenny smiled again. "Women skier falls to her death off of a cliff. It took three days for officials to find her body, because she went skiing alone when the ski lodge was closed. It was the fifth such incident to happen this year."

Jessica only stared at him and realized that was the reason he'd bought her the ski set in the first place.

Kenny nodded and read her mind, "Oh, yes," he began to cough, "I've been planning this for awhile."

Kenny's cough grew louder as he began to perspire through his shirt. He batted his eyes rapidly when his sudden cough began to grow uncontrollable. When he looked at his hands, they were speckled with blood. He looked up toward Jessica who was now smiling wickedly at him.

She spoke to him in French. "I overheard you tell your uncle over the phone that you had just put the poison in my drink just now. When you turned your back, guess what I did?" Jessica nodded her head and continued, "I switched my drink with yours."

Kenny's eyes grew wider, and when he saw his fate, he panicked and reached over the table and began choking the life out of Jessica with all the strength he had left. Jessica fought, but he was too powerful as the air in her lungs began to diminish and the whites of her eyes began to burst bright red. She could no longer fight as her eyes began to fall to the back of her head. She felt life leaving her body when suddenly she gasped as air once again returned to her body.

The first thing Jessica saw when she opened her eyes was her friend Vonda, who had her cradled in her arms. The next thing she saw was Chubby brutally beating Kenny to a bloodied pulp.

"No, Chubby!" Jessica managed to scream. "He's dying anyway, and I don't want you to be blamed for it."

Chubby looked down at Kenny as his chest heaved in and out as he spat on him.

"I never liked your pretty ass anyway!"

They told Chubby that he had to leave before they call the police because of his extensive record and it would not look good for any of them. Vonda stayed to provide Jessica with support. The local police arrived and took Jessica's statement and collected the evidence. After they took Kenny's body away, they took them both to the station to continue their investigation and ran both of their records. It didn't look good for either of them at that point.

Suddenly, a lawyer appeared in the room where they were being kept and showed the detective his credentials. He announced that the two girls were his clients and were not answering any more questions. He waved for the girls to follow him.

He handed his card to the lead detective. "Here's my card. If you want to contact my clients for anything else, you call me."

As they walked out of the sheriff's office, the lawyer shook both their hands and said, "My name is Irwin Greenberg and I was hired by a man that only went by the name Mr. Chubby. He supposed to be your brother?"

Vonda raised her hand and said, "That's my brother."

"Oh, he said both you were his sisters, but, he is a good man. He came to my office about few hours ago and paid me two thousand dollars cash and said his sisters were in trouble and make it go away."

Jessica quickly asked, "So we won't be charged with anything?"

Mr. Greenberg stopped in place and said, "For what? Defending yourself against a suspected murderer?"

Jessica and Vonda were confused and Mr. Greenberg explained further. "They failed to inform you the deceased was under investigation for the murder of two of his former real estate partners who died under mysterious circumstances. They both were found to have potassium cyanide in their systems at the time of their death. There was a clause in their partnership that if any partner would happen to die, his share of the property would revert to the remaining owners, who happened to be Kenneth Duboise and Langston Duboise, Kenneth's uncle."

Jessica quickly said, "I gave a bottle of the same kind of poison to the police."

He shook his head, and said, "They already know you are innocent, they just don't get too many actual murders in these parts, and I guess they wanted to play policeman for a change." He gave them a smile and said, "You are free to go. Do you want me to give you a ride back to the cottage?"

They suddenly heard a honk and it was Chubby who was parked across the street in Vonda's car. Mr. Greenberg simply waved to them and drove off.

When they arrived back at the cottage Jessica wanted to leave it immediately and began packing up her luggage. As she packed, she found Kenny's wallet sitting above the fireplace mantle. She was going to throw it in the garbage but she decided against it.

After driving in silence on their way home, Vonda tapped Jessica on the shoulder and handed her Tiny's letter to read. Vonda reached over and clicked on the side light so she could read it.

Dear Jessica and Vonda,

Y'all are in extreme danger. You been set up by Jessica's boyfriend Kenny. I heard him speaking on what I think was a walkie-talkie while I was in the hospital. He thought I was unconscious, but I heard everything he said. He was talking to a man and told him that he set up everything and that they would clear out the building that night and was sure that some of you wouldn't make it out the building alive. I knew that you were pregnant, Jessica, and I couldn't allow you to chance it and be part of that so I dropped a dime on you and ratted you out to your P.O. I hope you ain't too mad at me, but that was the only way I knew to keep you away from that shit. I'm going to the building now to watch my girl Vonda's back, so nothing would happen to her either. I ain't got long to live, but I'm going use what little time I have left for the people I love the most, so don't feel sorry for me, just remember me forever just as I am.

Tiny
GET IT GIRLS

Jessica bit down her lip to prevent herself from crying, but she lost. She cried like she'd never cried before as Vonda hugged her and began to lose it too. Chubby could no longer focus on the highway because his eyes began to water as well. He pulled off and got out the car to release his emotions so his sister and friend would not hear him. Vonda stepped out of the car, followed by Jessica, and walked over to Chubby. The three embraced in a circle as they cried together in the middle of nowhere while the snow rained down upon them.

Epilogue

Three weeks later, Jessica, Ms. Jones, Vonda and baby Silver were at the bus terminal in Times Square, eagerly waiting on a person they hadn't seen in nearly two years. They watched the bus pull in and could barely contain themselves when he suddenly appeared smiling from ear to ear when he spotted them. It was Jessica's brother Jordan, who'd been away in Minnesota in a long-term treatment facility for the past eighteen months.

If it wasn't for his smile they would never had recognized him because he'd packed on so much weight. Ms. Jones was brought to tears as she embraced her son who she hadn't hugged in four years since he first began using drugs. Vonda hugged him next and then introduced Jordan to his niece.

Jordan held his niece in his arms and kissed her gently as he told her, "I'm your uncle Jordan."

Jordan finally looked up from Silver and spotted his big sister Jessica and handed Silver back to Vonda. He approached her slowly with his head down and he looked up when they were eye to eye. Jordan suddenly reached out and embraced his sister and cried as he whispered in her ear.

"Thank you, Jessica. Thank you for saving my life. I know why you did what you did, and I understand it now."

Jessica nodded and embraced her baby brother as she cried happy tears, knowing God delivered him back to his family. They pulled away and wiped away their tears.

Jessica said, "Ok, let's go home, Jordan."

"Hold on," said Jordan, "I still got to get my other bags from off the bus."

They watched the driver unload the passengers' luggage from the side of the bus and waited for him to retrieve them. When Jordan walked away it was then did Jessica notice for the first time that he now walked with a permanent limp.

She thought back to the night she'd last seen him in the abandoned building and told Shooter to shoot him four times in his legs but not to kill him. It was the only way she knew to get him off the streets long enough to be away from the drugs and enter a long term drug program. Jessica visited him in the hospital not long after while he recovered from his wounds and reminded him again that before he caused their mother another day of pain, she would do whatever it took to prevent that from happening. She gave him an ultimatum to either die a slow, miserable death from the drugs, or die a quick death from a bullet if he continued using. At that moment, Jordan looked his sister's eyes and knew she was deadly serious and made the smart decision then and there to go away as long as it took to beat his addiction.

Since Vonda received her Master's in Sociology she went on to run not-for-profit crisis centers for women and girls who were either addicts, homeless, or battered women and provided treatment and temporary shelter until they found permanent residency or long term treatment. Her work hadn't gone unnoticed as Vonda received millions of dollars of donations from people all over the world who recognized her unwavering dedication to humanity and her community. Not long after she opened her first crisis center, she was able to finally convince members of Tiny's family to seek treatment, including her mother, and they been they was able to beat their addiction and all have been working at the center clean and sober ever since.

Needless to say, two years after Tiny's mother sobriety, Vonda gave her a certified check for one hundred thousand dollars and told her it was a gift from her daughter. Vonda saved thousands of lives, but she was unable to save the ones closest to her—her other four brothers over the years lost their lives to the battle of addiction.

Chubby never missed a beat and remained the person he always was. Every Sunday over the years, including holidays, Vonda, Chubby, Tiny's mother, Cleveland, Sweets and his family, and the entire Jones clan, would meet up at Ms. Jones house and eat Sunday dinner together and have a ball. They would ask Chubby, when he will become a changed person and settle down and have a family instead of being terror in those streets.

Chubby would normally rock back and forth, but this time he got honest and admitted, "I gave that life up long ago, but I am what I am, I love my family and I will do anything to protect you. If you get in trouble with the law, you'd call a lawyer, if you get sick, you'd go see a doctor, but if you get in trouble with these niggas out here, you call on Chubby. I'm a gangster and you can't change a lion into a lamb."

As much as they wanted to change him, they knew he was right.

Chubby broke the silence and smiled. "But don't worry about me, because I'm a businessman now, I don't bother nobody." Chubby was in fact a businessman, and was actually well off and had many legitimate businesses, and secretly had enough money to last him a lifetime, but he chose to remain in the same neighborhood, same apartment, and same small room with his mother and walked the streets of Harlem like a king. But, what Chubby truly loved the most were his god-children, Silver Jones and Chancellor Haze.

It was no surprise when Jessica found out her mother and Cleveland had become an item, and soon after they sat her down and told her they were getting married. Jessica couldn't have been happier for them. A few years after they got married, Cleveland and Ms. Jones moved to Florida and brought a nice house and have been living happily ever since.

It took Jessica nearly two years to finally find the strength to contact Kenny's family in New Jersey. A year earlier, Jessica went through Kenny's wallet that and found several contact numbers, one which had above it "Mother." But she never had the nerve to reach out to her.

But the older Silver got, the more she realized how important it was to know the other side of her family, so one day, out of the blue, Jessica dialed the number and made arrangements to meet them at their home in New Jersey. The day she was supposed to meet them, Jessica did not know what she would be walking into because of Kenny's connection with his uncle, plus the fact she'd never met any of his family members. So, she asked Chubby to come with her.

When Jessica pulled up in front of the large, Victorian-style home in a beautiful suburban neighborhood, she felt a little more at ease. She looked at Chubby. "I'm going to ring the doorbell first to see if everything is ok, and if anything wrong should happen, forget about me and just get my daughter out of here safely."

Chubby remained silent and just stared at her.

"Chubby, I'm serious. Get my daughter out of here!"

Chubby reluctantly nodded and got into the driver's seat.

Jessica took a deep breath and proceeded up the walkway. Before Jessica could make it to the door, it had opened and an older couple stood at the doorway smiling. Jessica introduced herself and they eagerly shook her hand and hugged her. Jessica was overwhelmed by their by their friendliness and knew it was genuine.

The woman spoke first. She was in her late fifties with smooth, radiant skin. "Hi, Jessica, I'm Kenneth's mother Deidra, and this is my husband, Kenneth's father Leland."

He took off his dark glasses to get a good look at her and it was then, did Jessica saw where Kenny got his hazel eyes from— his father eyes was just like his.

Still excited, Kenny's mother asked, "So, where is the baby at?"

Jessica took a quick peek inside their home and said honestly,

"Is it possible I can come inside and talk to you first?"

The couple sensed something was wrong and welcomed her in. After nearly twenty minutes went by, Jessica emerged from the home smiling and waved for Chubby to bring the baby out. Chubby went to the rear door and brought out Silver and carried her up the walkway. The couple shook with anticipation as they approached. When they saw Silver's face, they knew instantly that she was their first and only grandchild.

Jessica found out that his parents knew nothing of their son's child until one day Kenny had called and told them he had a daughter and that the baby's mother had died and he had custody of her and wanted them to raise her. They told Jessica that they were happy to take their grandchild, but he never contacted them, and shortly that they were notified that he died.

When Jessica asked about his uncle, Kenny's mother's eyes turned cold and she explained that he was arrested for murder and died before he could be sentenced nearly a year ago. She always blamed his uncle for Kenny getting mixed up in his side of the business because he was a bad man. Jessica decided against telling his parents everything that went on with her son to spare them more heartbreak.

Over the years, Kenny's parents enjoyed their time with their only grandchild and pampered Silver as if she was a princess. Since Silver was Kenny's only biological daughter, his entire estate, which included five residential buildings throughout the city of New York, including the infamous Castle of Greyskull, were transferred over to Silver as the owner, and her mother Jessica and uncle Jordan now ran them.

Almost twenty years to the day four impressionable teenagers got charged with a murder they didn't commit, the case was reopened when Nikki of the Lenox Avenue crew came forward and turned herself in and told the authorities the whole truth that had been weighing her down for years. She apparently found God and told her pastor of her past atrocities and he simply advised her what was stated in the bible in John 8:32—"Then you will know the truth, and the truth shall set you free."

As a result, Tay-Tay was found and arrested, and she made consistent statements backing up Nikki's claim. A month later Jessica and Vonda learned through the District Attorney's office that they were exonerated of the crime they were charged with twenty years ago. Nikki and Tay-Tay, who were now productive citizens with families of their own, avoided jail time only after Vonda and Jessica spoke on their behalf at their sentencing. When Jessica got her turn before the judge to make a plea on their behalf, she removed a letter and opened it.

"Twenty years ago, me and my three best friends, Vonda Williams, Claresse Maynard, and Lynise Davis, had our whole lives ahead of us. We went to our prom and found love, or what we thought was love and decided to become women that night and give away what was sacred and holy—our virginities. Because of that decision we made a secret pact to keep it between the four of us, which it was our right to do.

"Unfortunately, the most memorable night in our lives also turned into the most tragic—a girl was murdered. To make a long story short, four innocent young girls, still in their prom gowns, were all charged with the murder. Because of this pact we made, the only truth we left out to the authorities was that we all were in a hotel to spare our parents the embarrassment. The one fatal omission also proved to be a life changing error and cost us six years of our life.

"The day we were convicted, we made another pact, that no matter what happens when they close those gates on us, we would stick together and do whatever was necessary to make it out of prison alive. I stand before the same court, twenty years later, to tell you that we failed at our pact and two of our best friends didn't make it out alive. They died the same day they entered prison. They would die a miserable death years later, but it was all the same, because of the injustice that would ultimately suck away their souls.

"One would wonder why, after so much pain, after so much hurt, why I would defend the very people that played such a role in ruining our lives? The answer is simple, I already have too much blood on my hands, and I refuse to bloody them any further and take another person's life by doing the same thing the penal system did to us. They suffered equal burdens over years, I'm sure, and salvaged their lives the best way they knew how and became productive citizens.

"We ask you, to not weigh down our burden any further. Today we chose life over death. So, Your Honor, on behalf of Claresse Maynard, Lynise Davis, myself, and Vonda Williams, the four of us still stand by our pact. We still stand collectively together in spirit, for we are and forever will be, the Get It Girls!"